HUNTRESS ADEPT

HUNTRESS ADEPT

HUNTRESS CLAN SAGA™ BOOK 5

JAMIE DAVIS

DISRUPTIVE IMAGINATION

Copyright © 2020 Jamie Davis
Cover Art by Jake @ J Caleb Design
http://jcalebdesign.com / jcalebdesign@gmail.com

LMBPN Publishing
PMB 196, 2540 South Maryland Pkwy
Las Vegas, NV 89109

First US Edition, July, 2020
eBook ISBN: 978-1-64971-043-7
Print ISBN: 978-1-64971-044-4

THE HUNTRESS ADEPT TEAM

Thanks to the JIT Readers

Diane L. Smith
John Ashmore
Dorothy Lloyd
Deb Mader

If I've missed anyone, please let me know!

Editor
The Skyhunter Editing Team

CHAPTER ONE

For a young woman who'd had her share of crazy nights, this one had topped them all. Quinn ducked beneath the swipe of an enormous clawed paw and yelled, "Mom, I could use some help over here."

"I'm a little busy, dear," Naomi replied.

Quinn spared a quick glance in Naomi's direction. Her mother delivered a pair of lightning-fast slashes into the body of what could only be described as a giant slug—that is, if slugs had circular gaping maws filled with multiple rows of dagger-like teeth.

A chittering snarl from in front of her snapped Quinn's attention back to her foe. The giant squirrel, easily the size of a horse, looked like any other squirrel except for the glowing red eyes and the carnivorous-looking teeth behind the glistening yellow tusks jutting from its upper jaw.

The creature's rear legs bunched up, tensing for a leap. It was barely enough of a warning for Quinn to launch herself backward into a handspring that catapulted her out of reach of the freakish thing. It propelled itself forward in a charge at where she'd been standing a split-second before.

Thank God the thing wasn't too bright. It appeared a little confused to find she was no longer where it had landed. Quinn took advantage of the pause to dart in and slash at the neck, digging in deep with her Bowie knife before dodging back to safety.

She almost made it.

One of the claws raked at her back, and Quinn cried out at the burning pain. She managed to break free before the paws gripped her shoulder and pulled her in to get at her with its teeth. She wanted to avoid that.

The evasive move put her only a few feet from her mother, who was still battling the giant slug. It had to be nearly the size of a small car.

"Wanna trade?" Quinn said as she tried to catch her breath.

"What would be the fun in that?" Naomi replied. "By the way, aren't slugs supposed to be as slow as snails?"

As she finished the sentence, Naomi jumped to the side as the slug swung its front end around to snap at her with its multi-toothed mouth.

"Never mind," Quinn said. "I take it back."

She had to find a way to get rid of both creatures as soon as possible. Whoever had cast the spell that created them was probably getting away.

"Mom, I've got an idea."

"I'll take whatever you've got. My sword's doing very little lasting damage that I can see."

Quinn leaped straight up to dodge a grab at her ankles

by the squirrel. "Get as close as you can to it and get it to roll this way."

"I'll try. I'm not even sure this thing has eyes to see me. What's the plan?"

Quinn ran at the squirrel, ducking under a swipe at her head, and slashed at the whiskered face just above its mouth. "You'll see. Just be ready to get out of the way."

When Quinn's blade scored a red line across the creature's sensitive nose, it let out a roar that would have made any lion proud. "Uh-oh," she said, then ran in the direction of her mother and the giant slug. "Here I come."

The squirrel's hot breath raised the hairs on the back of her neck, spurring her to draw down more stamina to boost her speed.

The clack of snapping teeth right behind her told her it was just in time.

Ahead, Naomi had managed to get the slug to pivot toward her. She turned to face Quinn. Her eyes widened when she realized how close her daughter and the snarling squirrel were.

"Dodge *NOW!*" Quinn shouted. At that instant, she gathered all her remaining strength and vaulted to the left. Her mother leaped in the opposite direction.

Behind her, Quinn felt more than heard the collision between the monstrous beasts. As she landed and spun, ready to defend herself, she smiled. The plan had worked.

Squirrel and slug were locked in a death grip. The slug's circular teeth bored into the squirrel's chest and gut, while the squirrel's jutting tusks and razor teeth tore away hunks of slime-covered slug flesh. It was over in seconds. The slug succumbed first. The squirrel stumbled a few feet, entrails dragging on the sidewalk. It stopped and swayed, staring up at the moon before falling over with a crashing thump.

Quinn scanned the area for Naomi but didn't see her. "Mom?"

"Up here."

Quinn turned her gaze up to Naomi, who was perched on a lamppost next to the slug. No, scratch that, it was where the body of the slug had been.

"What the— Where did they go?"

The bodies of the slug and the squirrel were gone. There was no sign the fight had taken place, other than the injuries on her and Naomi.

The vampire jumped down from her perch and crouched to examine the sidewalk, then pointed at something there on the pavement. "Not gone, just small again."

Quinn walked over and stared at the spot where her mother pointed. A tiny slug lay there, looking like something had chewed through the top half of it.

"If that's here, then…" Quinn turned and took a few steps to where she'd last seen the squirrel. "Yep, the squirrel's here, disemboweled just like the bigger version."

Naomi searched the empty city streets around them. "No one nearby. Whoever cast the spell must have run off. That's why the animals went back to normal."

Quinn pulled up her HUD and enabled the transparent map overlay. She scanned it for any of the tell-tale red blips that would indicate a known enemy nearby. Nothing.

"It's a good thing whoever it was didn't launch the attack while we were on the way to the club earlier," Naomi said. "There were a lot of people out tonight. It would've been hard to hide it from the ordinary public, or protect bystanders."

Quinn nodded. Her mother was right, they were lucky. Anyone out at this time of night had either been lucky enough or smart enough to stay away from the battle.

She nudged the dead squirrel with the toe of her boot. It looked completely normal now—just a harmless little creature common in the city. He'd never done anything to deserve this.

Quinn ground her teeth together. "It's not fair. I want this guy, Mom. I'm tired of the secret attacks and random spells they're casting all over town."

"At least we know it's centered on you," Naomi said. "That makes it likely someone working with Gemma, or maybe Filippa." She pulled out a cloth and started wiping down her blade. Her face screwed up in a frown as she rubbed away the slug slime coating the metal.

Quinn remembered her Bowie. If she left blood on it for too long, it would etch and pock the magical steel and silver alloy. She pulled the bottom of her t-shirt from out of her jeans and worked at cleaning her own blade.

The mother-daughter team began walking east toward the neighborhood where they lived. Quinn and Naomi had been trying to spend at least one night out together ever since Avery left. Avery, who was Quinn's new love interest, had an urgent quest: she searched for other women like her, raised as Huntresses by the Fae for their nefarious purposes.

Naomi had suggested she and Quinn hang out more together to take her mind off Avery's departure. It was also an effort to build on the connection they had started. Mother and daughter had many years to catch up on.

While the encounter with the squirrel and the slug had been terrifying, Quinn had been glad to have her mother along. Strange things had been happening to Quinn for several weeks now, and when she'd reported them to her friends, she'd gotten the impression they didn't believe her. She couldn't blame them.

It had started with minor and seemingly random occurrences that when taken alone, could have been discounted as coincidences. However, things had started to add up, to the point that Quinn was sure someone was targeting her. When all the food she ate for two days straight spoiled the minute she touched it, Quinn had decided someone was out to get her. Tonight's attack was the boldest attempt yet.

Naomi sheathed her sword across her back beneath her blazer, the hilt reaching her right hip. A clip held the blade in place but could be released with the flick of her thumb.

"Based on what you've described," Naomi said, "I'd say whoever is after you has moved from annoying to murderous, yes?"

Quinn nodded. "Up until now, it's been inconveniences. It wasn't too bad when all the pans and utensils on my stove turned to paper and cardboard." Her only frying pan had burst into flame around the grilled cheese sandwich she'd been making. So did the cardboard spatula she'd been holding. She'd avoided getting burned only because she'd dropped it all on the floor and stomped on the burning mess until the flames went out.

Naomi shook her head. "This is a major escalation. You've had at least one of these incidents—"

"They're attacks, not incidents. Someone is out to get me."

"Sorry. I mean, you've had at least one of these attacks each day since Avery left, yes?"

Quinn nodded while her mother continued.

"That makes me wonder if Gemma left the city like we thought she did."

"I agree, but both Taylor and Miranda say this doesn't match with Gemma's school of arcane arts. Besides, you and Clark scoured the city for a week to try to track her down, and you were sure she'd left. Now you're not certain?"

Naomi shrugged. "If not her, then maybe someone working for her." She hooked a thumb over her shoulder. "Someone powerful enough to transform living cells and increase mass at the same time. I'm not the expert Miranda is, but it sounds like that would be incredibly difficult to pull off." She glanced at Quinn, "I don't suppose you thought to switch on your arcane sight during the fight?"

Quinn bit her lower lip. That ability might have picked up on the source of the magic controlling the creatures. "No, I should've thought of it, but I didn't."

Naomi nudged her with an elbow as they walked. "Don't beat yourself up about it. We were a little busy at the time. Next time this happens, try to pick up on where the initial flows are coming from. We might get an idea of where the mage stood when they cast the spell. Any clues we can gather could help us locate them."

"That's a good idea. I'll try to remember." Quinn didn't

want to have a "next time," but at this point, it was fairly certain she would. That worried her since the attacks also endangered her friends and family just for standing next to her.

"There has to be a connection or pattern of some sort," Naomi continued. "It can't be as random as you say it is."

"If there's a pattern, I haven't figured it out."

"Let's start at the beginning and go through each attack until this one. Describe them all to me while we walk. You focus on each one in turn, and I'll try to look for the common thread. There has to be one."

"Okay," Quinn agreed. "The first one I noticed was when I got back from taking Avery to catch her flight."

"That was the floor thing?"

"Yes, the wooden boards in the hallway outside my apartment got soft, I guess. My foot sank in up to the ankle like it was mud. Then it solidified, holding me in place. If someone wanted to launch an attack, that would have been the time. I couldn't go anywhere until Clark brought Paddy up with a power saw and a chisel to cut me free."

"Okay, what was next?" Naomi asked. "Tell me everything you can remember."

Quinn kept going, outlining each incident and ticking them off on her fingers. Each appeared random, and they seemed to have no connection. Tonight was the first time she'd been in any real danger. Until now, the attacks had been merely annoying. She told Naomi as much when she finished relaying the details of the last one before tonight.

When she finished talking, Quinn looked around. She was surprised to see they were almost home.

Beside her, Naomi said, "Well, if there's a pattern there, I don't see one." She'd been taking notes on her phone, and she scrolled through what she'd written while Quinn talked. "It's almost as if…" Her voice trailed off as she shook her head.

"Almost as if what?" Quinn asked.

"If you weren't the obvious target, I'd call this an outbreak of wild magic in the city. But that's so rare it's ridiculous."

"What's wild magic? Isn't all magic wild?"

"Miranda can explain this way better than I can, but the short answer is no. Magic has rules like the things that govern the natural order of things. You can manipulate certain things but only within some basic laws of physics and chemistry. A mage or witch pulls in the energy and uses it to influence a shift in the natural order. The bigger the shift, the more energy required."

"Yeah, I get that. But what makes these attacks different?" Quinn asked.

Naomi sighed. "This is just a hunch. I really need to talk to someone with more magical skill. The things happening to you are different from each other and seem random, but all have to do with a shift in natural rules."

When Quinn said nothing and just stared at her mother, Naomi shrugged. "Each is a sort of matter transformation or transmutation. That sounds a lot like how I understand wild magic manifests."

"You still haven't explained what wild magic is."

Naomi shook her head. "I guess that's because I don't know. It's more of a legend than anything else. I don't know anyone who's seen it. This sounds like the way legends describe it: mostly as random changes in the natural order occurring in a localized geographical area."

Quinn started to ask another question but stopped when she realized they'd turned down the alley leading to the O'Malley's basement entrance. Quinn's apartment could be reached from a stairway inside.

They pulled open the outer doors and walked into the vestibule, greeting the doorman Jonah with a nod. Quinn said, "I guess I need to sit down and follow this line of thought with Miranda and Taylor."

"It can wait until morning," Naomi said. "You said things haven't happened too close together, usually just one a day. Go to bed. There'll be time to revisit all this in the morning. Maybe that'll give us both a fresh look at the problem."

The inside of the bar was relatively quiet. The band had already packed up and left. Only the diehards remained; three of the local leprechaun tribe were seated at the bar. Juni, the owner's daughter, waved at Quinn and Naomi as they entered from where she stood behind the bar, chatting with her patrons.

The two women waved back as they split up to go their own ways. Quinn headed to the apartment stairs leading to the second and third floors of the row home above the club. Naomi turned off to go to the storerooms and the long underground tunnel that led to the old Hunter chambers located nearby. Her converted vampire lair was down there.

Quinn rubbed her right hand. Every time she talked about the attacks, her hand itched and tingled. It was more annoying than painful. Tonight it had been bugging her ever since the attack. It was one more thing to track down about this person who was after her. Maybe something would come to her or her mother in the morning after they talked to the others. Quinn was ready to lead an offensive against whoever it was doing this to her, but not right now. Now, she needed rest.

CHAPTER TWO

When the alarm on her phone went off, Quinn switched it off without really waking up. It was an off-day as far as Clark's never-ending training regimen went, so she decided to sleep in. About an hour later, just before nine, her phone went off with a continuous series of alerts spaced a few minutes apart.

"Go away," Quinn groaned as she rolled over and pulled the other pillow over her head to hide from the incoming messages.

The alerts stopped for a little bit, and she drifted off to sleep again. Booming thumps on her apartment door jerked her upright, though. She rubbed her eyes with the heels of her hands to wake up, then she grabbed her phone to check the time.

It was 9:15.

Someone banged on her apartment door again, and a muffled voice called out. She couldn't make out who it was or what they were saying.

"All right, I'm coming already." Quinn swung her feet to

the floor as she stood. Wary at the way she'd been awakened, and remembering the attack the night before, she grabbed her Bowie from the sheath hanging on her headboard and walked out to the living room.

"Who is it?"

"It's Taylor. Open up, Quinn. We need you downstairs. You have to see this."

Quinn unlocked the door and pulled it open a crack before turning around to fire up her coffee maker. Behind her, Taylor burst into the room.

Seeing Quinn grab a mug from the sink and begin to rinse it out, she said, "No time for that. Go." Taylor took the cup from Quinn's hand and nudged her toward her bedroom. "Get dressed in your best badass Huntress outfit. You need to look the part before you get downstairs."

"What the hell is going on?"

"Just get dressed. I'll tell you as we head down."

Quinn pointed to her mug. "I need coffee."

"Fine, I'll make you a cup. Get dressed."

Quinn waited until Taylor started the process before she went back to her bedroom. At this point, curiosity propelled her to see what was going on. It wasn't an attack. That would have set off her amulet to warn her. Her hand drifted up to brush the silver medallion hanging around her neck. It was body temperature, which meant it was something else, but she had no idea what that could be.

She slid on a pair of blue jeans, black knee-high leather boots, and swapped out the t-shirt she'd slept in for a clean one. She also grabbed her shoulder rig for her knife. The last piece of her usual ensemble was her waist-length leather jacket, which was draped across the sofa in the other room where she'd left it last night.

Quinn walked back into the living room and picked up the jacket from the night before. The back had been shredded by the squirrel's claws. She hadn't remembered it being so torn up.

"Never mind that," Taylor said. "I found another in your closet. You should buy stock in those things." Her best friend stood waiting by the door with a steaming mug of coffee in one hand and Quinn's spare jacket in the other. After slipping on the coat, Quinn took the mug and followed Taylor out the door.

"Okay, T, what's so urgent that you cut short my hard-earned beauty sleep?"

Taylor laughed. "You're gorgeous enough, believe me."

"Seriously, what's going on?"

"The bar's full of people, all looking for you?"

"Me? What the heck did I do to that many people to deserve a lynch mob showing up here at breakfast time? The bar's not even open yet."

"They're not here because they're angry with you, they're here because they need your help."

Quinn stopped walking and stared at her friend. It took Taylor a few steps to realize Quinn wasn't behind her.

"Quinn, this is serious, keep up."

"If they're not angry, what do they want help with? Why come here for me?"

Taylor rolled her eyes. "Because you're the Huntress, Quinn. They're here because they're scared and they need your help."

That shut Quinn up. She remained silent the rest of the

way down the stairs to the basement. The buzz of voices on the other side of the door leading into O'Malley's pub sounded like more than just a few people on the other side. When Taylor pulled open the door, it washed over her like a rushing wind.

Quinn was three steps into the bar before the people noticed. The rush of bodies in her direction took her by surprise. Each of them called out for help in one way or another.

"Quinn, Quinn, please, you have to find my son."

"Huntress, I need you to close the portal that just opened in my basement."

"Huntress…"

"Quinn…"

"Please help…"

So many voices at once threatened to overwhelm her. Finally, she couldn't take it anymore and shouted, "Enough!"

She hadn't realized what she'd done until the room fell silent, and she noticed the wagon wheel chandeliers swaying from the force of her command. Quinn's HUD had loaded on its own. She'd unconsciously drawn down her stamina and boosted her voice using an icon she'd never seen before. It looked like an old-fashioned megaphone.

Quinn started to click off the icon, then stopped. She wanted the people to hear what she said next. "Everyone listen. I want to help you, I really do, but let me get over to the bar and talk to my friends for a few minutes. I promise to hear you out and see what I can do."

Across the room, Paddy O'Malley jumped up on a chair,

pointed at the kitchen door, and mimed eating something. Quinn smiled and nodded.

"While you're waiting, why don't you get yourselves some breakfast? Paddy's opened the kitchen early, so grab a seat, and the servers who are here will try to get your orders as quickly as they can."

It took a few seconds for what she'd said to sink in. Slowly the crowd around her split up and moved to find a place to sit down.

"Nicely done," Taylor said. "What was that spell you used to amplify your voice?"

"Not a spell, at least not in the traditional sense. It just showed up in my HUD. I'm not sure how I activated it."

Taylor smiled. "You always find something new when you're stressed. It's like your brain knows how all this stuff works, even if your conscious self doesn't."

"I really wish we could find an instruction manual," Quinn said. "I'm tired of floundering through it."

Taylor tugged Quinn's elbow to start her toward the bar. "You don't seem to be having trouble innovating when it counts. I'd stop complaining. My guess is there isn't a manual and your mind is making this up as you go somehow."

Quinn could only smile. Taylor always dropped a perspective bomb on her when she needed it the most. She closed her mouth.

Clark, Naomi, and Miranda waited by the bar for the two of them. Quinn and Taylor joined them, and they all leaned in to talk.

"What's going on?" Quinn asked.

Clark answered after exchanging glances with Naomi

and Miranda. "Something happened last night to amp up the situation here in the city."

"You heard about the attack, then?" Quinn asked.

Naomi nodded. "I told him about it before all this came up."

"A single attack like you both faced is one thing," Clark said. "These people report separate events, though, all over the city last night. It all happened about the same time you two were attacked or soon after, based on what I can piece together so far."

Quinn glanced at the people in the bar. All were settled at or around the tables. A few groups talked among themselves, but every now and then, individuals would steal a glance toward Quinn. A mix of desperation and maybe a little hope showed in their eyes.

"Why did they come here, and why now?"

"I think I know why," Taylor said, looking up from something on her phone. "There were lively discussions overnight on social channels about what happened. No one knew what to do about it until about two hours ago, then someone posted a message that said:

Quinn threw her hands up. "Why would anyone assume this was something I could fix? That's insane."

Clark chuckled. "Goes with the territory. You wanted to revive the clans. This is what it was like in the old days. When there were supernatural problems, people sought out the Hunters living among them to get to the root of the problem."

Quinn twisted her head to look around. "Who are they all? They're here at O'Malley's, so they aren't members of the normal human population."

Naomi said, "There are people from all the corners of the supernatural community around the city. Judging by the variety, there hasn't been a corner of Baltimore untouched."

Miranda pointed at two groups nearby at adjacent tables. "Whatever has happened, it's got them spooked. Groups are sitting together that should be trying to kill each other. There's a group of Spanish Xana shifters sitting next to a western tribal Wendigo family. They've been blood enemies since the conquistadors landed in the American Southwest. It's weird even seeing them in the same room."

"All the more reason we need to get this resolved in some way," Clark said. "Quinn, you have to talk to them."

"Me?"

"Yes," Naomi said. "It's you they came to see. They've decided you can fix this, so whether or not it's true, you have to make them think you've got a handle on it."

"But you know I don't. None of us do, at least not yet."

Clark leaned close. "Lie to them. Then we can put our heads together and try to make sense of this. We can't do that with the whole world here watching us." He nodded to the side.

Quinn glanced that way and saw several people holding their phones up at the group. They were taking video or maybe live-streaming the whole thing. "Okay, that has to stop. It's the kind of thing that could make all our lives difficult."

"You have to do it," Taylor said. "We tried to calm them when they showed up this morning. They wouldn't listen to us."

Quinn sighed. She was barely awake. She lifted her mug, took a long sip of her coffee, and made a face. Taylor had put too much cream in it. She set the coffee down and turned, raising her hands up to get people's attention. As soon as she did, the murmur of voices petered out into silence. The only sound came from the occasional bang of a pot or pan in the kitchen.

"People of Baltimore, I want to help you. I've been aware of unusual occurrences around the city for a few weeks now."

"Why didn't you stop them?" a voice called.

"Because they were isolated and had no apparent cause. Last night was the first mass attack on the city. That's bad in many ways, but it has one benefit."

That brought a fresh swell of low voices as people tried to understand where she was going. Quinn wondered, too, but she kept talking. She was making this up as she went along.

"I know that doesn't make sense, but whoever was behind this has made a mistake by spreading the attack so broadly last night. Someone somewhere had to see something that'll be a clue as to who is behind this."

Quinn gestured to her friends. "These are all members of my clan. You can trust them as you trust me. We're going to talk to you all in small groups, so be patient. We'll get to everyone. We want to hear your stories about what happened to you. Try hard to remember everything you can. You never know what small detail will connect with something someone else said. Anything could be the critical clue that ties all this together. While you wait for us to come to your table, enjoy your breakfast and don't forget to tip your waitresses. They weren't expecting all of you to drop in this morning."

She turned and lowered her voice. "Everyone take a table. Ask them what happened. Take notes or record it on your phone if you want, but get a good description from each group. When you're finished with a table, ask them to finish eating and return to their homes. We'll meet back here at the bar once everyone leaves."

Clark nodded. "Good idea, Quinn. Very much the plan of a clan leader."

"We have to know what happened. This seemed like the best way to find out."

"Let's fan out from the bar," Naomi suggested. "Move straight across the room from this point until all the tables have been covered."

The others nodded and they split up, picking the tables closest to where they stood along the curved bar. Quinn headed to the table Miranda had pointed to with the Xana and Wendigo families. She knew a little about Wendigos from an old TV show. Most of it was probably wrong, but at least that was a start. She had no idea what the Xanas were.

Both groups looked up from where they sat at the round table. The Xanas were all women, beautiful in long, flowing dresses, though each had dark circles under her eyes. The four Wendigos, men and women, clearly showed their Native American heritage. They, too, looked worried and gaunt, like they hadn't had any sleep for at least a night, maybe more.

Quinn sat down and leaned forward. "I'm Quinn. Why

don't you have one from each of your groups tell me about what happened last night? Okay?"

Both sides nodded, and after glancing back and forth, each family chose an individual spokesperson. The tallest of the Xanas started telling her strange and harrowing tale about the pipes coming out of the walls and attacking them in their apartment. The oldest male in the Wendigo family occasionally interjected a comment after she started until the two families wove their tale together. Despite being from feuding clans, they lived in the same high-rise apartment building.

Quinn pulled out her phone and used her voice memo app to record what they said. Looking at all the expectant faces waiting their turn at the other tables, she realized they were going to be here for a while.

CHAPTER THREE

By the time the members of the Huntress clan had finished interviewing the final groups and sent them on their way, it was after lunch. As Quinn returned to the bar, Paddy O'Malley, the leprechaun owner of the pub, stood on the raised platform behind the bar, counting a stack of bills he'd pulled from the register.

"Sorry, Paddy," Quinn said. She leaned back on the bar and looked around. The place was a mess. Every table had dirty dishes and glasses on it. Juni and the other servers bustled about trying to clear away the debris.

"Sorry about what, me girl? I just did a week's worth of business in three hours." He giggled as he used a rubber band to wrap a bundle of bills and set it down next to several others.

"But Juni and the others..."

"Will be smiling once they see the count on the tips we collected. Don't worry about them, Quinn. You focus on figuring out the source of this mess. Not too quickly, though. I could use a few more mornings like this one."

"I'd like to avoid that if I can help it."

Paddy let out a maniacal cackle and winked at Quinn while he scooped up the cash bundles he'd made and scurried to his office in the back. She assumed there was a hidden safe somewhere back there, but who knew where a modern leprechaun kept his pot of gold?

Taylor, Clark, Naomi, and Miranda sat on the barstools on either side of her.

Quinn glanced at them and shrugged. "Well, did anyone make any sense out of anything you heard? Because there seemed to be no connection."

Naomi shook her head. "It's as if each story I heard was an attack by a different person, no common themes or incidents."

"I had an auto mechanic who had to lock himself in a storeroom all night at his shop," Clark said. "One of the cars he'd been working on went Christine on him."

When all he got was a blank stare from Quinn and Taylor, he said, "*Christine*? The Steven King story about the demon car?"

"So, it's demons?" Quinn asked.

"Not sure it is," Miranda said. The ghost shook her head and continued, "One of mine was a newlywed couple. They were in bed fooling around when everything turned into an elaborate musical song and dance number. Those two wanted to know how to make it happen again. That doesn't sound like demonic magic to me. They enjoyed themselves and called it magical."

"Maybe they're destined for divorce," Naomi suggested. "That would make a demon happy."

"I don't think so," Miranda replied. "There weren't any

warning signs I could see about their relationship. I can spot auras easily now that I'm a spirit. Those two were definitely in L-O-V-E, love!"

"What did you learn?" Quinn asked her mother.

Naomi said, "Not much of use. Three different stories, none of them linked in any way."

"What time did all this happen?" Taylor asked. "Maybe if they happened sequentially, we can track down the locations where the attacker moved through the city."

"That's a good idea," Clark said. "Can you pull up a city map so we can pin down each location?"

Taylor grinned. "Piece of cake. Come on down to my lab."

Taylor skipped across the pub to the storeroom door. Quinn and the others followed her. This idea seemed like the best option so far. Maybe it would yield results.

Taylor was already behind her triple monitors when the rest of the group entered her makeshift workshop down the long underground hallway behind the club. Quinn tried to move around behind her to see the screens.

"Oh, go back over there," Taylor said, waving Quinn away. "Don't all of you try to fit back here. There's no room. I upgraded the system with some leftover VirSync office equipment."

She turned on a power strip next to her screens and a small projector mounted behind the center monitor switched on, shining on a plain white sheet tacked to the far wall by the door. Quinn hadn't seen it when she entered.

Soon the makeshift screen filled with a map of the city, and Taylor looked up from her keyboard. "Okay, call out your encounters with time and locations as best you can. Start with you, Miranda."

The ghost started listing the information from her encounters. Then Naomi, Clark, and finally Quinn passed along what they knew.

Taylor pointed to the screen after she finished tapping something on her keyboard. "Here are the markers for each of you, along with the four groups I interviewed."

Quinn checked the projection on the wall. A series of map pins dropped into place, each with a text flag listing time and the name of the person who had given it. She had trouble making sense of it. There were over twenty pins across the map. The incidents ran from down by the harbor to a few blocks from O'Malley's.

Naomi walked over and tapped her chin. "Taylor, can you link them together so we can see them in chronological order, starting with the first encounter?"

"Sure, give me a sec."

The tech witch tapped on her keyboard for a minute or so and said, "Look at it now."

Clark pointed at the first pin in a chain linked by a glowing line. "That one. Whose was that?"

"Quinn and me," Naomi said. "That was our encounter with the giant squirrel and the slug."

"Ew!" Taylor groaned. "I stepped on a slug barefoot once. It squished between my toes. Made me throw up."

"You wouldn't have been able to step on this one, T," Quinn said. "It was the size of a small car."

"Sheesh, that's even worse."

Quinn walked over to stand next to Naomi. Something

about the path from the clubs down at Fells Point back to here at the pub seemed familiar.

Naomi glanced to the side at Quinn. "See it yet? I just noticed the pattern."

"Oh, my God. Whoever it was must have followed us home, or close to it."

"It sure looks that way," Naomi agreed.

Clark walked up beside them, staring at the projection on the wall. "Think back. Did you see anyone on the street or anything unusual on your way home? There couldn't have been that many people out and about at that time of night."

Quinn and Naomi looked at each other. Both shrugged and gazed at Clark.

Quinn said, "We were alone as far as I could tell. We walked all the way back here."

"It pisses me off someone tracked us like that without either of us knowing it," Naomi said. A hint of a growl sounded low in her throat, and she bared her fangs.

Taylor said, "They'd have to be pretty good to cause this much trouble along the way without either of you catching a glimpse of them."

Miranda floated over to stare at the map. "What if it was nobody?"

"That doesn't make any sense," Clark said. "Someone had to have orchestrated this."

"Not necessarily," Miranda said. "It would have taken someone with extraordinary power and magical resources to do even half of what we heard about this morning. On top of that, some of these things would have required a spellcaster's constant attention. Once they moved on to follow you two, the spell would have ended. How could they have been boosting the newlyweds' musical libido here for two hours and be six blocks away with the wino who nearly died from the never-ending bottle of Mad Dog 20/20?"

Naomi nodded. "They couldn't. You're right, Miranda. There's no way, especially not when you factor in all the other incidents."

Quinn asked, "Could there have been a whole gang of them?"

"And neither of us saw any of them all night?" Naomi asked. "Not likely. This would have taken how many mages or witches, Miranda?"

"Judging from the stories, at least ten."

"Ten?" Quinn asked. "There's no way ten people followed us all the way home. It has to be something else."

Miranda turned back to face them. Quinn swore the ghost looked paler and more transparent than usual. "There is another explanation, but you're not going to like it."

"What?" Clark asked. "If there's some sort of conspiracy going on, we need to know about it right now."

"I don't think it's any of the things we've come up with so far. It's far worse than that." Miranda paused and realized everyone was waiting for her to continue. She sighed and said, "It's wild magic."

"Oh, crap!" Clark exclaimed.

"I'll second that," Naomi added.

Taylor smiled. "Awesome."

Quinn looked at all of them. "Mom mentioned that last

night. I still don't understand how magic isn't inherently wild?"

Miranda shook her head. "Magic in normal circumstances is quite orderly and follows natural rules very closely. That is how spellcasters can manipulate it; they understand how the rules work and the orderly ways they can bend them."

"That's ridiculous," Quinn said. "If there are rules, how can you bend them?"

"It's like this, Quinn," Miranda said. "If a mage wants to fly, they have to understand basic physics and aerodynamics. Otherwise, the spell won't work. Only by knowing how the rules of nature apply can you subvert them in particular ways."

"I still don't see the difference. It seems totally the same as what happened last night to all those people."

"And to you over the last two weeks, remember?" Miranda added. "It's a matter of understanding all the rules. No one can remember all of it, so mages, witches, and other magic users have specialties—things they're better at when it comes to spells. Usually, those correspond to a particular school of thought like chemistry, physics, natural order, and biology. All of us who can cast spells are good with one or two areas, and we can dabble with simple spells in most areas. But one person can't do all the things we listed from last night, especially when coupled with all the things you've experienced. There's just no way."

"But it happened," Quinn said. "That makes it possible."

Clark nodded. "That's what points to an outbreak of wild magic. I think Miranda is right, and that's not a good thing. We're just lucky it has limited itself to Quinn and her immediate vicinity so far."

"Me?"

Naomi nodded. "It makes much more sense now. Somehow, someone has tagged you with some sort of charm or curse that is allowing the wild magic to break free around you."

Clark walked over to the map and stared at it for a few seconds before turning around. "No one died last night, right? None of your stories had any major injuries."

Taylor smiled. "You think it might be a benign outbreak?"

"There's no such thing," Miranda countered. "You are too young to remember the last outbreak, and you wouldn't have heard about it because you weren't part of the supernatural community until recently. It happened right after Hurricane Katrina hit New Orleans."

Clark shook his head. "It was bad. I heard it took several families of Cajun mages from down in the bayous to come up and sort it out. Apparently, someone owned an occult shop and died of a heart attack during the storm. They never got the chance to secure their shop against magical intrusion. The chaos of the hurricane passing over triggered one of the ancient artifacts she owned. When the storm passed, everyone assumed the worst was over. Then the wild magic struck and let loose a string of uncontrolled outbreaks. Some of them caused the pumps to seize up and the levees to fail."

"Thousands died," Miranda said. "All because of an outbreak of wild magic. And that one was contained after only forty-eight hours."

"Forty-eight hours?" Quinn asked. "This one has been going on for two weeks."

"That's why we're lucky," Clark said. "It's also why we need to track this down right away. We can't count on us staying lucky for much longer."

"You said it's centered on me?" Quinn frowned. "How could that be? Wouldn't I know?"

"Two weeks," Clark said. "That was when we sent Gemma on her way. Could she have left some sort of trap that caught Quinn without us knowing it?"

"I don't think so," Miranda said. "Quinn, think back to the fight with Gemma and the interval until the first incident happened outside your apartment. Did you notice anything unusual happening around you, maybe even within you, before your foot sank into the floor outside your apartment?"

"Like what?"

"It could be anything," the ghost went on. "Think. Was there anything strange that happened to you during the attacks? Maybe that could link back to a specific event you don't remember."

Quinn rubbed her hands together as she thought about it, then stopped and stared down at her fingers. "The tingling."

"What tingling?" Naomi asked.

"Ever since I pulled the spear out of Avery's back, my right hand has sort of tingled. Not all the time, just on and off."

Miranda said, "You never said anything about that. Tell us exactly how it happened from the first time you felt it."

Quinn explained how Gemma had magically launched

the golden spear at Avery. The shaft had pulsed with sparks of energy when Quinn gripped it to pull the head out of her friend's back.

"I realized at the time that I could pull in that energy and channel it to help heal Avery. I had no juice left in the tank, so I couldn't do it on my own. The spear held the only power source around, so I used it to replenish my mana supply."

"I need to see that spear," Miranda said. "Then we have to see if the archives in the Hunter chambers below have any information on how to contain wild magic once it's set free."

"You think it was the spear?" Naomi asked. "I've touched it. It felt like it might have magical properties, but nothing happened to me from handling it."

"You didn't draw spell energy through it the way Quinn did." Miranda turned to the Huntress. "Go get the spear and bring it here. We'll wait. I need to prep Taylor to do the divination spell so we can verify it as the source."

Quinn frowned. Was all this somehow her fault, even though she'd tried to do everything right? She pulled the door shut behind her and trudged up the hall that led to the pub.

She shook herself. There was no use moping about what might have been. At least they'd figured it out. Quinn stood up straight and put her shoulders back. A Huntress didn't shy away from trouble. If this was related to her, she'd find a way to counter it and make everything right again. She picked up her pace so she could get the spear back down and they could stop the wild magic once and for all.

CHAPTER FOUR

Quinn entered her apartment and froze. Someone or something was inside. A peculiar rhythmic scraping noise came from back toward her bedroom. Her door had been locked, and her silver Huntress amulet remained warm against her breastbone beneath her shirt. The lack of a chill from the magic charm didn't tell her everything, though. Apparently, it didn't warn her against wild magic attacks.

The scraping sound continued as Quinn took a few more steps inside and stopped. Whatever it was making the noise, it was back by the short hallway to her bedroom.

Quinn drew her Bowie and held it at her side, ready for anything as she walked into the hall. She checked to make sure the bathroom was empty and the linen closet door was closed. Whoever or whatever it was, they were in her bedroom.

The door was only open a few inches, so she couldn't see the whole room from the hallway. Quinn walked the final steps, pushed the door open all the way, and relaxed.

The football-sized glittering green egg spun like a top on the wooden floor beside her bed, its rock-hard surface scraping the boards on each rotation. While she'd seen it move on its own before, usually in reaction to her imaginary conversations with it, it had never been quite this animated before.

She crossed to it and knelt beside it. "Hey, you. What's got you all worked up?"

Quinn laid a hand atop the egg, finding that the shell was almost too hot to touch. She pressed down until the spinning egg slowed to a stop. Even though it no longer spun, it wasn't stationary. The egg vibrated to the point it almost hummed beneath Quinn's outstretched hand.

Concerned, Quinn picked up the egg and cradled it against her chest with both arms. She sat down on her bed and rocked the egg, cooing a soothing tune without words until the vibrations settled into a gentle, pulsing rhythm. That was better. She'd come to associate the rhythmic pulse with the little dragon inside falling asleep.

Quinn set the egg on her pillow, patting it once with an outstretched hand. "Must've been a bad dream," she said to herself. She chuckled. "If baby dragons dream, that is."

Making sure the egg had settled and wasn't likely to roll off the bed, Quinn went to the corner on the opposite side of the bed. The golden spear she'd taken from the Crystal Well was propped there. As she reached for it, she stopped. Her right hand tingled with that same pins-and-needles sensation she'd felt so often lately.

Quinn brought her hands together, rubbing her right hand and wrist with her left until the tingling passed. It took almost a full minute for the sensation to fade.

Knowing her friends were waiting for her, Quinn braced herself, reached out with her left hand this time, and gripped the golden wood of the shaft. She half-expected it to zap her with a shock of energy again, especially after the tingling she'd experienced.

Nothing happened.

Realizing she'd been holding her breath, Quinn let herself relax, releasing the air through pursed lips. She left her bedroom and headed for her apartment's front door. She dipped the leaf-shaped head atop the seven-foot weapon to pass beneath the doorframe and pulled the door shut behind her. She made sure it had latched and locked, then walked downstairs.

Minutes later, Quinn stood in Taylor's workroom with her friends. The rough wooden table usually reserved for sending Quinn into the magical virtual reality system was cleared of the VR equipment. In its place lay the golden spear, with the group gathered around it.

"So?" Quinn asked. "What now?"

Everyone turned to look at Miranda, their resident expert on the arcane. The ghost seemed surprised at the sudden shift in attention but gathered herself after a few seconds.

"First, we let Taylor cast the special spells I just walked through with her. We'll use them to identify if this is the source of the wild magic outbreak."

"I guess that means the next move is mine," Taylor said. She grinned. "Here goes nothing."

Reaching out with both hands, fingers splayed out like she was ready to palm a basketball, Taylor began chanting.

The words coming from her friend were unfamiliar to

Quinn. The strange language had a lilting quality to it so that the words sounded like a song.

Taylor's hands started moving in a sort of choreographed dance with her words. Quinn remembered she could see at least some of what her friend was doing. Enabling her arcane sight ability, the visible spectrum took on a new look, its usually crisp outlines now hazy. Everything had an aura around it, each with different colors related to the amount of magical energy contained within it.

Taylor's body emanated a purple glow, with ribbons and threads of multicolored energy flowing from her hands to the air about a foot above the golden spear. The others in the room also had auras now.

Clark and Naomi had bright white nimbuses surrounding them. Naomi's was different from Clark's since dark patches morphed through her aura. It was as if the darkness were trying to dampen the light energy emanating from within her. Quinn wondered if that was the death energy of her vampire self warring with the dominant Hunter powers she'd retained after her transformation.

Miranda's ghostly outline also had faint purple energy around it. It was similar to Taylor's energy signature, though not anywhere near as bright as the living magic Quinn's best friend displayed.

A sudden increase in the volume of Taylor's chants drew Quinn's attention back to the spell and the spear. The tech witch's voice strained to maintain the increased volume as she continued the sing-song progression of words to bolster her magic. The ribbons of energy flowed from her hands, but now the magical power flowed closer to the spear. It closed to about an inch away and stopped as if the twisted ribbons and strands had hit a glass barrier.

"What's wrong?" Quinn asked.

Miranda drifted closer to Taylor. "Keep going. The magic infused into the spear is resisting your spell. Keep pushing. No simple inanimate object should be able to hold off a divination spell like this."

Taylor moved her hands lower and increased the pace of the chant. Beads of sweat glistened on her forehead, and the strain of the casting was evident in every tensed muscle of her rigid form.

Something was wrong. Quinn called, "T, stop. We can do this another way."

Taylor pressed her trembling arms downward until her hands hovered a few inches above the spear. The space between her hands and the spear pulsed with light from the compressed flows. There was still space between the spear and the surrounding magic, though.

Taylor's chanting increased in speed and volume, her voice a continuous groan now. She stared down, eyes wide and unblinking.

"Stop her, Miranda. Tell her," Quinn pleaded.

"Quinn's right, Taylor," the ghost said. "Release the spell. This isn't working."

Taylor kept going.

"She can't hear us," Naomi said. "It's like the spell has taken over."

"No," Clark said. "Not the spell. The spear."

Quinn reached out to grab Taylor's shoulders, but her hands never reached her friend.

Taylor turned her face to Quinn, the chant continuing. Her eyes locked on the Huntress. A flare of light, this one blinding and golden, flashed from her irises, and a wall of force hit Quinn.

The energy caused her to stumble back several steps, and she nearly fell to the floor. Clark and Naomi moved close to reach out for Taylor, too.

Again, Taylor's eyes flashed as she turned her gaze on the new intruders. The flash was even more powerful this time.

Clark and Naomi flew backward, blasted away from the table to slam into the wall on the opposite side of the room.

Quinn recovered her balance and searched for a solution. Taylor's hands still hovered over the spear, energy clearly flowing from the spear into her now. Quinn feared what would happen if Taylor didn't stop the spell.

Miranda shouted at Taylor, her ghostly face an inch from the tech witch's, imploring her to let go and stop the spell. The tech witch ignored the ghost's pleas.

After popping up her HUD, Quinn stared at the icons lining the borders, searching for some ability that might offer a solution. Her eyes kept coming back to the two green and blue bars at the top. The green bar was her stamina, her personal energy stores.

The blue bar was newer. It represented something called mana and was a measure of magical energy. She'd only used it once when she transferred power from the spear to heal Avery. Could it be used here?

Reaching out to the mana bar the same way she did when drawing on her stamina, Quinn siphoned off power and drained the bar until it only had fifty percent remaining. Her whole body tingled now from holding onto the magical force without releasing it in some way.

She still had her arcane sight enabled. A glance at her hands showed a deep blue glow outlining her fingers. Energized by the power, Quinn sensed she had to do something soon, or the energy from her mana stores would dissipate on its own. She could feel it leeching away.

Making a decision, Quinn raced forward and poured every ounce of the drawn power into her outstretched hands as her fingers closed around the butt of the spear. Ignoring the jolt like an electric shock, she yanked it off the table.

As soon as she did, all the power Taylor had built up around it erupted in a backlash that flung the short blonde across the room to crash into a pile of empty metal beer kegs. They flew out like pins struck by a bowling ball. Taylor landed in a crumpled heap on the floor amid the tumbling barrels.

In Quinn's hands, the spear bucked and tugged as if it were alive. She struggled to maintain her hold, discovering she could only do so by drawing off more mana and channeling it into her hands. It was like she wore gloves made of magic fibers that insulated her from the spear's magic.

Realizing it was a losing battle, and that her mana would soon run out, Quinn seized on a desperate idea. She spun in place, gripping the shaft in the center and raised the spear to her shoulder, then flung it at the stone wall by the door.

The weapon flew from her hands, traveling with more energy than her muscles could have provided, gold sparks flaring from it. The spearhead struck the stone wall. Instead of bending or deflecting away from the stone, it embedded deep into the rock. All but an inch of the golden metal sank into the wall.

A few remaining sparks played up and down the shaft for a few seconds, then it settled to stillness, the energy dissipating into the air. Quinn released the rest of the mana she'd drawn from her reserves and forced her tense muscles to relax.

Then she remembered Taylor. Quinn rushed to her friend's body on the floor. A muffled groan from the girl sent a wave of relief through the Huntress.

Quinn rolled her friend onto her back.

Taylor's eyes met Quinn's, and she smiled with a slightly crazed expression on her face. "That was a rush."

"What?" Quinn asked, her voice rising in pitch and volume. "I thought you were dead. You weren't listening. Why wouldn't you stop?"

Taylor sat up and rubbed the back of her hand across her forehead to wipe away sweat. "I guess I couldn't. I mean, I could hear you, sort of, but my body wasn't listening to my mind anymore. It was like the spell took over control."

Miranda floated over. "Wild magic from the spear; that has to be it. This time the flare-up made Taylor's magic go haywire."

Taylor shook her head. "I don't think so, at least not completely."

"What do you mean?" Naomi asked. She and Clark had recovered from being thrown across the room. They clustered with Quinn and Miranda around Taylor lying on the floor.

"I could sense the wild magic. It resisted my attempts to touch it. It wasn't coming from the spear. It felt like it was a layer on top of the spear's magic."

"I don't understand, T," Quinn said. "If the wild magic wasn't coming from the spear, where was it coming from?"

Taylor shrugged. "I don't know. Something the spear had been in contact with, maybe?"

Clark offered, "I wonder if the wild magic came from the Crystal Well? It's possible the spear soaked up some of it while it hung there all those years."

"That's a thought," Naomi said. "Quinn, you talked to the guardian before he died. You were there longer than any of us. Did he say anything about wild magic?"

"No. All Upwood said about the magic of the place was that it was to be used as both a gateway between dimensions and a way to pinpoint incursions from the netherworld. I suppose that would require powerful magic, though. Possibly even wild magic, right?"

"Maybe," Miranda said. "Taylor, you said the wild magic was a layer on top of the spear's inherent magic?"

"That's what it felt like."

Miranda shook her head. "Then I doubt the spear is the source we're looking for. It might have absorbed some of the wild magic, or this might just be another random manifestation of magic gone haywire."

Quinn didn't like the sound of that. "Damn, so we're no closer to an answer than we were when we started. I feel like we need to talk to an expert. Who do you go to when there's an outbreak of wild magic?"

Clark shrugged. "Usually the local Hunter clan would have a house mage steeped in arcane knowledge to deal with the outbreak. They would instruct the Hunters about what needed to be done."

"Well, our mages are tapped out," Quinn said with a glance at Taylor. "What else do we have?"

"I have an idea," Naomi said. "But I'm not sure how we'd pull it off, or even if we want to."

Quinn shrugged. "Don't have another option. What's the idea?"

"We ask a demon."

Clark shook his head. "We can't summon a demon, even for something like this. It's too dangerous."

"Why is a demon something we'd want to bring into this situation?" Quinn asked.

"It's rumored that wild magic was used to imprison the demons in the netherworld long ago. It plays across the boundaries of their prison, and they're intimately acquainted with its power."

Taylor let out a wry chuckle as she sat up. "Too bad we killed all of VirSync's demon-kinder. Those possessed dudes could have answered our questions if we'd captured one. I don't suppose any are left in hiding somewhere?"

Clark shook his head. "We killed them all, or Quinn and Naomi did. It's better we did. It's never a good idea to leave a demon alive, either in possessed form or a real manifestation."

Quinn smiled. "Maybe we can find a way around that problem."

"What are you thinking, Quinn?" Naomi asked. "I don't like that smile. It usually ends up meaning trouble. You heard Clark. No matter how badly we need it, we can't conjure a demon. It's too dangerous."

"I think I have the perfect solution. We won't have to summon a demon, or at least not a new one."

When her friends stared at her with puzzled and concerned expressions, Quinn said, "Trust me. I have a plan."

CHAPTER FIVE

Quinn glanced at Clark as he pulled into a short driveway leading to closed iron gates. It was just after nine at night. A single overhead street lamp illuminated the area around a small unoccupied guard shack. The formerly immaculate landscaping had become overgrown with weeds. They'd stopped beside a card reader sitting on a pole at the same height as Clark's driver's window.

"I still don't like this, Quinn," Clark said.

"Unless you know of another demon we can talk to, this is the only option."

Taylor leaned forward from the back seat, where she sat beside Naomi. "What if Jared isn't down there anymore?"

Quinn shrugged. "We come back up and figure out a new plan. Come on. He's harmless now. Remember, we trapped him inside that magic pedestal. He can't hurt anyone."

Naomi shook her head. "Demons are always capable of

causing harm, Quinn. They can never be trusted, even when you think they're trapped."

"Mom, I promise, this one's as harmless as a demon can get. He's locked inside the stone in the middle of a cavern no one knows about."

Quinn glanced at Naomi, who didn't look convinced. "You'll see."

Clark nodded at the gates. "How do we get inside? I don't feel like climbing the wall."

Taylor handed him a keycard with wires running from it to the laptop on the seat beside her. "Try this. The red light on the swiper is on, so there's power. I think I can hack it."

Clark took the card and checked to see where the magnetic stripe was. He repositioned it, then held the card out the window between his thumb and forefinger and passed it through the reader on the post. A second later, the gate jerked open. It groaned in a way that told them it hadn't been opened in a while. Slowly, it slid to the side until there was room for their car to drive through.

Clark passed the card back over his shoulder, saying, "Lucky."

Taylor smiled. "Nope. Pure skill." She detached the connector holding the wires to the card. "Hold onto it. I left the programmed code in the strip. It should open the doors into the building up there, too." She pointed up the hill at the darkened VirSync building.

The place had been vacant since Quinn and the others had disrupted their operations, stealing their VR technology to stop their plans to let demons into the world.

Weeds had started taking over, growing through the cracks in and around the parking lot. The once-carefully-landscaped and manicured grounds were now overgrown. No one had been here in months.

Clark drove up the circular road off the main parking lot that passed the entrance and switched off the engine, pocketing the keys.

Quinn popped open her door. "Let's go."

The others climbed out and joined her on the sidewalk.

"No lights on," Taylor said, gazing at the empty building. "This isn't creepy."

"Oh, you can't see in the dark," Quinn said. "I didn't think of that. Maybe Clark has a flashlight."

"I'm good. My werewolf side can make do in a pinch, but it's not the same as a real light. Don't worry, I can figure something out." Taylor raised one hand beside her head and traced something in the air. She finished and snapped her fingers. A glowing blue-white orb about the size of a grapefruit hung just above her hand.

"How's that?" she asked.

"That's great," Quinn said. "Your magic is getting better all the time, T. My night vision ability is cool and all when there's no other option, but nobody's around now, and I can see better with that light."

"Let's get this over with," Clark said. He held up the hacked keycard. "The sooner we get in there, the sooner we find out it's not going to work."

Quinn walked past him, snagging the card from his hand as she did. "You don't have any faith in my ideas—until they work out, that is."

Clark grumbled, Taylor laughed, and Naomi shrugged. The vampire leaned in as she passed Clark. "She's not wrong. Come on, let's see what she's got up her sleeve with this trapped demon."

Quinn glanced back as she headed for the front doors. Clark followed at the end of the quartet with his usual grim expression. She decided to let up on him a little. He'd been through a lot, living on his own for so long. He still wasn't used to having a clan around him again. She had to remember that.

Taylor's hacked card worked like a charm, opening the outer doors and both sets of inner doors on the first floor and basement levels they needed to pass through to get to the freight elevator down to the underground caverns.

The building was in a poor state of repair inside, too. There was evidence that looters had been in here and cleaned the place out, probably breaking in via one of the back doors. Light fixtures had been removed; even a few water fountains had been stripped from the hallways. Hopefully, the looters hadn't been able to get into the secured areas. It didn't look like they'd gained access to the basement and the caverns below.

The freight elevator creaked and groaned quite a bit as it descended the dark shaft to the caverns. Quinn hoped it was a question of needing lubrication and nothing else. She wasn't sure how they'd get back up if it broke down. There was no cell service down there.

The descending car finally jerked to an abrupt halt about two feet above the ground at the bottom. Quinn and the others waited to be sure the elevator car had really stopped before they lifted the wire mesh gate and jumped the rest of the way.

Quinn bent down to look under the elevator car and saw that small boulders from a cave-in had rolled into the bottom of the shaft. The car had come to a stop on top of them.

Clark spotted them, too. "I hope that doesn't mean this place is getting ready to cave in."

"Boy," Naomi said. "You're just a joy to be around tonight, aren't you? These caverns look like they've been here forever. We'll be fine. You can stay here to guard the elevator if you don't want to come with Quinn and the rest of us."

"Oh, I'm coming. I'm just a realist," Clark said. "Someone in this group has to be."

Quinn started down the sloping passage, with Taylor right behind her. Memories of coming down here the first time washed over Quinn. They walked past the room where Taylor had laid in a coma all those months ago. A shiver ran down Quinn's spine at the thought of how close things had been. She didn't know what she would have done if she'd lost Taylor that day.

Taylor's floating ball of light did an excellent job of illuminating their way. The old electrical lights strung on cables down the passage weren't all working. About half of them had burned out, leaving broad sections dark.

The pervasive smell of rot and death was the first indicator that they were getting close to the bottom of the passage. Despite her confidence in the plan, the smell forced Quinn's doubts to the surface. She'd seen a lot of dead bodies by this stage in her time as the Huntress. She shouldn't be squeamish. Her return had her stomach in knots by the time she arrived at the end of the tunnel and stood at the opening to the ceremonial cavern.

Taylor stopped beside her, waved a hand in the air, and muttered some words Quinn couldn't make out. The illuminated globe floated into the center of the room and up toward the ceiling, stopping about ten feet off the ground. It brightened, filling the room with blue-white light.

In the center of the large open cavern stood the waist-high stone pedestal. Covering the floor in all directions for at least ten feet lay the partially desiccated bodies of the former VirSync VR candidates. The memory of fighting them as they reanimated into zombies shook her. She'd been friends with some of them.

Taylor said, "Okay, now what?"

"I don't know exactly," Quinn replied. She could feel her friends' eyes upon her. "Look, you knew a certain amount of this was going to be improvisation. We don't even know if Jared's demon soul is still trapped in there."

"He hasn't acknowledged our presence," Taylor said. "Maybe you're right and he's gone."

Naomi pointed at the floor of the tunnel in which they stood. "Or, he can't sense anything outside the room in which that rock stands. Look, the floor in there is worked and flattened to form a disk around the pedestal."

They could stand here arguing the how and why all night, but Quinn needed answers now. She took a deep breath and stepped into the room. When nothing happened, she turned and looked at her friends, shrugging.

She jumped when Jared's voice boomed across the cavern.

"I knew you'd be back, Quinn. I told you that when you left the last time."

"How's life in the pedestal, Jared?" Quinn asked. "Everything you dreamed of and more?"

Jared let out a cackling laugh with a hint of insanity in it. "I have spent my time awaiting the one who might set me free. I was surprised it is you who's come to do so."

"I'm not here to set you free, Jared. I have come with questions for you."

Another brief burst of laughter was followed by, "I have no desire to answer any of your questions, girl."

Clark stepped over the line into the room and moved to stand beside Quinn. Naomi and Taylor joined him.

"We know how this has to work, demon," Clark said. "You'll answer our questions, or we'll go and seek out information elsewhere."

"Quinn," Jared replied. "You brought your friends. How delicious. It doesn't matter, though. Unless you have something to give me, or better yet, plan on setting me free, I don't think I want to play along with your little game."

Quinn searched for something she might use in trade for what Jared could tell them. She glanced at her friends, shaking her head.

Naomi spoke up. "Demon, I heard what happened to you. Quinn didn't banish your soul into this chamber for all time. Others were involved. Perhaps you'd like to know their fates."

For a few seconds, there was no answer. Then Jared said, "I suppose it might be nice to know if they met a fate worse than my own. Perhaps a trade, then. A question for a question?"

Quinn smiled and nodded a thank you to her mother. "That is acceptable, but we go first."

"Very well, ask your first question. Make it good. I bore easily."

Quinn paused, searching for the answer they needed to know more than any other. She couldn't just ask for random information on wild magic.

Taylor came to the rescue. "There's an outbreak of wild magic in the city."

Jared replied, "I sensed a taint of it on you when you entered. What is your question?"

"We seek its source. What is the best way to track down wild magic so we can contain it?"

"Your smart little friend seems to be misinformed, Quinn," Jared said. "Wild magic must run its course once released unless the source decides to rein it in. It won't be contained."

"That's ridiculous," Quinn said. "How can a spear rein anything in?"

"Oh, no, you don't," Jared replied. "That's a second question. It's my turn."

"Fine, ask your question."

"You said something about Myles Hickman and the demon-kinder he created. I know you killed some here when you escaped that first time. What happened to Myles and the others? I hope it was painful."

Quinn suppressed a shudder at the bloodthirsty anticipation in the demon's tone. "We defeated them. I don't know what you want to hear. They're all dead, including John Handon and his cabal of vampires."

"That's no way to tell a tale, girl. Your friends must

consider you boring as hell. What really happened? I want all the details."

Quinn smiled. "As you pointed out a minute ago, that is another question. My turn."

"Oh, hellspawn, you're going to drag this out for the entire night at this rate. I tire of this game."

Quinn shook her head. "You made the rules. If you're more forthcoming, I could give you the details since I killed them all or watched them die at the hands of others. It's up to you."

"That's a little better," Jared said. "Ask your next question."

Taylor said, "You said the magic must be held back by its source. In our case, that source is a golden spear used to activate the Crystal Well. It's not alive, so it can't rein in the wild magic."

"It's simple, child. Wild magic is the oldest of the magics. It dates back to the chaos that predates the formation of the universe. It was contained by the only one who could when the creator brought order to things. Specific ancient races can harness the trapped wild magic. It's only released during times of great stress or life change, such as death. Has anyone important in the supernatural world died lately?"

Quinn glanced at Clark and Naomi. Both shrugged, and Quinn said, "No, not to our knowledge."

"All right," Jared said. "You promised me details. I want them, and don't leave a single scream or spurt of blood out of it."

"You didn't help us with anything," Taylor said. "Don't give him what he wants, Quinn."

"An agreement was made with you, Huntress. You must abide by it."

The last thing Quinn wanted was to relive the near-death experiences she'd had fighting John Handon, Myles Hickman, and all the others. However, she'd made this bargain. The only way she'd discover anything else was to give Jared what he wanted, no matter how many nightmares returned to disrupt her sleep.

The more she dredged up the old memories, the angrier she got at herself for letting the demon manipulate her into this. It was like he'd known the effect it would have on her. Quinn's arms started trembling as she clenched her fists. She thought over the battles in her mind.

"I'm waiting, Quinn. Tell me every juicy, bloody moment. I want the gore, all of it."

Quinn took a step toward the pedestal, raising her hand with her forefinger pointing at the pedestal. "You want gore, you filthy demon, you've got it."

She never got any farther. The earthquake stopped her and everything else in the cavern. The shaking quickly became so violent that it knocked everyone from their feet. Rocks broke free from the ceiling, railing down on those below.

Jared shouted, "You brought it with you, you foolish humans. You'll destroy us all."

"What are you talking about?" Quinn yelled over the rumbling. "We came alone."

"I can sense it. One of you carries the taint, and it's set off a new wave here in the—"

Jared's voice cut off as a colossal boulder broke free of

the ceiling and crashed to the cavern floor, crushing the pedestal into fist-sized rocks and dust.

"We have to get out of here," Clark called. He'd crawled back to the cavern's entrance. "It might be localized to this part of the caves."

Quinn nodded and started crawling toward the tunnel leading back to the elevator. She didn't want to think about what this earthquake might be doing to their only route back to the surface. There was no way she and the others could climb that shaft to the basement.

She was the last of the group to reach the relative safety of the tunnel. The shaking was less here, but as Quinn crawled into the passage, the rock changed beneath her. The unyielding surface of stone had taken on the consistency of a mattress.

"What the..." Quinn got to her knees and probed the floor with her fingertips.

Clark bent down and pushed the soft tunnel floor. "Don't stop to worry about it. We have to get out of here."

"I don't think they're going to let us," Taylor said.

"What are you talking about?" Quinn asked. She followed Taylor's pointing finger back up the winding tunnel. Four man-shaped figures rose from the passage floor, their skin the same color as the surrounding stone.

"Rock elementals," Naomi shouted. She drew her sword and charged at the nearest of the four creatures. "We must kill them before they mature and their skin hardens."

Quinn stood and drew her Bowie. The rumbling had let up, but a new threat stood between them and the surface. Quinn raced after her mother, with Clark behind her. Taylor started chanting as she readied a spell.

Quinn led with her blade, slashing at the creature closest to her. She expected there to be nothing but sparks when the edge struck the elemental's skin. Instead, the knife opened a long gash, and a muddy brown liquid oozed from the wound.

The beast howled in pain and reached out to pull Quinn into a giant bearhug. She didn't have to know anything about fighting elementals to understand that embrace would be the end of her.

She danced back, evading the outstretched arms and scoring two more attacks, one on each arm while she dodged.

The skin seemed like softened clay, not stone, but she knew her mother was probably right about what would happen if they allowed that skin to harden. Quinn dove back in, launching another attack, working as quickly as she could. She had to kill this thing fast.

She scored another hit and danced away, dodging the clutching arms once again.

"Duck!"

When Taylor's shout registered, Quinn dove for the floor, landing beside Naomi and Clark. Ice-cold wind rushed over them.

The magically chilled air struck the elementals, and ice crystals started to form instantly. The sudden layer of frost cracked the flash-frozen skin and slowed the elementals almost to a standstill.

"It worked!" Taylor exclaimed. "Quick, get past them. We can make a run for the elevator."

Before Quinn could get up, Taylor darted past her, weaving between the frozen elementals while laughing at her magic's effect. Quinn smiled and ran after her, followed by Naomi and Clark.

The four of them dove into the elevator when they reached it. Quinn sighed with relief as the car jerked upward, rising back to the surface. They'd made it out.

CHAPTER SIX

Quinn let the double glass doors shut behind her as she left the VirSync building with the others. "I hope that boulder destroyed Jared's demon soul along with the pedestal. I'd hate to think of him roaming around now, looking for a new host."

"We should be rid of him," Clark said. "Usually, when a magical locus for a spirit is destroyed, the spirit within is also destroyed."

"'Usually' doesn't fill me with confidence," Quinn replied. "We don't need another random piece of evil roaming around right now."

"Clark's right," Naomi said. "The demon is gone. Even if he was somehow freed, he'd need someone to inhabit to move on before his energy fades. That's not going to happen any time soon, with those lurking elementals down there."

They all got into the car, and Clark started driving home.

Quinn was quiet for a few minutes, trying to make

sense of what little they'd learned from Jared. He'd said the wild magic was focused on or around a few ancient races. The more she thought about it, the surer she was she had an answer.

"I think I know who's responsible for the attacks," Quinn told them.

"Who?" Taylor asked. "Jared didn't give us a lot to go on before everything fell apart down there."

"Think about it. He mentioned ancient races. That has to be the Fae, right? I think this is Filippa's way of getting back at us for screwing up her plan to control the Crystal Well."

Naomi shook her head. "I know you think she's the root of all the evil in the world, but we have no indication this is a result of Fae magic."

"Filippa wasn't down in that cavern with us, Quinn," Clark said. "The only person who has all the incidents in common is you."

"Me? You think *I'm* doing this?"

"Not doing it," Clark replied. "Hear me out. I'm not blaming you. I'm trying to understand what's in play here. Something about you is triggering these events. You might not even be aware of it."

"Clark's right," Naomi agreed. "What were you doing or thinking about right before the tremors started down there?"

Quinn fought down her objections to this line of questioning. There was a logic to their thoughts she couldn't deny. She went back in her mind to when they were down in the cavern. What had she been thinking about when the earthquake began?

"I guess I was angry at Jared for making me remember the fighting that defeated Handon and the others. I didn't want to go there, but Jared forced me to."

Clark glanced over his shoulder at Naomi. "What do you think? Would that be enough?"

"Maybe. None of us knows enough about the subject to be sure. We just lost the best resource we had on wild magic, so we need to go back to square one. What was it the demon said about the spear?"

Taylor said, "He said it couldn't be the source of the outbreak, even though the evidence points to it."

Clark shook his head. "I can't shake the feeling we're missing something. I don't know what. We need to start from scratch and throw out any suppositions we have. Maybe then we'll see what we've overlooked."

Quinn didn't respond. Everyone had thought she was obsessed with what Filippa was up to until Quinn had uncovered evidence that the Fae princess was behind something, which had happened more than once. She'd have to keep her mouth shut until she unearthed the proof she needed.

It was late, and the group fell into silence for the rest of the drive. When Clark finally pulled into the alley outside O'Malley's, they got out, lost in their thoughts. Quinn wanted to get some sleep and planned on going straight up to her apartment once she got inside.

They all walked down the steps and entered the entryway for the club. The thumping rhythm section of the night's country-western band filled the tiny foyer, even with the doors closed.

Jonas, the giant who acted at the bouncer for the bar,

nodded at them. "Quinn, someone's here to see you? They're waiting at the bar."

"Who is it?"

"You should see for yourself. I don't want to be the bearer of bad tidings. It makes me grumpy."

"You big baby," Taylor said. "Come on, Quinn. It can't be that bad. Jonas would never let anyone dangerous into the bar."

Quinn let Taylor tug her along by the elbow. The music washed over her. The place was jumping, and the area between them and the bar was filled with patrons, many of them dancing to the current song.

Quinn and Taylor worked their way through the crowd. Clark and Naomi were right behind them.

The mass of people finally thinned enough for Quinn to see the bar. She knew right away which one Jonas referred to. The tall, thin woman wore some sort of riding outfit, complete with a crop tucked under one arm. She sat atop one of the barstools, sipping a frozen cocktail.

Filippa spotted Quinn at the same time Quinn spotted her. A big grin spread across her face, and she raised her drink in a toast.

"Aw, hell no!" Quinn exclaimed. She turned and glared at Clark and Naomi. "One of these times, you're going to listen to me when I tell you my hunches. We'd have avoided a whole host of problems over the last year if you'd done that."

Clark shook his head. "Let's hear what she has to say."

Quinn's jaw dropped.

Clark held up a hand to stop her from responding further. "I'm not disagreeing with you, but now that she's here, let's play this smart and see if we can find out what she's up to."

Quinn grimaced. "That's kind of like a doctor telling someone to just let cancer run its course. You know that?"

"O'Malley's is neutral ground, Quinn," Naomi reminded her. "You can't attack her here, and she can't do anything to you. Clark's right. We need to know what she wants."

Quinn glared at the Fae princess, who sat beaming at her across the room. She had to see the expression on Quinn's face, but she didn't seem to care. That woman's smug self-assurance was one of the things Quinn hated the most.

Shaking off Clark's hand on her shoulder, Quinn strode over to Filippa. She could feel Clark and Naomi following, ready to stop her from doing anything that would violate O'Malley's neutrality.

"Quinn, darling, it's so good to see you. You look so much better than the last time I saw you."

Quinn forced a half-grin onto her face and said through gritted teeth, "Considering a room full of cultists and vampires was trying to kill me at the time, I'm not surprised I look better. It's a shame a spare blade didn't slip and slash out in your direction."

"My, my, you're not still carrying a grudge about that, are you?" Filippa took a long sip from her drink and set it down on the bar. "I was in no position to intervene. Had I tried, they would have killed me for sure. Besides, you obviously had everything in hand. Look, you and Clark survived, and you were reunited with your mother, too. I'd call that a win."

Quinn realized she wasn't going to catch the princess in

an admission of guilt. She wasn't sure what good it would do if she did.

"What do you want, Filippa? You came out from under your rock for something. What was it?"

"Why, to come see you, of course. I would have thought that was plain. Why else would I have come here?"

"All right," Quinn said. "You've seen me. Now leave."

Clark stepped forward. "Quinn, rudeness won't solve anything." He turned to Filippa. "If you have something to say to us, let's have it. We have urgent business to tend to."

"Is it about the wild magic that's broken loose? I can help you with that."

Quinn had had enough. "Of course you can. You're behind it, just like you were behind Gemma coming here to try to run me out of town."

"Gemma? Gemma Beckingsly? I haven't seen or talked to her for a few years. I used to help her out from time to time following the purges. I did the same for Clark. It was the least I could do, considering everything that happened to the clans. Gemma and I had a falling out, though. Why, what has she been up to?"

"We know you were behind it, Filippa," Quinn said. "Aurora filled us in on your desire to find the Crystal Well."

Filippa waved a hand in the air. "My cousin talks too much, though she is right. I've been searching for the Well's location for years. I dropped that particular passion project recently for more pressing matters, though. Don't tell me you located it?"

Quinn let out an exasperated groan. "Agh, I can't talk to her anymore." She turned away from the princess and crossed her arms.

"My, my, Clark, she *does* have a flair for the dramatic. I came to offer my help. Rumblings of a wild magic outbreak are rippling throughout the world. Several of my royal cousins have asked me to come here and look into it. Based upon Quinn's reaction, you people have not had much luck locating the source."

"You're correct," Clark agreed. "We had a source of information, but it fell through before we got the answers we need."

"Then you need me," Filippa explained. "I have a way to determine the source so you can isolate it and control it until it dissipates. It's far too dangerous, given the current state of things."

Taylor asked, "What do you want in return? You don't strike me as the kind of person who does anything for free."

"The ritual you'll have to perform is difficult, though your little clan here has the necessary talents to pull it off. If it's successful, I'll ask a small favor of Quinn."

Quinn spun. "I don't want to owe you anything. I won't be beholden to you so you can hold it over me later on."

"What I want is quite simple. I'll tell you what it is upfront if that's what you want."

Quinn nodded. "Good, tell me. Then I'll tell you if we want your help."

Filippa smiled, her pearly, iridescent teeth showed for a second, making it look more menacing than friendly. "It's simple, Quinn, my dear. I want you to promise to come to me first when the time comes to imprint the dragon egg when your year is up. Promise to do that, and I'll help you find the source of the wild magic."

JAMIE DAVIS

Quinn started to refuse reflexively, but Clark stopped her. "We can live with that. Aurora can do what she needs to do to get it back from you if she wants it badly enough."

"Clark, we told Aurora we'd offer it back to her," Quinn reminded him. "We can't go back on that."

"She shouldn't have put us in the middle of a Fae custody battle." Clark turned back to Filippa. "How long have the two of you been passing that thing back and forth?"

"Oh, it has to be several centuries now. We've both possessed it many times at this point. If my cousin wants it back, she has her own ways of accomplishing the task without involving you."

Clark nodded. "Then we have a deal. Help us nail down the source of the wild magic outbreak, and we'll give you first dibs on the egg a few months from now when Quinn's year is up."

"Excellent." Filippa grinned and nodded as if ticking off a box on a to-do list in her mind. She slid off the barstool, then gave a little wave with the raised fingers of one hand. "I have some errands to run. I left my phone number with Juni. Contact me when you're ready to begin. I'll start making arrangements to acquire what we need."

The princess left her spot at the bar and walked toward the exit as she sketched a simple rune in the air with a finger. The crowd parted as if they'd choreographed it beforehand, allowing her a direct route to the door. None of the patrons even glanced her way.

As soon as she left the club, Quinn turned to Clark. "The egg's not yours to bargain with. That was my decision to make."

66

"Quinn," Taylor asked, "what's the big deal? You were just holding the egg for Aurora anyway. Let the Fae royals battle it out. We're better off without it."

Naomi had been staring at Quinn for some time now. Quinn sensed her mother's eyes on her and said, "What's your problem, Mother? Why don't you pile on me like the rest of them?"

"No one's piling on you, Quinn. There's something you're not telling us, though. Why have you become so attached to the dragon egg? I know it's rare even to see one, but let's face it, they're just pretty rocks until they're ready to hatch. There hasn't been a new dragon born in a century, maybe more."

Quinn started to answer and stopped. She didn't know what to tell them. One thing was sure: her dragon egg was not just a pretty rock. The dragon inside was pretty animated for a baby in a shell. Realizing everyone was waiting for an answer, she explained, "I've become attached to it. It's nice to have around."

Taylor laughed. "You don't talk to it like a plant, do you?"

As Quinn felt the heat rising in her face, Taylor spotted her blushing and blurted, "You *do*! Oh, Quinn, sometimes I think you missed out when none of your foster families got you a dog growing up."

"Sometimes it's nice to talk things through," Quinn said, realizing this was a way out of the conversation. "It's not like I take both sides of the conversation or anything."

Naomi smiled. "Well, I suppose that's good. Do let us know if you start hearing dragon voices answering you."

"I'll make sure to do that." Quinn pulled out her phone

and glanced at the screen. "It's late, and tomorrow's a training day. I need to get some sleep. Can we talk more about how to handle Filippa in the morning?"

"That'll work," Clark agreed. "We also need to mull over what little information we got from Jared tonight. We know the source isn't the spear, so if we can localize it ourselves, we don't have to use Filippa's help."

"I like that option best," Quinn said. "See you all in the morning."

The others waved. Quinn headed for the stairs up to her apartment above the club. As late as it was, she realized she had too much swirling through her mind to go right to sleep. Maybe talking things through with the egg would help her them out so she could get some rest.

She smiled as she thought about the dragon egg. Holding it always settled her mind and gave her a sense of well-being. There was no way she was giving that up to a conniving Fae princess, no matter which one it was.

CHAPTER SEVEN

Quinn woke up the next morning to the warm, soothing vibration of the egg against her back. She imagined the tiny dragon inside snoring while asleep, generating the gentle trembling transmitted through the shell.

She rolled over and laid her hand on the egg. "Morning, you. Did you have a good sleep?"

The smooth vibration stopped, then the egg gently trembled once and went still.

"Good. I did, too, thanks to you. At least I won't be tired for this morning's training exercise. Clark and Mom are probably going to blast me with something hard since I've been off for a few days."

The egg vibrated twice.

"You don't think so? I hope you're right." She glanced at the phone on the nightstand. She still had time to get some breakfast.

Quinn stood up and looked down at the egg. "You want

to come out and watch me eat, or do you want to go back to sleep?"

A double vibration brought a chuckle from Quinn. "I don't blame you. I'd want to sleep in, too. Okay, I'll see you when I get back later. Sleep tight."

She knew the responses were probably all in her imagination. How could the tiny thing in there even hear her through the thick shell? It was probably just a random series of ordinary movements she was putting voice to.

Quinn shook her head. She didn't care. As far as she was concerned, the little creature inside was listening to every word she said. Padding out to the living room and kitchen in her bare feet, Quinn fired up the coffee maker and got her first mug going while she tried to decide what she wanted to eat.

She still had cereal and milk, and a few hard-boiled eggs from the batch Paddy's cook had made for her a few days ago. She decided to have one of the eggs right now and shove a couple of protein bars into her pocket to snack on during rest breaks.

Having figured out her breakfast, Quinn went back into her room with her mug to get showered and dress for the day's activities. Fifteen minutes later, she started downstairs with a peeled egg in one hand and a cup of coffee number two in the other.

The crowd in the club at 8:30 in the morning surprised her, then she recognized several faces from the other day when everyone came to ask her for help.

Juni walked by, and Quinn stopped her. "What's up with all the people? Did something happen again?"

"No, but Da told them he'd fire up a new breakfast

menu if they came back every day. I told him he was crazy, but once again he's proved me wrong."

Quinn laughed. "I'm learning that parents can be pretty annoying when they're right. Speaking of which, have you seen Naomi this morning?"

"She was here when I got in earlier, but she left. The sun's out now, so I figured she'd gone to sleep or whatever it is vamps do in the daytime."

"I don't think they really sleep. I know she's not this morning. She and Clark have another training day ready for me."

Juni shook her head. "I don't know how you do that day in and day out. I don't mind a bit of sport, but you're going like you're prepping for the Olympics."

"This is where Clark would say something prophetic like 'there's no second place in a fight to the death.' To be honest, though, I don't mind it, even though I complain about it. I've always liked being active, and I was at my best when I was training for whatever sport I was playing. This is kind of like that."

"Whatever suits you." A table nearby called for the waitress. Juni smiled and nodded at them. "I gotta go. I hope it's not too bad."

Quinn smiled as the leprechaun left to tend to the customers. It was nice to have a group of friends and a place to call home that was really hers.

Her phone buzzed in her back pocket, and she pulled it out. It was a text from Clark.

Quinn slid the phone back into her pocket, popped the last bite of egg in her mouth, and headed for the storeroom door. She wasn't going to complain if she didn't have to start the day's workout right away. Whatever they had going on with Taylor would take up at least half an hour of training time.

A few minutes later, Quinn opened the door to Taylor's domain and stopped when her eyes landed on an unwanted visitor.

Filippa stood in the center of the room with Clark and Naomi. Taylor and Miranda were back by the computer rig.

"What is she doing here?"

Filippa smiled and said, "Clark called and invited me. He wanted me to take a look at the spear you found and see if I could use it to find the source of wild magic since it was connected in some way."

"And?" Quinn asked.

Clark shook his head. "The answer is no."

"Not exactly, Clark darling. The full answer is, the spear only links to the source in a tangential way. I'm not sure I can use it to track directly back over the link."

"So, like I said, no," Clark said.

Filippa shrugged. "Potato, potahto."

"So, why did you need me?" Quinn asked.

"Because," Naomi explained, "Filippa thinks since you're the one tied to the spear, she might be able to use you to track down the source."

"Me? I don't have anything to do with all this, other than that it seems to be following me around."

"Exactly, my dear," Filippa agreed. "The wild magic has somehow linked itself to you like it has the spear. It might be because of your tie to the spear. It also might be something else. Either way, if we can track that link, we'll have found our source."

"We thought the source might somehow be linked to a Fae," Quinn said. "You wouldn't know anything about that, would you?"

"Why would you think it's one of us?"

"Another source told us the wild magic is linked to a few of the old races. He seemed to think that would be a place to start looking for the source."

"We stopped playing around with wild magic millennia ago, my dear." She waved her hand. "Far too dangerous and unpredictable for anything needing a reliable solution. No Fae I know has so much as dabbled in it for centuries."

Quinn didn't believe her; she still thought Filippa was playing them. That woman knew exactly who was behind all of this, she was sure.

"Filippa," Clark said, "what do you need from us to get this spell set up?"

"I need Quinn to go get the spear where it's stuck in the wall and bring it to the center of the room. Then your little techy-mage friend should come over."

"I'm a tech witch," Taylor corrected as she stood and walked to the center of the room.

"Of course you are," Filippa replied.

Quinn wanted to smack the condescending grin off the woman's face. Naomi must have spotted her daughter tensing up because she stepped between Quinn and the princess.

"Quinn, bring the spear so we can get this over with. Then Filippa can go about her day."

"I don't know what makes you think I can pull that thing out of solid stone."

"You're the only one with both the link and the strength, of course," Filippa explained. "I'd have thought that would be obvious, even to you."

Grumbling under her breath, Quinn walked to the corner and grasped the spear. Despite being in this cold basement room all night, the shaft was warm to the touch. She tensed against what she expected to be a spear stuck in stone, but to her surprise, the gold blade slid out of the rock easily.

Quinn returned to the center of the room, ignoring Filippa's know-it-all expression.

Taylor took a position opposite Quinn, then directed Filippa to move until she was opposite Clark. They stood at four points around a loose circle.

"Taylor," Filippa said. "I'll start the magic flow, but you'll direct it like I just told you. Focus your attention on the spear. I'll do the same with Quinn. The goal is to highlight any magical link between the two. Then we should be able to follow that link back to the source of the magic."

Taylor nodded, and Filippa started chanting in a sing-songy language Quinn assumed was Fae. Taylor joined in with her own chant, though hers sounded like Latin, providing a sort of rhythmic counterpoint to the princess' spell.

In Quinn's hands, the spear vibrated and began glowing with a soft golden light. As the spell progressed, the nimbus of light expanded to outline Quinn's hands and forearms.

There was a flash, and Quinn found herself back in her

apartment. For a second, she thought she'd been somehow teleported there, but then she realized this was a vision of some sort. Her view of the room had a golden haze overlaying it.

A voice behind her made her jump, and she turned toward it. She saw herself standing beside the window in her living room, staring at the alley below. Quinn knew what she saw. This was the day Avery left for the airport. An invisible force sucked her into her other self to participate as a sort of passive observer.

Avery came up from behind and wrapped her arms around Quinn's waist and let her chin rest on her shoulder. "If everything goes as planned, I won't be that long."

"I know," Quinn said. "But I'd hoped for one more day."

"One day or a hundred, the sooner I go, the sooner I'll be able to return." Avery let go, walking to where the golden spear was propped against the wall. She reached out and brushed her fingertips down the smooth shaft.

Quinn shifted her gaze from Avery to the dragon egg, which was perched atop a pillow on the chair. The golden spear rested against the wall beside the chair. She chuckled. "I seem to be gathering quite the collection of rare and magical artifacts."

Avery laughed. "Just be careful. There are legends about what happens when items of great power get too close to each other. You wouldn't want an explosion of arcane energy on your hands."

"Yeah," Quinn agreed, laughing. "Don't want to cross the streams and all that nonsense. Don't worry, the egg isn't mine. I'm only watching it for a little while longer.

Soon enough, it'll be going back to Aurora, where it belongs."

Quinn from the past stared at the egg for a few seconds and then said, "I guess it's time to go. Come on. At least I can ride with you to the airport. You'd better keep in touch while you're over there. Tell me if you run into any trouble, and we'll gather the troops."

"I'll be fine," Avery said, starting for the door. "Let's go. The others are waiting."

Quinn nodded and followed Avery out of the apartment. Quinn's past self let her anger manifest in slamming the door a little too hard. The impact jolted spirit Quinn back into the center of the now-empty room.

The slamming door jarred the room a little. Against the wall, the spear slid down to bump the chair beside it.

On the way to the floor, the spear's blade kissed the dragon egg's shell. It wasn't much, but it turned out to be enough. Gold light flared in the darkened apartment, transferring from the blade in a cascade of sparks that surrounded the shell. Quinn, inside the spell's vision, shielded her eyes from the burst of light.

The exchange between the spear and the egg only lasted a second before the shaft rolled off and clattered to the floor.

On the pillow, the egg rocked violently for nearly thirty seconds while golden sparks shot across its surface. Then the energy dissipated, darkening the room again as the egg settled to stillness.

Quinn tried to walk over and check on the egg, but she couldn't move from where she stood. Then the golden haze around her coalesced into a thick mist, and she found herself back inside the workshop.

She looked up and realized everyone stared at her, varying levels of shock registering on their faces. Quinn glanced down, and her jaw dropped. Golden light outlined her.

Taylor stopped chanting when Filippa did. Their spell ended, and the magic around Quinn faded after a few seconds.

"Well, well, this is a surprise," Filippa remarked, staring at Quinn.

The Huntress shook her head. "I don't know what you're thinking, but I'm sure it's not what it looks like."

"It looks like you're the source of the wild magic, darling," Filippa told her. "That's a problem because channeling it should kill an ordinary human."

"Filippa," Clark said, "you're talking in riddles. For once, say what you're thinking in plain language."

"Very well. Your little protege here has somehow opened a connection to wild magic. If we don't break the connection or find her a way to control it, sooner or later, she'll destroy herself and take down everything and everyone around her for miles in every direction."

"Well, that's not ominous-sounding," Taylor commented. "What do we need to do to break the connection?"

Filippa said, "We must destroy the source to do that. During the spell, Quinn, did anything lead you to understand where you came in contact with wild magic?"

Quinn's mind whirled back to her vision. She realized

what they'd have to do if she told the truth, and she had to protect the egg at all costs.

Looking at her friends, she shrugged. "I have no idea. I guess we'll have to go for option two. How do I train to control wild magic?"

Filippa fixed Quinn with the evilest grin she'd ever seen. "I have no idea. You see, my dear, no human has ever survived the process."

CHAPTER EIGHT

Quinn stared out the window at the trees and farm fields passing by. Clark drove along the interstate through the countryside an hour west of Baltimore. The address Filippa had given them the night before came up as a property along a lake in western Maryland.

"You ever been out here?" Quinn asked.

Clark shook his head. "No, not to this location. I've driven past this lake on my way to West Virginia, but I never stopped there."

Quinn's anxiety had kicked in early that morning as they loaded up and left the city. She'd been raised in an urban setting, so she had little experience approaching a rural or wilderness area.

Filippa had offered little information when she'd texted the address to them following her departure the night before. All she'd said was that it was the home of someone who might help her learn to control the wild magic. The Fae princess said she'd meet them there in the morning.

"I don't trust her, Clark. She's been trying to get rid of

me for a while now. What's to stop her from staging an ambush out here in the middle of nowhere?"

"It's not her style to be directly involved in anything as messy as a murder. People know she led us here. I think that makes it safe to come out and see what we can learn. If something changes, I'll warn you."

When she didn't respond, Clark glanced her way. "Don't take what Filippa said last night seriously. She was trying to break your self-confidence. She might not be the type to kill you outright, but if you die during the rigorous training, that's another matter entirely. You have to trust yourself and your skills to handle this. If she gets into your head, you lose."

"Easy for you to say. You're not the one who's head is on the chopping block of potential failure."

Clark grunted. "Why don't you tell me what you wouldn't tell Filippa last night? I know you hid something when she asked you what you had learned during the spell."

How did he know? Quinn had always considered herself pretty good at hiding her feelings. It was a necessary survival trait the times she'd lived on the streets. You had to keep everything to yourself.

Clark waited, and when she didn't answer, he said, "Suit yourself. I suspected it last night, and the way you reacted, including your refusal to answer me, confirms my suspicions."

Quinn remained silent, struggling to decide whether she should share what she'd seen in her vision.

"Suit yourself," Clark repeated. "If you think it's best to

keep silent for now, I respect that. But you should apply that determination to your confidence in handling whatever Filippa has planned for you out here. I've seen you find a way out of many impossible situations, so I know you can handle a little Fae deceit. Trust yourself, and you'll be fine."

"How much farther?" Quinn asked to change the subject.

"About a half-hour. I figured we'd stop and get something to eat at a rest area close to the interstate before we head into the backcountry."

"That works. I could eat something."

Clark laughed. "I've never known you *not* to be hungry. Hunters all burn a lot of calories, but you take it to a whole new level."

"I'm a growing girl," Quinn replied. "Every new ability draws more energy when I use it. I gotta replenish somehow."

Clark smiled and flipped on his turn signal to get off at the next exit. The sign showed several fast food places and gas stations.

Twenty minutes later, they were back on the road, driving away from the interstate highway on a county road. Quinn finished the final bite of her foot-long Italian sub and took a sip of her soda.

She tucked the wrapper into an empty bag and held it up for Clark. "Any trash?"

"Yeah, here." He handed her his empty burger wrapper. "We're almost there, according to my phone. There should be a lane somewhere up ahead on the right."

"I've seen signs for the lake but no water yet."

"I think it's through that forested area, hidden from view. Take a look at the map on your phone."

Quinn pulled it up and saw that Clark was correct. She followed their dot down the road. A right turn down an unnamed road showed about a quarter-mile ahead.

"It should be the next right."

"I see it." Clark slowed and turned onto a gravel road passing through the thick trees lining the main road. "The app says our destination is a half-mile ahead. You ready?"

Quinn forced a smile onto her face and nodded. The food had helped her mood, but she had lingering doubts.

The gravel lane ended at a small cabin amid a cluster of pine trees. Beyond the trees lay the shores of what must be the lake. Clark parked by the cabin and got out.

Quinn climbed out of the passenger side and looked around. No other cars anywhere in sight. "We must be the first ones here."

"I wouldn't count on it," Clark said. He gestured to the cabin. A thin plume of smoke rose from the metal stovepipe poking through the wood-shingled roof.

Quinn shrugged and walked over to the small porch, stepping up to the front door. She raised a hand to knock, but the door swung open before she could rap on it.

"You two made good time," Filippa said. She wore jeans, a cream turtleneck, and a puffy down vest. She held a tin mug with steam wafting off the top. Quinn could smell fresh breakfast tea.

"Where's your car?"

"I had Alistair drop me off before tending to another errand I had for him. He'll be back before lunch."

"Is your magic teacher inside?" Quinn asked, peering

past Filippa. All she could see was a rustic wooden table and four chairs beside a black metal cookstove.

"He went down to the lake to catch something for us for lunch. He should be back soon. In fact, let's go down to the shore to meet him."

Filippa stepped onto the porch and pulled the cabin door closed. Quinn and Clark followed her down to the lake's edge. The deep blue waters stretched out, with gentle waves lapping the shore.

The distant treetops of the far shore peeked through the mist rising from the water. The sun hadn't burned through the haze overhead yet.

A bulge of water in the middle of the lake drew Quinn's eyes. They widened as the surge of water started in their direction. Something huge moved just under the surface, pushing a wave ahead of it toward the shore.

Quinn took a step back and reached for her Bowie. Clark laid a hand on her wrist.

He said, "Easy does it. This makes sense now."

"What does?"

"You'll see."

Filippa's satisfied grin widened.

Quinn wondered what the two of them weren't telling her. Clark didn't seem scared, so she took her cue from him and tried to assume a relaxed pose as the bulging wave approached.

That lasted all of two seconds until an enormous reptilian head rose from the water. A long curved neck covered in smooth blue scales arched down into the water. As the creature drew closer, the body became visible through the water.

The creature, bigger than a small delivery van, walked onto the shore supported by four short legs ending in webbed claws. A long tail with a double fin at the end emerged from the lake last.

Filippa nodded at the creature and gestured at Quinn and Clark. "Gil, this is the girl I was telling you about. The other one is called Clark. She's his ward."

Quinn bristled at the description but didn't get a chance to say anything. In two seconds, the giant reptile shrank and shifted into a man about five and a half feet tall. He had shoulder-length white hair surrounding his mostly bald head. A slightly pointed ear poked out from the hair on one side. He carried a length of rope from which hung three large fish.

He studied Quinn for a second before saying, "So, you think you can learn to deal with wild magic?"

"I do," Quinn replied.

He nodded as if she'd given the correct answer. "We'll see, we'll see. Come on up to the cabin so I can get these ready for frying. While I'm at it, you and your gruff friend can try to convince me why I should take you on as a pupil."

Gil marched toward the cabin, Filippa by his side as the two of them chatted quietly about something to do with the fish.

Quinn turned to Clark. "What was that?"

"He's a lake dragon. I didn't know there was one out here, but apparently there is."

"What's a lake dragon?"

"I'm not sure of the lore," Clark said. "I know you've

heard of them, just not by that name. You know, like the Loch Ness Monster, or the Brosno Dragon?"

"I've heard of Nessie, I guess. Not the other one."

"From what I recall, they're cousins to the other dragons, the real ones. Probably not a good idea to make too much of that, though. It might offend the guy."

"Why bring me to him?" Quinn asked. "I thought there'd be a magic teacher, not a dragon."

"I think it's because he can work wild magic. Dragons are among the most ancient races on the planet, along with the Fae. It makes sense they're one of the creatures Jared referred to."

Quinn thought back to her dragon egg and connected the dots. If this lake dragon could wield wild magic, her baby dragon could, too. However, the egg had channeled the wild magic through her. She now had the chance to learn to control it. Perhaps she could pass on the lessons to the tiny dragon, at least enough to keep anyone from hurting it.

Quinn walked back to the cabin with Clark. The door was ajar, and Quinn went inside. Gil stood at a wooden sink with a filleting knife in hand, cleaning the fish.

"Come in and make yourself at home. I'll just be a minute or two. Then we can talk about what you want me to do."

Filippa had already sat down in one of the chairs by the table. She lifted a kettle. "Would you like some tea?"

Quinn decided to play nice and nodded, taking a seat across the table from the princess. The Fae reached behind her to a shelf along the wall and grabbed two more of the tin mugs. "Clark, I know you'll want this. Gil found a remarkable blend somewhere."

"With a description like that, I have to try it," Clark said as he took one of the remaining seats.

Filippa picked up a metal ball with holes in it to infuse the tea. She opened it and spooned some loose tea leaves from a ceramic crock in the center of the table. After depositing them in the infuser, Filippa closed the ball and dropped it into one of the mugs.

She poured steaming water in and slid the mug toward Quinn. "There are sugar cubes in the bowl beside the crock, but no cream, I'm afraid."

"Black is fine with me," Quinn replied.

"Really?" Filippa said, an amused smile appearing on her lips. "Perhaps you're not the barbarian I thought you were. I so hate to see people ruin a nice cup of tea with too much cream and sugar."

"Growing up, I didn't usually have anything but the tea bags. That's how I grew to like it, I guess."

Quinn bobbed the infuser for a minute or so, then lifted it out of her mug by its thin chain. Filippa passed over a small bowl, and the Huntress set the ball down in it.

The princess had already produced a second infuser and poured Clark a cup, too. Quinn lifted the cup and sipped at the hot tea, her eyebrows rising in surprise at the pleasant aroma and taste.

"Is that cinnamon?" Quinn asked.

"It seems like it," Filippa said. "Did you detect mint, too?"

"I did."

Clark said, "It is quite remarkable." He set his mug down, a pleased grin on his face.

"Gil refuses to tell me his source. I think it's because he likes to know I'll visit for a cup whenever I'm in the area."

Over by the sink, Gil laughed. "It works, don't it?"

"If you don't like living alone, darling, why don't you move back to the city? You have the house there next to the reservoir, after all."

"I don't like all the people around nowadays. Besides, I'm a lake dragon, not a reservoir dragon. Whoever heard of that?"

Filippa shrugged. "Suit yourself. Don't complain about being lonely then."

Gil stared at Filippa. "When have I ever complained about that? I said I wanted a companion. That's not the same thing as wanting full-time company."

"Whoever heard of a lake with more than one dragon in it? It would be scandalous." The princess winked at Quinn, and despite the way she felt about the woman, she found herself smiling.

Gil turned back around and picked up a wooden platter with prepared filets of fish arrayed on it. "It happens from time to time. Where else are baby lake dragons supposed to come from?"

"Like I said, scandalous," Filippa replied.

Gil shook his head but didn't respond to her. He turned to Clark instead. "Would you mind scooping some of the coals from the wood stove into that metal bucket? We'll cook these outside while we chat about your girl there."

Clark got up and grabbed the small metal bucket beside

the stove. A pair of leather gloves rested on the bucket's rim, and inside was a small hand shovel.

Putting on the gloves, Clark opened the front of the stove and scooped several shovels full of red-hot coals into the bucket.

"Here, Quinn. Carry this out to Gil."

Quinn took the bucket and went outside. Gil had settled by a small fire pit, where he'd taken out six narrow wooden planks of some reddish wood. Using a small hammer and a few nails, he tacked a filet to each of the planks.

"Dump those in the center of the pit, girl. Then add small split wood blocks atop them."

She did as he asked and then settled down on the ground to watch as the wood on the coals blazed to life. Gil walked around the pit, setting the planks of fish in a circle around the blaze by jamming the ends into the dirt until the wood stood upright.

When he finished placing the fish, Gil crouched beside the fire opposite Quinn. He picked up a metal rod with a wooden handle from the ground and used it to stoke the coals, repositioning the chunks of wood so their burning sides faced outward.

The wave of heat radiating outward surprised her. She didn't think it would take the fish long to cook.

Beside her, Clark said, "I haven't had planked trout in a long time. This is going to be delicious, Quinn. It's a real treat."

Filippa stood. "Clark, come help me put together a salad with the wild greens I collected this morning. That should give Gil and Quinn a chance to get acquainted."

"Sounds good." Clark stood and followed the Fae princess back into the cabin.

Gil poked the fire a few times. Without looking up, he said, "You're playing with fire, girl."

"My name is Quinn."

"Very well," Gil agreed. "Quinn it is. So, Quinn, Filippa told me you've managed to absorb some wild magic and need to learn to control it. I want to know why you lied to her."

Quinn shot the old man a stern glare.

He held out a hand palm down to calm her. "Relax. I doubt she knows, but it's plain to me you're lying. I can smell the taint of wild magic on you, but you're not the source, nor have you absorbed enough of it to be more than a nuisance."

Gil's eyes came up from the fire and met hers. "It's another dragon, isn't it?" His nostrils flared, and he drew in a deep breath through his nose. His smile broadened after a second of thought. "A young 'un, then. One near hatching if I don't miss my guess. How'd you come by that? The Fae guard all the remaining dragon eggs I know of."

Quinn shrugged. Clearly, there was no point in hiding anything. "It was an accident. The egg imprinted on me before I knew what it was."

Gil let out a cackling laugh. "Was it hers?" He hooked a thumb toward the cabin.

"No," Quinn said. "At least, not right now. She and Aurora have been passing it back and forth, I think."

"Well, you did the right thing by keeping this from her. If she knew that egg was about to hatch? Well, let's just say she's a vindictive one. Don't get me wrong. I enjoy her company once in a while, but I wouldn't wish her ire on anyone."

"That ship has sailed, I think."

"Maybe, but she brought you here, so she doesn't want you dead just yet. That means she doesn't know about the egg." Gil went back to poking the fire. "One thing I don't understand. Usually, it takes a mature dragon to conjure the amount of wild magic to do what Filippa tells me has been happening. You have any idea of how the young 'un became so energized?"

Quinn thought about keeping it to herself, but Gil had been straight with her. She paused for a few seconds, then told him about her vision during the spell the night before.

He shook his head, a frown on his face and his brow furrowed with concern. "That's not good. I had hoped whatever transferred the power was still in contact with the egg. Then it would be a simple matter of reversing the flows. Since the initial transfer contact was interrupted, though, things are dicier. This could kill that little dragon and you along with it since you're linked. It could also cause quite a bit of havoc along the way."

"No," Quinn said, fearing for the little dragon. "You have to save it. I mean, I'd like to live too, but that little one didn't do anyone any harm. It should get to live its life."

Gil smiled. "Good answer. You have a good heart, and while that might be enough to make this work, it won't be easy." His eyes met hers again. "You get that, right?"

Quinn nodded. "Nothing about my life has been easy. Why start now?"

Gil chuckled. "Good. We'll eat lunch and then send your man and the princess on their way. What we have to do requires privacy. I don't teach what I'm going to teach you in front of prying eyes."

"How long will it take?"

Gil's eyes turned as cold as ice, and a deep blue glow emanated from them. "Long enough that you'll either learn or you'll die. Once you begin, there can be only two possible outcomes."

Quinn squared her shoulders. She wasn't going to allow him to intimidate her. "Bring it on."

Gil's eyes softened again, and a slight grin crossed his lips. He nodded and went back to tending the fire.

CHAPTER NINE

Quinn took the duffel bag from the trunk.

"You've got your phone," Clark said. "Call, and I'll come back out to get you."

"I will. Gil didn't say how long it will be."

"At least you're with someone who knows how to help you. I recommend you be honest with him, even if you won't tell me everything that's going on. He's a powerful creature, and I suspect he won't take well to someone lying to him. Remember that."

Quinn nodded and followed Clark to the driver's side of the old sedan.

Inside, Filippa leaned over from where she sat in the front passenger seat. "Clark, darling, we need to be going if we're going to get back to the city by nightfall. I have another engagement this evening, and I sent Alistair back after you said you'd give me a lift."

"Coming," Clark said, a wry grin on his face. He whispered to Quinn, "You got the better end of this bargain." He pulled out his keys and slid into the driver's seat.

"I heard that, Clark Hunter." Filippa tapped her pointed ear. "Fae hearing, remember? I might have to come up with a penance for you on the way back to Baltimore."

"Oh, joy," Clark replied as he closed the door.

Quinn moved back a few steps as the car backed up and turned around. She watched them drive down the lane until they turned a corner and moved out of sight.

Lifting the duffel bag with her clothes over her shoulder, Quinn headed back to the cabin. Gil waited for her down by the lake. He'd told her to meet him there after the others left, saying to be ready for a swim. She hadn't packed a suit, but she did have a pair of running shorts and an extra sports bra. It would have to do.

She went upstairs and changed in Gil's loft bedroom. He'd offered her a padded pallet mattress on the floor in the corner downstairs, which was fine with her as long as she could change in private.

When she came back downstairs, she left the duffel atop her mattress with all her clothes. She took a few seconds to reconfigure the sheathed Bowie knife onto a nylon web belt, then snugged it around her waist with the leather sheath resting against her left thigh. She tied the loose leather thong around her leg to keep the knife from flapping around when she ran or swam.

Realizing she'd been procrastinating, Quinn took a deep breath and headed down to the shore to get started with whatever the lake dragon had planned for her.

The old man was nowhere to be seen when she got down to the lake. She stood on the shore with her hands on her hips and looked around. Wondering if he'd gone ahead into the water, Quinn took a step forward to stand ankle-deep in the cold mountain lake.

"Don't dive in yet. I want to try something with you first."

Quinn barely managed to keep herself from jumping in surprise. Gil had snuck up behind her and was standing there with a big grin on his face.

"I thought you might have gone into the water when I didn't see you right away. Where were you hiding? There's nothing for a dozen yards in any direction."

Gil laughed. "A lake dragon that don't want to be seen won't be seen. It's one of the ways we harness the natural aspects of wild magic."

"So, you used a wild magic spell on me?"

"No," Gil replied. "You don't use the wild magic the same way people have harnessed the formal arcane forces. Wild magic does whatever it wants, so you have to convince it to do what you want."

"Wild magic has a mind of its own?" Quinn asked. "You can reason with it?"

"Oh, no, there's no reasoning with wild magic." Gil looked around and bent over to pick up a flat stone. "Think of it this way. Can you walk on water and cross the lake to the far shore?"

"No, of course not. I'd sink or have to swim."

"Exactly. You can't unless you know a trick to use the lake's properties to your advantage without actually changing anything."

Gil brought his arm back and threw the flat stone side-armed at the lake. The spinning stone skipped three, four, five times before it disappeared beneath the waves a good hundred feet from shore.

"That stone should sink every time, but if you know the trick, you can make it pretty far out before the lake's properties resume dominance and stop supporting the stone. Wild magic is the same. You can fool it sometimes to do what you want, but you must not press your luck because it's an unforgiving mistress that will swallow you whole if you're not careful."

Quinn bent down and selected a stone. She'd never done this before, so she picked up a smooth and very round one. She tried to mimic Gil's toss.

Ploop. The stone hit the water and sank out of sight. "Okay, there's a trick to this, then."

"Yes, but hopefully, with a little practice, you will get a stone to skip a few times. Practice more, and you could theoretically get it to the far shore."

Quinn looked at the dim outline of the distant shore. "You've skipped a stone all that way before?"

"No, of course not. Why would I need to do that? There are plenty of stones over there." He frowned. "You're missing the point. The problem most humans have is that they have to be in control all the time. It's one of the reasons they are so good with the formal magical arts. When you touch wild magic, you're never in control. That's what the stone teaches, too. The wild magic will always win in the end."

"I thought I was here to learn to control the wild magic coming from the egg? You're telling me I cannot do it, and the harder I try, the more dangerous it will be. If that's true, why am I here?"

Gil walked to the edge of the water to stand beside her. "You must learn to guide your young dragonling until it learns to flow with the wild magic passing through it. I have to warn you that this is uncharted territory. It's perilous stuff. I know of no other instance of a dragon that young accessing wild magic. It shouldn't be possible until it fully matures."

"So, what do I do?" Quinn asked.

"I'll train you the way I'd train a young lake dragon. Our kind doesn't have the power of our greater cousins, but I can show you the basics. You'll either get the hang of it, or you won't. In either case, I'll have you out of my hair, one way or another, within a few days."

The old man's form shimmered, and the massive lake dragon stood there. His voice now spoke directly in Quinn's mind. *Let's go for a swim. I want you to see something out in the lake. If you survive the trip, you might have what it takes to save your young dragon.*

The dragon surged forward, slipping into the water with an ease that didn't match his bulk. Barely a ripple remained above the surface to show his passing as he swam toward the middle of the lake. Quinn waded forward until the chill water passed her waist. With a gasp, she dove in and swam after him.

Quinn considered herself a strong swimmer, but it had been a while since she'd swum any distance. Her muscles and lungs burned before long with the strain of trying to keep up with Gil. He had pulled so far ahead that she could only just make out his form through the clear blue water ahead.

This is your first lesson, Gil whispered in her mind. *The wild magic is present in the lake's waters like it is in many large fixtures in nature. It is one reason I choose to live here. Reach out to it and picture yourself belonging to the water. See yourself as a native in a world, unlike the one you came from.*

She pictured herself as she was, swimming with ease across the lake's surface.

No, girl. Don't see yourself within the constraints of your human form. You can already assume that shape. You have to be one with the lake's other denizens.

Quinn tried shifting her vision to see herself as a fish version of a woman. Her mind pictured a cartoon mermaid from her youth.

You cannot be one of the merfolk, girl. You have to see Quinn, the real you, the one that would be at home in the lake.

Quinn's lungs ached with every breath she took between strokes now. Her exhaustion distracted her, and the next time she turned her head to breathe, she opened her mouth too early and took in a massive gulp of water.

Coughing spasms wracked her body as she stopped swimming and tried to clear her throat while struggling to tread water.

Focus, Quinn. You're trying to push when you should let the magic pull you where it wants to go.

Quinn coughed and shouted, "You said the wild magic would kill me."

No, I said you'll kill yourself trying to control something that cannot be controlled. The wild magic knows you better than you know yourself. Give in to it and let the magic take over. Give up control to gain access to it.

If Quinn hadn't been struggling to not drown, she'd have rolled her eyes. What Gil had said made no sense. She tried to gauge how far it was back to shore. Having trouble locating it from the middle of the lake, she brought up her HUD and attempted to engage the map function. She stopped when she spotted a new purple icon in the center of the upper edge of her visual field.

The new icon had three vertical wavy lines that pulsed in variations of indigo, violet, and dark purple. Reaching out with her mind, Quinn clicked the icon. She gasped for one last breath as something tugged her body and dragged her underwater.

Quinn fought back, reaching down for whatever pulled her toward the depths, but found nothing gripping her feet. She stroked and kicked with all her strength, trying to return to the surface. She struggled without success as the blue light above her dwindled and the darkness of deeper water closed around her.

She kept resisting, using up what little oxygen she had remaining. Her lungs ached with the buildup of carbon dioxide.

As a last-ditch effort, Quinn accessed the HUD and tried to reactivate the icon. The three wavy lines glowed uniform indigo now. It would not change, resisting her efforts to click on it.

She ran out of air and her head pounded from lack of oxygen, her vision narrowing as she started to lose consciousness. Without realizing it, she opened her mouth and gasped for a breath of air that wasn't there, sucking in water.

Instead of coughing as she would have expected, her body pushed the water through her chest. As it coursed through her, the ache and need for air dissipated. Warmth passed her sides. Her vision cleared, and her headache lessened. She didn't have the burning need to breathe anymore.

Well, that wasn't entirely true. Floating in the depths of the lake and able to see more clearly than before, Quinn sucked in more water and once again felt a warm flow at her sides beneath her arms.

She twisted her head and looked down, eyes widening at the triple flaps of skin just below her sports bra. She drew in more water through her mouth. A second later, the flaps opened as water flowed out. A glance showed similar flaps on the other side.

I have freaking gills! Quinn thought. She couldn't say it aloud, after all. No air passed over her vocal cords.

Very well done, Quinn, Gil said in mindspeak. *For a little bit there, I was afraid you'd fail to figure it out. The wild magic knew what was needed to sustain you down here. You had to trust it to do what needed to be done.*

But what if it had decided I didn't need gills but instead put lead weights around my feet?

Then you'd have died. That is the lesson here. The wild magic will not be controlled or coerced. However, if you extend your trust, it will often give you what you need rather than what you think you want.

So, now what? Quinn asked.

Now we swim. You're finally built for it.

Gil's monstrous form circled her once with effortless grace. Then, with a thrash of his long tail, he darted into the distant darkness. Quinn pushed at the water to follow and noticed her feet had elongated into fins, and webbing stretched between her fingers.

Kicking with her new, more powerful limbs, Quinn swept through the water at a speed she'd never thought possible for a person. Of course, she wasn't a person, was she? She was Quinn, the super fish girl.

Gil took her on a tour of the lake over the next two hours, showing her sunken motorboats on the bottom. He took her to the surface to show her a collection of human homes built on the lake's shores. She stared at them with nothing but her forehead and eyes above the water. He also pointed out a deep underwater cave. Quinn started to swim toward the cave's entrance, but Gil veered in front of her, halting her progress.

That is not for you right now. I show it to you merely to make sure you stay back from it.

What's in there?

It's a warren of twisting caves and caverns that run under the mountains to the north, but you're not ready yet. I haven't decided which way your studies should turn. Should you survive the other things I have planned for you, we will see if this is something you should do before returning to Baltimore.

Wow, Quinn thought. *Cryptic much?*

Gil's mind projected glee at her. *This is turning out to be much more fun than I expected. You have surprised me, and there is little in this world that manages to do that anymore.*

I'll take that as a compliment. Quinn turned in the water, enjoying the freedom her finned limbs allowed her in this underwater world. *So, what next?*

Next, we see if you survive the transition back to the surface. It is getting late. Come with me.

Quinn hadn't considered there would be a problem going in the other direction. She followed Gil as he swam toward the shore, realizing they'd made a full circle and were close to where she'd entered the lake.

Gil surfaced and moved onto the banks. Quinn swam until she could go no farther underwater, then pressed her webbed hands into the muddy bottom and lifted her head into the cool evening air.

As soon as her face left the water, Quinn's vision shifted, becoming distorted and out of focus. No matter how hard she tried, she couldn't see clearly. Standing and walking toward the shore, water flowed down her sides as her gills drained.

Pain flared in her chest when she sucked in air and she doubled over with cramps, aching agony radiating throughout her chest. She fell to her knees in the last few inches of water along the shoreline and struggled to pull in more air, trying to understand why she couldn't breathe again.

Gil, now back in human form, stood on the shore a few feet away. "You've forgotten already. Perhaps you're not suited to this after all."

"No," Quinn croaked. It wasn't speech in the usual sense. She forced air over her vocal cords using her abdominal muscles since her lungs weren't working.

For a moment, Quinn considered going back into the lake to replenish her oxygen, but something told her if she returned, she'd never come back. Instead, she forced herself to remain where she was and tried to make herself change back.

Nothing she did worked, despite concentrating on being as human as she could manage. Then, in another moment of clarity, Quinn opened her HUD. The top center icon was active again and glowed in rotating shades of tan, gold, and saffron. Quinn clicked on it and relaxed when her dizziness and cramping went away.

Her hands had returned to normal. The skin on her flanks was smooth and unbroken by gills, and her eyes now focused normally in the differing medium of the air.

"You surprise me again, young Quinn."

Quinn looked up at Gil and smiled. "I have my moments." Her stomach churned, the gurgle audible to both of them. "I'm suddenly starving. Did you have more fish at the house?"

"I have a ham curing in the cellar, along with some things I picked up at the market in the village nearby. We have plenty to eat.

"Good, because I feel like I'm about to pass out. Lead on. I'm right behind you."

Gil chuckled and shook his head as he started toward his cabin. Quinn glanced back at the lake and then looked down at her body. It all seemed like it had happened to someone else, and she'd only been along for the ride.

Shaking her head, she realized while she'd passed the first two tests, she still had a great deal to learn about how to work with wild magic.

CHAPTER TEN

Quinn spent three more days with Gil, working on her transformation until she felt no resistance to the change to and from her aquatic form. On the last day, she and Gil spent the afternoon hunting.

The lake dragon required a tremendous amount of food, even though he spent most of his time with Quinn in human form. She swam with him and scared schooling fish in his direction. His neck snaked out, jaws open wide so they could snap down, catching two or three large lake trout at a time.

On the last run, when Gil was getting full, Quinn pulled out her Bowie. When a large trout turned to evade Gil's snapping jaw, Quinn used her powerful fins to propel herself forward with the blade held out in front of her. She angled toward the nearest of the scattering fish and skewered one on the knife.

The fish slid down the blade, resting against the guard, its tail lashing at the water in its death throes. She slowed and gripped the trout by the head, then slid it off her blade and tucked it into a canvas pouch she'd crafted a few nights before to hold the fish she caught for her meals. The dying fish settled into the satchel beside another she'd nabbed earlier. She'd never been a fan of fish, but there was something about catching your own and preparing it that made it taste delicious.

Well done, Quinn. Gil's voice echoed in her mind.

Quinn turned and responded in kind with her thought voice, her mouth busy drawing in water to pass down and over her gills.

I think I'm getting the hang of this.

I will miss our hunts together. You are an apt pupil.

Quinn knew she'd done well, but that was because of her unique HUD display and abilities. She was no closer to being able to do anything real with the wild magic. She had no idea how to stop the things happening back in the city.

Gil, while I enjoy this time in the water with you and have mastered this particular transformation, I don't see how it's supposed to help with wild magic outbreaks.

Disappointment radiated from her connection to Gil's mind. *It's all the same, girl. Have you learned nothing? You still think to 'manage' something uncontrollable.*

I adapted to aquatic form easily enough once I accepted it, Quinn said.

Gil's huge dragon head swung around until his enormous glowing, yellow eyes stared into hers. *You accepted nothing. You did nothing. It was the wild magic that did it. You only released your resistance. That is what must be done with all the wild magic until the little one is hatched.*

Hatched? When will that be? The thought of a dragon

growing up and lumbering around downtown Baltimore scared her.

I fear it will be soon. That is the final lesson I have for you, because without your assistance, the little green will have no chance of survival.

What must I do? Quinn asked. The idea of the dragon dying because of something she couldn't do frightened her.

Not now. Let us take the two fish you've caught and return to the cabin. There are a few last things we must discuss before you return to your home.

Gil's long reptilian form snaked away, gliding smoothly through the water to the west. Quinn slid the pouch on its shoulder strap around to rest on her back, then she kicked hard to catch up with the lake dragon.

They returned to the shore, emerging at the same time and transforming to human form simultaneously. The last of the water drained from her gills before the skin flaps closed, allowing her lungs to fill with air again. She drew a big breath, the most awkward part of the entire process. It was more than a little uncomfortable.

Gil caught her grimace as she sucked in air in two more gasping breaths. "You still fight it. It is not as easy as it should be."

"I think I'm always going to be the kind of girl who prefers walking around on dry land."

Gil shook his head and poked her breastbone. "That is why you risk failure in this venture. Because you resist and do not see yourself as the wild magic sees you, it is difficult to switch back and forth.

"I'm not sure how to deal with that. Maybe going through the exercises you taught me will help some."

"They might," Gil said, conceding her point. "The purpose is to attune you to listen to the wild magic that is linked to you. Until you can do that without pause, any transformation will be difficult for you."

"Oh, joy." Quinn liked a challenge probably more than anyone she knew. She took it personally when anyone dared her to do something, believing they doubted her abilities. This, however, had to be one of the hardest things she'd ever tried.

Typically, with magic or supernatural things or any of her secret abilities, Quinn could see, touch, or smell the source of the problem. In this case, she had to assume it was there, even though she couldn't do anything to verify it. She didn't sense the hidden flows until it was too late, and by then, they'd coalesced into something dangerous.

That was what she'd hoped to learn here: how to see what the wild magic intended. Gil had been telling her it was impossible, but she'd hoped that like the new icon, she'd be able to develop shortcuts for drawing in power so it didn't cause anyone harm.

"Gil," Quinn said, "I've appreciated your time teaching me. This is one area where I don't know if this is the right way to go about it. I've learned over the last year that when it comes to being the Huntress, I have to do things my own way."

Gil didn't answer, although she could see the disapproval on his face. They started working on preparing dinner. He'd taught her to scale, clean, and filet fish the first night, and she found she had a knack for it. It was dirty work getting started, but a nice filet with all the bones removed was a reward in and of itself.

Gil had a cast iron pan heating on the stovetop. When she brought the fish over, he scooped some bacon fat from a jar and dropped it into the pan. He let it melt and then took each filet and settled it gently into the hot oil.

The smell of the cooking fish set Quinn to salivating. All she wanted to do was stand there and drink it in until the meal was ready. Gil had other ideas.

"Go set the table. Put out three settings tonight."

"You expecting company?" Quinn asked.

"I have a feeling an old friend might drop by."

Quinn shrugged. She hadn't seen anyone else while she'd been here, or not up close. There were a lot of people out and around the lake, especially on the far shore. She and Gil had avoided them, hiding beneath the blue waters of the lake. Having a visitor, especially a supernatural one, would be a pleasant change of pace.

"I wish we'd caught more than the two we did. I don't know that there'll be enough."

Gil shook his head. "Whoever it is will likely bring in something as a gift since this is my home. We'll see what it is and incorporate it into our meal as best we can. It's the way in these parts. No one takes offense."

Quinn grabbed three of the tin plates and mugs off a nearby shelf and put out the place settings. She grabbed the stamped metal flatware too, so each had a knife, fork, and spoon.

She had her back to the door when it creaked open behind her. The scent of something similar to wet fur reached her. Quinn knew what that meant and spun to keep from having her back to a shifter. What she saw widened her eyes. The man who walked in wasn't just big.

He had to duck to come in, and his broad shoulders and barrel chest made it so he had to turn sideways to fit through the door.

Gil turned with a huge grin on his face. "Terrence! How are you?"

The man's voice was deep, slow, and rough like grinding gravel. "I'm well. Who's she?"

"That's Quinn. She's here learning a little something from me." Gil glanced her way and winked.

"She responsible for the ripples I've felt?" Terrence asked. He still stood near the door as if he weren't sure if he wanted to come in.

"She is," Gil replied. "I wondered as she blundered around, finding her way. Come in, for God's sake. She won't bite."

Terrence gave Quinn a side-eye glance and stepped farther in, shutting the door behind him.

"It's nice to meet you, Terrence," Quinn said. "I was excited when Gil mentioned we might have some company this evening."

The big man shrugged. "I had to come down this way anyhow. I needed to follow the ripples to make sure it was safe around my mountain."

"Ripples? I don't know what those are," Quinn said.

Gil laughed. "You should. That's what happens when you resist your shifting back and forth like you do. It resonates as the fabric of the world reorients around you, according to the wild magic."

"Yours are strong, stronger than most I've felt. I expected some destruction when I got here." Terrence turned to Gil. "How'd she stop it from killing her?"

The smaller man shrugged. "Not sure. She managed it, though, so I kept pushing her."

Terrence stared at Quinn for a long time and she became uncomfortable. She was unsure how to react, and Gil had turned back to tend to the fish.

Finally, she couldn't wait any longer. "Terrence, we're having fish tonight. I hope that's okay?"

"Gil always has fish. Except when he doesn't."

The obviousness of the statement made her grin. "Do you perhaps have anything to add to the meal? I'd be happy to put it on a platter or into a bowl for serving."

Terrence reached into his heavy coat and pulled out a sack about the size of a standard pillowcase. He set it on the table.

Quinn walked over and opened the top, peeking inside. It was full of blackberries. She could smell the juice's sweetness.

"These look delicious. Let me go over and rinse them, then I'll get a bowl to put them in."

"Could just use the sack."

"I suppose we could," Quinn replied, laughing a little. "However, let's splurge since we're inside at a table and all."

The big man shrugged and sat down.

Quinn went over to the wooden sink and worked the pump handle up and down until the water flowed from the well. She carefully dumped the berries into a large wooden work bowl and held it under the flow to rinse them, then drained them with her fingers as she transferred the still-damp berries to another container for the table.

Gil had already placed the fish on a large platter and brought it over to set by the berries. He pointed to a chair for Quinn and smiled. She sat with Gil on her left and Terrence opposite her.

"I'm thinking, Terrence, you might be able to help me with something for the girl. She has a little problem with wild magic. I figure you might be able to give her a different perspective since your take is so different from mine."

"What's the problem?"

Quinn shot Gil a look, unsure if they should be sharing her secret with this person she'd just met. He either didn't see her or ignored her glare.

"She's got a dragon egg that's about to hatch, and somehow she absorbed wild magic from the little one inside."

Terrence shifted his gaze to her. "Impossible."

"I thought so too, but you can smell it on her now that you've sat down with us, can't you?"

Terrence lifted his head to put his nose in the air. His nostrils flared, and his eyebrows shot up. "She shouldn't be alive. It should have torn her apart by now."

Gil nodded. "And yet here she is. I've done what I can with the lake's power, but I wonder if your mountain might have something to offer to her?"

"Maybe." Terrence kept his eyes on her as he took a bite of the fish on his plate. "How'd she do in the water?"

"Grew honest-to-goodness gills, if you can believe it."

"Really? Haven't heard that one before."

Gil laughed. "When have you heard of a human taking on this kind of power?"

"Fair enough." Terrence ate a few more bites, staring down at his plate without saying anything else.

Quinn worked on her own fish, using a spoon to move some of the fresh berries to her plate. The berries shouldn't have been in season, but Terrence had brought them as if they'd just ripened and he'd picked them that day.

"These berries are delicious, but they're early summer things usually. How'd you get them so fresh this far along toward fall?"

"The mountain provides as it will. I decided to come down to visit my friend, and these were along the path."

Gil nodded. "It's another manifestation of wild magic you might learn from, Quinn."

Quinn didn't know what to say, so she just smiled and returned to her food. The three of them finished the meal in silence. When they were all done, she rose and cleared the plates, washing them in the wooden sink. The other two remained seated for a few more minutes while she completed the cleanup. It was her role as the student in this setting, and she didn't mind.

Gil caught her eye and nodded at the seat beside him. She got the hint and came over to sit down. Terrence turned his gaze to her and held her eyes with his for almost a minute.

Then, without saying anything, he stood and walked back toward the door. He pulled the door open and started through, stopping before he closed it behind him. "Good dinner. Appreciate it. Send her over in the morning."

With that, he closed the door and left Quinn and Gil alone in the cabin. Quinn waited for a count of ten and then said. "So, that's it? You're sending me on to someone else?"

"I was going to send you back home until I sensed him coming. He's the spirit of the mountains hereabouts."

"He's a shifter, isn't he? Maybe a werebear?"

Gil smiled. "He's many things. He's also the current guardian of the wild magic in the hills, as I am here by the lake. I think what he can teach might be more akin to what you've been dealing with. The wild magic of the lake is fluid and doesn't have as many hard edges as the land magic does. Just as deadly, but not the same. Maybe you need the harsher lessons the mountain can teach you."

"So, am I going to learn to shift up there in his cave on the mountain?" Quinn asked.

"Good Lord, no." Gil started laughing. "I think you'll be surprised by his cave, too. I have no idea what you'll learn up there, but I don't think it'll be the same thing as down here. You've learned that lesson already. Now, you might want to get some sleep. His place is in the hills off the northern shore. It's a long trek there on foot. You'll want to be rested."

Quinn nodded, unsure of what awaited her in this next phase. Terrence didn't seem like he'd be much of a teacher. She shrugged and went over to her pallet on the floor.

Gil took the lamp from the table, checked to make sure the cabin door was secured, and then went up the stairs to the loft.

The speed with which she fell asleep surprised her again. Even with the uncertainty swirling in her mind about what awaited her tomorrow, the work of swimming with Gil and shifting to and from aquatic form had worn her out. She was asleep within a few minutes of her head hitting the makeshift pillow of her duffel bag.

CHAPTER ELEVEN

Quinn's eyes popped open in the darkness after midnight as a hand clamped down over her mouth. She reached for her Bowie beneath the duffel bag but stopped as Gil's face came into focus. He held his finger against his lips, urging her to be quiet.

When she nodded, he took his hand away. He whispered, "Get up. Hurry."

Quinn sat up and started looking around for her jeans. She wore shorts and a sports bra to sleep in, but if there was trouble somewhere, she wanted to be fully dressed.

"No time for that." Gil batted her hands as she fumbled to pull clothes from her duffel bag. "You need to go now!"

"What's going on?" Quinn hissed.

"Fae magic all around the house. Whoever they are, they've put up a dampening field to stop magic and electronics from working. That points to someone expecting trouble."

"Fae? Why?" Quinn asked.

"They have to be here for you. I don't know why or

who it is, but you have to run for it. I'll create a diversion and make a hole in their perimeter. Head for the lake. You should be able to lose them in the water."

"Where am I supposed to go? We're in the middle of nowhere."

"Remember the cave?"

Quinn nodded.

"Head there if they follow you and hide until it's clear. Don't go inside any more than a few feet. It's too dangerous in there without me to guide you. After they stop searching, head for the lake's northern shore and hike toward the tallest of the hills there. Terrence will find you and take you in. The Fae won't know you're there, and you should be safe. I'll send word to you once I figure out what's going on."

Quinn shoved her phone in the duffel bag's side pocket and zipped it shut. It was supposed to be water-resistant. She was about to discover how resistant it really was. She slipped her arms through the drawstrings, so it rode between her shoulders like a backpack and buckled on the belt with her Bowie last of all.

"I can fight, Gil. You don't have to face them alone."

The old man shook his head. "It's you they want. Once you go, they'll leave me alone. They don't want to tangle with an enraged lake dragon." He showed his teeth at the last statement.

Quinn nodded and went over to stand by the door. "Okay, I'll head for the lake. You say when."

"Let me go out first. When you hear me roar and the fighting start, run for the shore. Hopefully, we'll get lucky, and you'll get away clean. I think you're fast enough to make it before they see you. If you run into someone, don't stop to fight. Just break free and make for the water."

"Got it. Good luck."

"You too, girl." Gil pulled open the door and raced out into the darkness.

Quinn opened her HUD and drew down her stamina bar, adding to her strength and speed. The last thing she did before going out the door was whisper, "Damn it, I need to see."

The darkness of the cabin's interior brightened as her night vision kicked in. It was just in time. A defiant roar filled the silence of the forest around them, followed by gunshots, of all things. There was also a bright explosion of blue-white light as if a lightning bolt had struck and sent surges of electricity arcing across the nearby trees. Quinn pulled the door open and stepped out onto the porch. More gunfire sounded, and she spotted muzzle flashes amid the trees between the cabin and the lake.

Quinn sprinted across the porch, vaulted the rail at the end, and ran into the brush beside the cabin. She didn't see anyone nearby, and she could make out moonlight on the surface of the lake through the trees.

At enhanced speed, Quinn bolted for the shoreline. All she had to do was get into the water.

She almost made it.

A dark form lunged from behind a tree at her, knocking her to the ground. Quinn came up, Bowie drawn and squared off against not one but two dark-clad attackers.

It was a male and a female. Their slim forms and angular features told her they were Fae without seeing their ears. The two spread out as soon as she stood, trying to draw her attention in two directions at once.

Quinn remembered Gil's instructions as more shots and explosions went off in the woods. Another angry roar sounded in the night. She couldn't waste time fighting these two. She was close to the water, and if she didn't get away, all that Gil was doing would be for nothing.

The pair on either side of her charged in at the same time. They must have wanted her alive since they made no move toward the sidearms on their hips.

Quinn had been ready for something like that. She spun in place, grabbing for the hand reaching for her on the right. At the same time, she slashed at the attacker on her left with her blade.

Her enhanced speed caught them by surprise, and she managed to grab the wrist of one attacker while cutting a deep gash in the other's leg.

The woman she cut cried out and twisted to get away. Quinn tugged at the wrist she held in her right hand, pulling the off-balance attacker past her and into the woman. Both fell to the ground, the woman with both hands pressed to the wound in her leg. The second Fae tumbled over his companion and fell to the ground beside her.

Quinn could have finished them both off but remembered there were probably more like them around. Instead, she raced the rest of the way to the shore, then leapt out until she was in over her waist. A spotlight switched on and swung around to momentarily blind her in the darkness. Voices shouted at her to stop.

Two boats bobbed on the lake about twenty yards from

the shore. Quinn cursed and looked for a way out. The Fae had been waiting for her to escape this way. Did they suspect what she'd learned from Gil? There was no way to be sure, and she couldn't go back the way she'd come. More shouts from the shore behind her told her that route was blocked. Maybe they didn't know everything she could do.

Shots rang out from the boats, and bullets kicked up water around her. She guessed they'd given up on taking her alive.

Opening her HUD again as she dove into the water, Quinn activated her aquatic form. She opened herself to the wild magic around her and gave in to the pull shifting her to another form.

Bullets splashed into the water, zipping past her beneath the surface. She kicked her powerful fins, propelling her into deeper water. She'd be safe from the bullets there.

She increased speed as she passed beneath the boats, smiling at how easy it was to evade them.

Except it wasn't.

She swam into the net hung like a curtain between the boats at full speed. If she'd been looking for it, Quinn might have spotted it in time, but it was too late. She made the mistake of twisting to change her direction. Instead of helping her escape, her thrashing caused the netting to catch her hands and feet. The strands twisted around her.

Realizing her error, Quinn stopped struggling. That kept her from getting more tangled. Instead, she relaxed and tried to work her left arm loose enough to reach for the knife at her waist.

She almost reached it, but the net tightened around her. The Fae on the boats had started pulling in the lines. They must have felt someone struggling.

Quinn didn't have much time. Her hand was only a few inches from the hilt of her blade. If she could grab it, she'd make short work of the net's nylon fibers.

She struggled to remain calm so she could free her hand without panicking. She glanced up, judging the distance to the surface. It wouldn't be long before they pulled her to the top. Then she'd be an easy target for them to kill or capture at their leisure.

Resisting the urge to push with brute strength for the hilt, Quinn continued to slowly twist her arm free of the netting.

Almost there.

Almost there.

Got it!

Drawing the blade, she slashed the net, freeing herself just in time. Her head broke the surface for a few seconds and lights swiveled to shine her way, then voices shouted warnings. She dove and propelled herself into the midnight water, beyond the reach of the Fae pursuing her.

Quinn couldn't go as fast as she was used to with the drag of the duffel bag on her back. She'd gotten past the two motorboats but had no idea if they had others out on the surface looking for her. Taking a few seconds to get her bearings, Quinn twisted and shot away in a new direction, aiming for the cave Gil had shown her that one time.

Behind her, the buzzing of propellers crossed the surface as the vessels above started searching for her. An occasional splash sounded as the boats passed over. She glanced up and saw the forms of people in the water outlined against the moonlight. They had divers coming down to search for her. Quinn smiled. Let them come. They had no way of knowing her capabilities in this form. They could spend the whole night searching for her. She'd be far away by the time the sun came up.

At least she thought she would be. She'd forgotten to check the time when Gil awakened her. She had no idea how long it was until dawn. Speeding up, Quinn felt the urgency of making it to the north shore before first light,

She had to stop twice more as boats swept by, dragging their nets behind them, trying to snare her or maybe her body. More divers dropped into the water to look for her. They didn't know if she was dead or alive, but they weren't taking any chances.

It ended up taking her over an hour to reach the cave. Diving all the way to the bottom, Quinn approached the dark cave. Even with her night vision and aquatic form, she couldn't see much beyond the entrance.

Heeding Gil's warning, Quinn swam only a few feet inside the entrance. She figured it was enough to keep her out of sight, and drifted down to sit on the sandy floor to wait for things to die down.

It only took twenty minutes for the first of the divers to swim toward the cave, an underwater flashlight illuminating the entrance. Quinn considered lying in wait and killing the intruder but changed her mind when four other divers arrived. As the first approached, she understood why. The full facemask of the diver's breathing gear allowed them to talk to each other, and the muffled voices carried through the water.

Quinn looked back into the cave's darkness. She couldn't escape past them at this point. Despite Gil's warning, she swam farther inside until she could see nothing but blackness. She became disoriented and couldn't tell which way was up or backward for a few seconds, then she remembered to pull up her HUD and its map overlay.

The layout of the cave and tunnels around her appeared. She was the blue dot in the center. The five red dots clustered at the cave's entrance represented the divers. It looked like others were on the way. There was a way forward, at least for now. If she was willing to risk it, the tunnels opened up somewhere she could escape.

Quinn swam for at least an hour. Even with the map overlay, the going was difficult, just as Gil had warned. The map did little to help her squeeze through the narrowest parts of the caves, and she left more than a bit of skin on the edges of the rocks as she wriggled through.

The good news was the divers had opted not to come in to search for her. Instead, they'd been content to post guards and boats around and above the cave entrance. Judging from the map, the Fae had decided this was her probable location.

Since she couldn't go back, Quinn pressed onward. The twisting narrow passages started sloping upward and opened out into the lake through a crack in its bed through which she barely squeezed herself. She swam until she surfaced in four feet of water on the northern shoreline. Surprised by where the tunnel came out, she scanned the shore for any signs the Fae might be waiting for her. The images were blurry because her aquatic vision distorted light in the air. Thankfully, the bright moonlight helped.

When she didn't see anything moving, Quinn decided to take a chance and sneak onto the shore so she could shift back to human form. Working her way forward, Quinn reached the point where she crawled the last few yards, staying as low in the water as possible.

Her gill flaps opened to air, and she coughed water out. While trying to stifle the sound, Quinn disengaged from her shifted self, transforming back into a human again. Taking a deep breath, she reactivated her night vision and stared at the beach nearby. Shrubs grew almost all the way to the lake here. Anyone could be hiding in there and she'd never see them, even with her enhanced sight.

Realizing she'd have to take a chance, Quinn rose to a crouch and darted toward the nearest copse of trees, which was about thirty yards away. She reached it and heard no sign of an alert or someone spotting her.

Quinn got behind a tree in case one of the boats out on the lake happened by. She could see them going back and forth in the distance, most likely circling the area above the cave. Their spotlights played on the surface. There were four boats in all.

She slipped out of the strings holding the duffel bag on her back and opened the top to retrieve her sodden tennis shoes. She didn't relish wearing wet sneakers up the mountain trails tonight, but it was better than going barefoot in the dark.

Quinn dug out her shoes and a pair of socks. She wrung out the socks, drying them as best she could, then pulled them on, followed by the sneakers. When she stood, her feet squelched, squeezing water out of the soles. It wouldn't be quiet, but hopefully, no one was nearby to hear her. They couldn't have enough people to surround an entire lake this size.

Looking at the moon where it filtered through the trees to check her position, Quinn started uphill as the early morning hours passed. Time to search for Terrence and continue her wild magic training.

Quinn glanced one last time over her shoulder to look and listen for pursuit. For the first time, she spotted a fire burning across the water. After a few seconds, Quinn realized it was in the area of Gil's cabin. She hoped that didn't mean he was dead or injured. She owed him a lot for helping her escape. Quinn decided she'd get payback on his behalf as soon as she was sure who was behind this.

Knowing there was nothing she could do at this point to help him, Quinn started into the darkness to find the only help she knew of nearby. She hoped Terrence was ready for her. Things had just become a lot more urgent than they'd been the night before.

CHAPTER TWELVE

The sun crested the hills to the east a little more than two hours later. Quinn sat down beside a sizable boulder and put her back against it, then bent down and pulled off her still-damp shoes, peeling off her socks next.

The blisters on the heels of both feet had broken open and were rubbed raw. She didn't know what she could do about her injured feet. She couldn't afford to pull any ley line energy from the earth with the Fae searching for her. It would be like firing a flare gun to announce her position.

That left her with more conventional methods. She didn't have any dry socks, which might have helped. Deciding to walk barefoot for a little while, Quinn tied the laces of her shoes together and hung them around her neck. She tied the socks around the loops on her duffel bag's drawstrings and dangled them behind her until they dried.

Satisfied that she'd come up with at least a partial solution, Quinn pulled her phone from her bag and tried to turn it on. It didn't power up, and she wondered if she'd ruined it forever. She returned it to the bag and stared down at the lake through the trees. Boats still crisscrossed the surface. She couldn't tell if all of them were the Fae attackers searching for her. The human residents who lived in a small community on the eastern edge of the lake took their boats out often in the early morning hours to fish.

Able to see a game trail leading up through the trees, Quinn began picking her way over the rough ground. She made sure to remain inside the cover of trees and shrubs so no one could spot her from the lake. She winced as the occasional rock or sharp twig poked into her feet from beneath the covering of leaves on the path. The going was slower than before, but at least her shoes weren't rubbing her feet raw.

Quinn turned a bend in the trail an hour later and stopped to rest while she removed a thorn from between her toes. As she pressed at the injured area with her fingertips to try to lever the tiny barb free, a deep voice behind her said, "Not very prepared for this, are you?"

Letting go of her injured foot, Quinn spun, reaching for her knife. She stopped when she saw Terrence standing downhill on the trail.

"Oh, thank God. I've been looking for you."

"Well," Terrence replied, "you found me."

"Technically, you found me." Terrence's eyebrows lowered and he glowered at her. She hastily added, "But I guess that's a minor point, right?"

"What happened down there? I heard guns and saw the fire."

"Fae attacked the cabin while we slept. Gil took the

fight to them and told me to run for it. I swam away and then came here to find you."

"Why would Fae come out here and attack old Gil, or you, for that matter?"

Quinn didn't know how much Gil had told Terrence other than what she'd overheard. However, she knew it wouldn't be a good idea to do anything to make Terrence think she was untrustworthy.

"As I said last night, I have a dragon egg back home. It's the reason I have the connection to wild magic that I do. It used to belong to two of the Fae princesses. I think they might have discovered the wild magic outbreak in the city is related to my connection to the egg."

"Makes sense," Terrence said. "Kill you, and the egg is free to bond with one of them."

Quinn nodded. "That's why Gil wanted me to come here. He hoped I'd learn enough about wild magic through the earth to help me stop the outbreaks in the city."

"Not sure what help I can be. I don't know much about dragons and such. I mostly keep to myself up here away from everyone else and their problems."

"Does that mean you won't help me?"

"No. I told Gil I'd do it, and I will, but you'll be doing most of the work. If you survive, I'll do what I can to help you."

Quinn shrugged. It was the best she could do, and without a working phone, Terrence was the only help she had out here in the wilds of western Maryland.

"Follow me," Terrence said and marched off, working his way through the brush. He left the trail, cutting across the face of the mountain.

Quinn picked her way after him as best she could in bare feet. Terrence stopped every little while and waited until she'd caught up. He'd start walking again as soon as she'd reached him, giving her no chance to rest. After a few hours, they came around the far side of the mountain and began working their way down into a tiny valley nestled between two rounded peaks. A small stream wound through the valley and lush green grass grew on either side up to the tree line at the base of the slopes.

When they finally walked onto the open grass of the valley, Quinn spotted a large structure nestled against the opposite hillside. It was made of logs, but to call it a log cabin wouldn't do it justice. This was a large home by any standard. Floor-to-ceiling windows looked out over the valley and likely filled the house with warmth from the sun as it passed overhead.

"Just a little farther. That's my home."

"Nice place," Quinn said. "Build it yourself?"

Terrence only grunted, which Quinn couldn't interpret as either a yes or a no. Her guide had started out again. She shook her head and picked up her pace to follow him. This was going to be a long few days without anyone to talk to. It was clear to her that Terrence didn't like chit-chat.

When they got closer, the rear of the home revealed an array of solar panels angled toward the south on metal posts. A pair of small satellite dishes mounted on a single post sat next to the solar farm.

Quinn's eyebrows shot up in surprise at the advanced technology and she glanced at Terrence, questions swirling in her mind. There was a lot more to this silent shifter than she'd initially appreciated.

Terrence led her to the back door, where he lifted the metal cover on a small rectangular box attached to the wall, revealing a touchscreen about the same size as her phone. Her host pressed his thumb against the pad, then the screen flashed green, and a virtual number pad appeared. He tapped in a sequence, and the door popped open with a click.

After opening the door, Terrence gestured for Quinn to enter. The small mudroom inside the door had a washer and dryer on the left, with a washbasin next to them. A bench with several pairs of shoes and boots beneath it sat against the wall opposite the appliances.

Terrence sat to remove his hiking boots. "I'll get you something to wear. Then you can get your belongings washed and dried."

"Sure. Is there someplace I can change?"

"Inside. There's a spare room."

Quinn nodded and waited until he'd removed his shoes, then followed him into the house. The mudroom opened on a short hall with a kitchen on the left and a large great room with a vaulted ceiling with long log beams on the right. Terrence walked through the big room past a sitting area with one of the largest flatscreens she'd ever seen mounted on the log wall above a fireplace.

There was a sophisticated multi-screen computer system set up on a desk in the corner. Taylor would positively drool over the layout. It looked brand new. Quinn tried to assess the wealth she saw on display here. It wasn't like there were gold fixtures or anything like that, but the room's elegant furnishings and design spoke of wealth and comfort at the same time.

"Are you coming?" Terrence stood by a hall on the other side of the great room.

"How did you get all of this up here? There's no road."

"Wasn't easy," Terrence agreed. He walked down the hallway to the first door on the right. "This one's yours. I'll bring you some clothes."

Quinn walked over and peeked into the room he indicated. A double bed sat against the far wall between two windows. There were two nightstands, a dresser with a mirror mounted on the wall above it, and an upholstered chair. Everything matched, from the fabric on the chair to the bedspread to the drapes.

Terrence returned a minute later with a pair of stretch denim leggings, thick socks, a t-shirt, and a plain green wool sweater. None of those things would have fit the big man.

"Thank you. I'm surprised you have things in my size."

"They're my wife's."

"Oh, is she around?" Quinn said, understanding the decor in the home now. "I'd like to thank her."

"She's dead, but she was about your size. I'll be in the kitchen." Terrence pulled the door shut as he left.

Quinn chided herself for being insensitive. She couldn't have known about his wife, but that didn't remove the unease at bringing up a touchy subject.

After stripping down, Quinn pulled on the clothes Terrence had provided. They were a little tight but served well enough. She picked up her dirty clothes and stuffed them in the top of the duffel bag with the damp clothing already inside. She retrieved her phone and shoved it into her back pocket after checking to see if it would turn on. It didn't.

Quinn took her stuff with her and went to the kitchen. Terrence had started laying out sandwich fixings on a small table.

"The clothes are great, thank you. I'm sorry if I—"

"It's good to get some use out of them. She would like that I've shared them with someone. Put your things in the washer. There's detergent on the shelf above the appliances. Use the scoop on the hook to measure so we don't flood the lake with phosphates."

Quinn nodded and returned to the mudroom, where she followed his instructions and got the single load going in the washer. Her stomach growled, and she realized how hungry she was. The shifting to and from aquatic form, along with the long swim and the climb up the mountain, had taken a toll on her. She needed to eat something soon, or she was going to collapse.

Terrence had already made himself a sandwich and was eating at the small round table in the corner when she got back to the kitchen. She sat down and pulled a loaf of brown bread closer to cut two thick slices from it. Terrence had carved extra slices from the hunk of what looked like roast beef. There were pickles and salad greens, and even a tomato to slice.

By the time Quinn had finished assembling her sandwich, the stack had grown so high she wasn't sure she could take a bite from it.

Terrence noted it. He finished the bite in his mouth and said, "This, I have to watch. I think your eyes are bigger than your mouth and stomach."

Living up to the challenge in his tone, Quinn took the knife and cut the sandwich in half diagonally. Lifting half, she twisted her head to one side as she opened her mouth and pressed the bread together with both hands to contain the ingredients.

It was a tight fit, but she managed a sizable bite, filling her mouth with the first food she'd had in over twelve hours. Terrence shook his head and returned to his own sandwich. Quinn noticed the hint of a grin on his face. It was the first crack she'd seen in his surly demeanor.

Quinn wolfed down the first sandwich and half of a second one before she started to feel like herself again. Terrence began cleaning up the food, putting most of it away in the refrigerator. The appliances were all matched to the kitchen cabinets and looked brand new and hardly used. If she didn't know how remote a location this was, Quinn would have thought she was in an upscale suburban home's kitchen in Baltimore.

After she finished her second sandwich, Quinn asked, "So, what now?"

"I need to double-check to make sure none of the Fae decided to come looking for you up here. Most supernaturals know to stay away from my mountain, and there's no reason to think they know you're here, but I'd better be sure."

"I could come with you."

Terrence shook his head. "No. I'll move faster on my own. You're welcome to watch something on the satellite while I'm gone. Stay out of anything else. I will only be gone for a few hours."

"I'd like to reach out and text my friends back in the

city. They need to know what happened. My phone isn't working. I had to swim to get away and reach your side of the lake. I think it got too wet, despite it being water-resistant." She pulled it out and tried to turn it on again.

"No, don't do that. There's a possibility they could use it to determine if you're still in the vicinity. They won't localize you here at my house, but they'll know you turned it on if they're watching for it. I have a dampening spell in place over my home to mask my electronic signature. It's not enough to keep your phone from pinging the tower on the other side of the lake."

Quinn once again marveled at the level of tech and knowledge Terrence had compared to Gil. She filed that mystery away for later. "I need to let them know I'm okay, or they'll come looking for me."

"Wait until I get back. I'll open a secure line over my satellite broadband connection. You can email or text them then. Give me your phone. I'll put it in the food dehydrator and see if that revives it."

Quinn gave him her phone, and he slid it onto a tray on a small, round appliance on the counter. He turned it on and left the kitchen. A few seconds later, the back door opened and closed. Quinn rose to rinse her dishes in the sink. Terrence walked past the kitchen window, stopping when he reached the open field at the center of the valley. He reached out with both hands like he was grabbing the air with clawed fingers. Then he shifted, catching Quinn by surprise. He didn't change into a bear as she'd expected. Instead, a magnificent bald eagle hopped across the grass where the big man had stood moments before.

The raptor beat its wings and soared up and across the

valley toward the lake. Quinn watched in awe, marveling at the magnificent creature until it disappeared over the trees.

Quinn finished cleaning up her dishes and went back into the great room. Terrence had suggested she watch TV, but she didn't feel like it. Instead, she picked up a book from the shelves beside the fireplace. The paperback tech-nothriller's cover looked interesting, and according to the back cover's description, it was an action-packed thrill ride. She settled down on the leather sofa to read and was asleep less than five minutes later.

When she sat up in the darkened room, awakened from a deep sleep by a deep voice, Quinn initially didn't know where she was. It took her a few seconds to orient herself. Terrence stood at the other end of the couch by her feet.

"I'm sorry," Quinn said. "I was asleep, what did you say?"

"I said, dinner's almost ready if you want to freshen up beforehand."

Quinn nodded. "Yes, thank you. That's a good idea." It was dark outside the floor-to-ceiling windows. She reached for her phone and remembered where it was. "What time is it?"

"Almost eight. I usually eat late, and it took me longer to get back than expected."

"Was there trouble?"

Terrence shrugged. "A few of the Fae ventured farther up my mountain than I thought was courteous without permission. I received an appropriate apology when I returned the unconscious trespassers to those on the shore by the lake."

"They didn't take issue with that? They fought Gil outside the cabin."

"They have no reason to think I have you, though they did ask. I told them I hadn't seen you, and if I had, I'd have done the same to a nosy little girl as I did to their men."

"Thank you," Quinn said. "I know this isn't your fight. You could have given me up to them if you wanted."

"I invited you here. You're my guest. That gives you certain protections. That's all. I'll do what I can to teach you. Then you'll have to leave."

Quinn understood. He was fulfilling a promise to Gil. He owed her nothing. She walked down the hall to a small bathroom across from her bedroom and splashed water on her face, then shut the door so she could use the toilet.

The table was already set and dinner ready when she arrived in the kitchen. A whole roasted chicken and green beans occupied a platter in the center of the table. Quinn sat down. "Thank you for dinner. I wish I was awake. I could have helped."

"I don't mind cooking. You can clean up."

"Fair enough." Quinn reached out and pulled off the leg and thigh portion closest to her. The chicken had been cooked well, and the meat practically fell off the bone.

"When do we start the training?" Quinn asked between bites.

"Tomorrow. Gil said you have promise, but there are some things I want to see for myself. After dinner, I'll fire up the computer and open a secure connection to message your friends. Then it's off to bed. I don't like to leave the lights on too long at night. It draws down the batteries."

Quinn smiled and went back to her food. She

composed a message in her head to let Clark and the others know what had happened. They'd be worried without more information, but she didn't want to tell them about Terrence. Better to protect his privacy and involvement with this, especially after what had happened at Gil's the night before.

Terrence didn't say anything else for the rest of the meal, and Quinn respected the silence. He lived alone in a secluded place on purpose, so he probably preferred it. Instead of talking, Quinn tried to imagine what made wild earth magic different from the water magic of the nearby lake. She'd thought when she came here that wild magic was the same thing everywhere. Now she knew differently. She'd proceed with a lot more caution tomorrow than she'd used with Gil a few days before. She knew she had a lot to learn.

CHAPTER THIRTEEN

Quinn stood on a shelf of rock jutting from the side of the mountain and took in the forested landscape below her. In the distance, she could make out a few open patches where farms dotted the land.

"You ready?"

Quinn turned back to Terrence. "What do you mean? You woke me up and brought me up here. Is there something I'm supposed to do?"

"We'll see. Gil said you took to the lake like a fish to water. Things aren't so easy up here in the mountains. The wild magic up here isn't as forgiving as it is down there in the lake's cool blue waters."

Quinn shuddered, remembering her first run-in with wild magic in the lake. She'd almost drowned, trying to get a handle on how it worked down there. She wasn't sure if that meant she had to master another skill in her HUD, so she pulled up the display in her mind. The single rounded square icon with the wavy vertical lines was still there at the top.

"Where'd you go?" Terrence asked.

"What do you mean?"

"You got a faraway look in your eyes, then your focus shifted back to me. It was like you went somewhere."

Unsure of how to describe what she could do, she said, "I remembered how I adapted to the wild magic underwater. I wondered if I could use something similar up here."

"What did your little trip down memory lane tell you?"

"That I don't know what the heck is going on, to be honest."

Terrence chuckled. "That is probably the wisest thing I've ever heard anyone say about wild magic."

"That's a strange reaction from someone who's an expert on the subject."

Terrence shook his head. "Ain't no such thing. Let's just say the magic and I have come to an understanding. It's like if you come face to face with a hungry bear. You stand there facing each other, neither one moving. That's how I feel when I face wild magic up here. Maybe I can just turn around and walk away, with the bear going off and eating its fill of honey and berries, or maybe this is the day he's decided he wants a little meat. So far, it's been berry time, but one of these days, meat will be back on the menu, and then the wild magic will take me."

"That's dark and fatalistic."

Terrence shrugged. "I'm ready to die if it comes to that. I miss my Maggie. Seeing her again won't come too soon."

The big man got a misty, glassy look in his eyes, then he blinked a few times and wiped them with the back of his hand. "Okay, Quinn. Gil says you have what it takes to figure this out. Ready to see if he's right? It's your funeral."

Quinn didn't like the sound of that, but she nodded and steeled herself for what came next. Instead of doing anything to her, Terrence walked over to the edge of the cliff.

"Come join me. I want to show you something. This is where I first met the wild magic."

Quinn walked over to the edge, stopping with her toes even with the lip of the drop-off. Good thing she wasn't scared of heights. It had to be several hundred feet down to the rocks on the slope below.

Iron fingers gripped Quinn's neck. She tried to twist away.

"What the hell?"

She shut up and gulped when the hand pushed. She found herself leaning out at a forty-five-degree angle and kept her body rigid as the fingers dug into her neck. The only thing holding her up was the firm grip on the back of her neck.

"When the cancer took Maggie, I came up here to this ledge, to the place she loved more than anything. My internet billion didn't mean anything to her. All she wanted was a place in the mountains. She wanted to live away from all the things we'd accumulated building our business. She got sick just after the house was finished."

Terrence pushed Quinn out another inch or so. "You ever lost anyone you loved, Quinn?"

"I grew up an orphan in foster care, so I guess you could say I've never had anyone in my life."

Terrence snorted. "You're better off than most of us. I sold off almost everything I had after she died. None of it could bring her back."

"You came up here to die." Quinn croaked, afraid any movement would loosen his grip.

"That was the plan." His voice took on a dark, growling tone. "This bastard of a mountain had another plan for me, though."

"The mountain told you to live?"

"Not exactly. It just won't let me die. I keep waiting for it to let me go at last so I can see her again. That's what's so vile about wild magic, kid. It doesn't care what you want."

She brought up her HUD. The icon at the top was grayed out. She stared down at the ground. Crap, drowning seemed peaceful compared to getting smashed to a pulp on the rocks down there. Quinn wondered what she was supposed to do.

"Uh, I'm not feeling any magic. Maybe it's not here right now."

"Figure it out. You're outta time."

The fingers let go. Quinn's arms windmilled, swiping at the air while she tried to dig in with her toes through the soles of her sneakers. All she ended up doing was pushing herself away from the ledge as she began falling.

She figured she had only a second or two. Staring at the HUD, Quinn willed time to slow so she could think.

The air rushed past her face, and she screamed.

Quinn sucked in another breath to scream again, and the blue mana line in her HUD depleted a little bit. Pouring her soul into the next sound to come out of her mouth, Quinn let out another shout at the futility of dying this way.

This time, the blue line drained almost to zero. The

wild magic icon at the top turned from gray to a brilliant blue, like a crystal-clear sky on a crisp winter day.

Quinn clicked the icon, and everything stopped: the rushing wind, the sound of her screams, everything. Realizing she'd squeezed her eyes shut against the inevitable impact, she opened them. She stared at the ground twenty feet below from her position floating in mid-air.

Twisting, she rotated in the air until she stared back up at the ledge from which she'd come. Not fallen. She'd been pushed.

Terrence looked down at her and then launched off the ledge. He plummeted almost to the bottom before shifting to eagle form.

The magnificent wings flapped as he caught the updraft and flew in a wide, lazy circle around Quinn, who was still floating stationary in mid-air.

A voice sounded in her mind—Terrence's voice. *Figured it out just in time. I thought you were dead for sure.*

She answered him in kind. *The way you fell without shifting, I was sure you were going to splatter all over the rocks yourself.*

The eagle banked in her direction, fixing her with its yellow-irised eyes. *Every time I do it, I try to resist shifting. I'm tired of this world. The wild magic forces this on me. Because of that, I have no choice but to soar over these mountains and see them in a way my wife never could. It's not fair, but that's wild magic in a nutshell.*

Quinn rotated and stared at the ground as the eagle landed a short distance away. *Um, how do I get down?*

"You'll figure it out," Terrence said aloud. He'd shifted back to human form. "I'll meet you back at the cabin. I figure it's worth splurging and thawing some venison steaks for tonight. I was sure I'd be eating alone. Old Gil knew what he was talking about."

The big man started down the slope, leaving Quinn floating twenty feet off the ground behind him. She wanted to scream at him to come get her down, but she knew that wouldn't do any good. A minute later, he was out of sight, and she was all alone.

Quinn sighed. She rolled over again and stared at the sky, then back at the ground. Okay, she could move but only in this location. On a whim, she twisted to the side and managed to rotate on her center axis horizontally until her head pointed in the direction her feet had seconds before.

Taking stock, she had learned she could move in two planes, rotating horizontally and vertically around a single point. She couldn't tilt her body off the horizontal axis, though. She glanced at her HUD. The icon glowed blue, but did it look a little fainter than before? She looked at the darker blue mana bar. It had drained even more. Quinn wondered what would happen when it reached zero? Nothing good, she guessed.

A fall from twenty feet up wouldn't kill her. She'd jumped as far in Huntress mode. But she'd never have enough time to rotate her feet down so she could land on them, and she didn't relish the idea of slamming down face-first. That wouldn't just hurt, it could seriously mess her up.

The mana bar dropped more, and judging by the rate of decline, she had only a few minutes of air time left. She had to think of something. She could click the icon and hope the magic faded slowly. That was wishful thinking, though. Everything she knew about the wild magic told her it wasn't likely to give her an easy way out.

Maybe, though, Quinn could click the icon and let it up slowly. Could she do that with her mind, like pressing a button, so it clicked and then releasing the virtual spring beneath gently?

The bar ticked down again, and Quinn had no more time to think about it. She focused her attention on the icon and pressed, not clicked. She concentrated on holding the icon button down and releasing it in micro-increments.

Quinn realized she'd shut her eyes again and forced them open. The ground was closer, only about ten feet away now. She sank lower by the second. In less than a minute, she was lying on the rocky slope below her.

She released the icon and her full body weight returned, pushing a little of the air out of her chest with a *woof*. Bringing her arms around in front of her, Quinn pushed up and twisted until she sat with her arms resting on her knees. She stared at the mountains for a long time, drinking in the stark beauty of the rocks, the forest, and the mountain air.

Quinn sat until she noticed it was getting dark and the sun had settled against the peaks to the west. She stood, orienting herself to where she was. Terrence's home was off to the left. She'd have to walk around the hill and through some woods to get there.

That was strange.

She glanced around. How did she know where his house was so precisely? Trying something else, Quinn thought about Gil's place by the lake. Her mind focused on the house and she knew exactly where it was, as well as the best path to get there from here. There were two routes in her mind. One followed the shore, but the fastest route was to go straight to the lake and shift forms to swim the rest of the way.

She'd never been so connected to a place. Quinn sensed life all around her. When she focused on any of the tiny points of light representing them in her mind, Quinn could see what each thing was. A fox trotted across a meadow in the next valley over. It was hungry and thought about a rabbit it had hunted earlier that day that had gotten away.

Quinn shifted her focus until she found Terrence. She tried to see what he was thinking about, but her mind ran into a wall so hard it almost physically hurt.

Get outta my head, girl. Since you're alive, dinner will be ready in a half-hour. Hurry up, or it's going to get cold.

Quinn backed away until she was in her body again. She hadn't realized that she'd sort of left it when she searched around her. She angled to the south, jogging across the slope toward the house. Spending all that mana had taken a lot out of her, and hunger pangs twisted her gut. Quinn's mouth watered at the thought of a hearty steak dinner.

CHAPTER FOURTEEN

Quinn spent another two days with Terrence on the mountain. Now that she had the connection to it, she didn't want to leave. He took her with him on his patrol to make sure everything was as it should be in his domain. She walked the mountain paths while he flew above the trees.

It was nearly nightfall when they found themselves down near the base of the mountain. Quinn quested out with her mind to search the land around her. Two blank areas stopped her sweep. They were located at the extreme edge of her search, just outside Terrence's property line.

"Terrence?" Quinn asked aloud. "Can you see those blank areas?"

He snorted, and a look of disgust crossed his face. "Those are likely a pair of Fae trackers from the group that was looking for you. My guess is they know you're hiding somewhere nearby and have left a few of their tracker teams to find you when you surface again. The Fae have their own way with the wild magic. They've created masking energy to let it pass over them."

"But I can see them anyway."

"Only because you're connected to this place the way you are. The wild magic of the mountain doesn't like them very much, probably because they're after you, so it highlights the absence there. That makes their attempt to hide look foolish."

"Will I be able to use this to evade them if I leave the mountain? I've got to go back eventually."

"Actually, Quinn, you have to go back now. I've taught you everything I know to show you. I think whatever the wild magic wants you to do has to be done back at your home."

"But I don't know what I'm supposed to do!"

Terrence laughed. "Did you know what you were supposed to do when I let go of you on the mountain?"

"No, I made it up as I fell."

"There you go. Wild magic doesn't have a plan. It just is. It's the ultimate in spontaneity. Remember that, and I think you'll be fine. I get the feeling that sort of thing suits you. Maybe you'll be the first wild magic adept, at least among humans."

"Where do I go from here? My phone is fried, despite your attempts to resurrect it. I don't have a way back to the city."

Terrence pointed south. "There's a convenience store off the highway about two miles through the woods in that direction. Send your friends a message to meet you there. It should only take them a few hours to come get you. Here's Maggie's old phone. I charged it and refreshed the software package for you. You'll have to evade the trackers and traps the Fae have left in your path, but that shouldn't be a problem. The mountain likes you, I think. Hold onto your link to it as long as you can. It'll help you get out. Oh, and here's your bag." He pulled it out from under his coat.

"I hope I can come back out here and spend more time with you. It's peaceful in a way I've never known."

Terrence shrugged. "Maybe. I might be here, and I might not."

Quinn placed her hand on Terrence's shoulder. "Maggie will wait for you. There's no rush. I think there's more good for you to do here and now."

He turned his sad eyes to hers. "Possibly, but I don't know that I have the strength to keep waiting."

"Let the mountain give you its strength," Quinn suggested. "It's the most patient thing around here. It's seen a lot in its million years of life. Lean on it. I think you'll be surprised at what you find."

"How'd you get so wise all of a sudden?"

Quinn smiled. "Near-death experiences, I guess. Kind of gives you perspective, right?"

Terrence smiled and nodded. "Goodbye, Quinn."

"Bye, Terrence."

Quinn started off to the south, heading for the edge of the mountain property. She glanced back once, but the guardian of the mountain had disappeared. She hoped he found peace at some point, even if it meant he would die. He deserved it.

Pulling out the phone, Quinn decided it was time to risk a phone call to Clark. He needed to get on the road so she wouldn't have to sit still and wait for too long. She had to keep moving to evade the trackers.

The phone rang only once before Clark picked up. "Where are you? We got your cryptic message, but then we couldn't get you again. I drove out and found Gil's cabin burned to the ground."

"Worried about me, Clark? I'm touched."

"Yeah, well, between what's been going on here and finding no sign of you or Gil at the cabin, I'm allowed."

"A Fae hit squad came out to get me. Gil helped me escape." Something else Clark said clicked. "Wait, what's happening back there? More wild magic outbreaks?"

"No, they stopped when you left, but what you said about the Fae makes sense now. Someone broke into your apartment and took the egg. They got the spear from Taylor's workshop, too. Juni mentioned a couple of Fae patrons acting strange in the pub earlier in the evening, but we never found out who they were. They must be connected."

The egg was gone? Quinn's heart sank. Everything was tied to it. "When did the egg and the spear go missing?"

"Three days ago. Why?"

Quinn nodded. "The day before, the Fae showed up here for me. I guess they figured out that the egg was ready to hatch, and they needed me for some reason."

"The egg is hatching? *That's* the reason for all this? Quinn, you need to start telling me everything."

"I can explain more when you pick me up."

"I'm not far from you. I've been hanging around, trying to find out who burned the cabin down. The locals don't know much about it, or they're not telling a stranger."

"I'm pretty sure there are still Fae trackers around, Clark. We have to be careful. I'm heading to a convenience store off the exit south of the lake. Can you get there?"

"I know where it is. I can be there soon."

Quinn drew on her connection to the mountain and judged the trail to the rest stop. "It'll take me about an hour cross-country to get there. I'm turning my phone off in case they can track it."

"Be careful."

Quinn hung up and shut the phone off, then slid it into her duffel bag and slung the bag across her back. She pulled up her map overlay and expanded the view until she could see the interstate. It might actually take more than an hour.

Darkness had started closing in, so Quinn muttered, "Damn it, I need to see." The forest around her lit up as her night vision mode kicked in. She scanned the overlay for any new blank spots that might indicate trackers nearby. She saw a few likely places, but they might also be open ground with no noticeable features. She didn't have time to examine them closely, and this far from the mountain, the level of detail was much lower. She'd try to angle around them.

Quinn drew down her stamina bar and boosted her speed, then set out. She loved running, and being able to go this fast through the forest exhilarated her. She leaped fences and raced through fields, neighborhoods, and parkland. By the time she arrived at the edge of the woods near the highway rest stop, it was just over an hour after she'd left Terrence's land.

She crouched in the brush amid the trees and scanned

the area. There was no sign of trouble, but Terrence had warned her the Fae could mask their presence. Her HUD map showed only the highway and buildings around her, none of the telltale red dots she'd expect from sighting known enemies nearby. Quinn turned from searching the trees and looked at the cars in the parking lot. She didn't see Clark's, but the far side of the building and parking lot were hidden.

Quinn started to circle around to check the other side but stopped when the faint crackle of a foot on dry leaves, coupled with the sudden chill of her Huntress amulet, warned her someone had come up behind her.

Spinning, Quinn drew her Bowie. She almost turned in time. A body slammed into her, carrying her to the ground as a humming whir buzzed past her head.

Quinn twisted and tried to stab at her assailant.

"Quinn, stay down," Clark hissed. "They have crossbows leveled at you."

Relaxing, she looked at the quivering bolt stuck in a tree trunk right where her head had been.

"I'm good. Get off me."

Clark rolled to the side.

Quinn pulled up her HUD map. The whole area around her was now blank. She lowered the display and asked, "How many are there?"

"I saw two moving this way from the parking lot. That was when I figured you must be close."

"That bolt came from behind me, so there are at least four of them. Terrence said they travel in pairs."

"Who?" Clark asked. He waved his hand. "Never mind. We're sitting ducks here. We need to move."

"At least they don't have guns like the ones that attacked the cabin."

"Fae don't like guns. They probably brought them to handle the dragon."

Quinn glanced around, trying to spot the trackers. "Let's split up. You go right, and I'll go left. Let's see if we can turn the tables on them."

Clark nodded and rose to a crouch. As he started moving away, he blurred out and became lost in the shadows. Quinn nodded and whispered, "Mist," dipping into the shadows herself. The trackers weren't the only ones who could hide.

Watching her step, Quinn brought up her HUD and engaged enhanced recon mode. A sixty-second clock started counting down. It should be enough time to get behind their assailants without being detected.

She picked up her pace under cover of the spell, moving silently despite the dry leaves of the forest floor. Thirty seconds later, she stood by a tree staring at the backs of two black-clad Fae trackers.

One held a crossbow leveled at the spot where she'd been hiding moments before. The other had a curved sword in his hand. Both wore dark masks to conceal their features and carried pistols holstered at their sides. They probably hadn't used them here since they'd be heard by someone at the convenience store.

Checking her timer, she had fifteen seconds left to cross the thirty yards between her and the two trackers— just enough time to put her hasty plan into motion.

Pushing off from the tree, Quinn charged at the crossbow wielder. He was the closest of the pair.

Even with her recon mode engaged, he must have sensed something because he spun and snapped off a shot that scored a burning graze across her neck.

Ignoring the flash of pain, Quinn dove at the man as he swung the spent crossbow at her head. She ducked under the swing and lunged with her knife, taking him in the chest.

Her Bowie sank in to the hilt as she rode him to the ground. The life already drained from the almond-shaped violet eyes behind the black leather mask. She pushed herself up and spun to meet the other attacker.

Quinn got her bloody blade up just in time to parry the downward slash from the curved sword.

The other masked tracker snarled and called out in a language Quinn didn't know. She hoped Clark had dealt with his pair and that there weren't others close by. There was no time to search in the middle of a desperate battle.

Quinn jumped backward to avoid a follow-up blow. The guy was as fast as she was, even enhanced with her stamina boost. He also had the advantage of a longer reach, both in arm and weapon.

Circling each other, Quinn tried several moves, but none of them scored a hit. Luckily, she fended off the incoming attacks.

She risked a quick look around for Clark. A clash of steel on steel to her left meant the Hunter was still engaged, so she was on her own.

Deciding to try something else, Quinn grinned at her attacker. "You should have brought more people. My guess is at least two of you are down, and my friend's about to finish off the other one."

"I am more than enough to take you, Huntress. My mistress no longer needs you alive. Your death will serve her needs just as well. Then the youngling will be free to imprint upon another."

"Filippa needs to stop obsessing about that egg. It's going to get her killed by the time I'm finished with her."

"You won't be there to do anything about it."

There was something familiar about the Fae's voice. She'd heard it before. Dodging an incoming lunge, she tried to remember who it was. She hadn't met many Fae and had only listened to a few speak.

Her thoughts distracted her enough that she missed seeing her assailant reverse his attack, switching it into a riposte. The tip of the sword caught her above the knee, cutting open her jeans.

Cursing under her breath, Quinn staggered back, limping as she fended off a series of follow-up blows. The Fae laughed, which fueled her anger and drove her to fight harder.

In a desperate move that Clark would have scolded her for had he seen it, Quinn let one of the slashing lunges come in by her feigned parry.

The tip of the sword cut into her side, but she twisted away before it went too deep. The move gave her the opening she needed. She reversed her false parry to chop down at the exposed wrist holding the extended sword.

The magically enhanced Bowie cut almost all the way through muscle and bone.

The curved sword flew from the useless hand, and the Fae tracker cried out in pain.

Quinn didn't wait. She drove forward despite her pain

and injuries, taking advantage of the unarmed attacker as he fumbled with his off-hand to pull the pistol free.

She kicked out, using the attack to knock him further off-balance, and followed up with a punch at the leather-masked face. The blow knocked him to the ground.

Quinn dropped on top of the struggling Fae, straddling his waist with her knees. She wanted to question him, but he'd managed to pull the pistol out and brought it around toward her head.

With only a split-second to act, Quinn shoved her blade into the Fae's chest, using all her might to twist it as it sank into his heart. He spasmed and lost his grip on the pistol. It fell to the ground beside him as he brought the hand over to grip at the hilt of Quinn's knife jutting from his chest.

She pulled the mask free and her eyes widened.

It was Zephyr.

"You weren't sent by Filippa. Aurora's behind this. Why? She's my friend."

"If the youngling hatches," Zephyr gasped between clenched teeth, "it only matters who imprints at that time. The dragon won't bond with anyone else, ever. She has to kill you to free it to bond with her."

Aurora's betrayal of what Quinn had assumed was a friendship irked her. She leaned into the hilt, twisting the blade again. Zephyr let out a gurgling gasp.

Quinn brought her head close to the pointed ears as the life faded from his body. "I've killed you, and I'm going after your mistress next. You can wait for her in hell."

Zephyr's lips moved as if saying something, but she never knew what. He died before answering her threat.

Quinn jerked her Bowie free and staggered to her feet.

She didn't hear any more fighting in the woods around her. Hopefully, that was a good sign.

"Clark, you out there?"

He stepped out of the shadows and walked forward. He had a fresh wound on his cheek. "You all right?"

Quinn pressed her elbow to the cut to her side to hide it from Clark. "I will be with some rest. I figured out who's behind all this." She nodded at the nearest body. "That's Zephyr. He's Aurora's man. She's got the egg. We need to retrieve it before it hatches."

"When's that going to be?"

Quinn shrugged. "I don't know anything about birthing dragons. It could've already happened for all I know. As long as I'm alive, though, that dragon is connected to me. We need to get it back."

"Come on, then," Clark replied. "The car's over here, and I've got a few things in the trunk we can use to patch us up before we get on the road."

Quinn nodded and limped after him toward the convenience store parking lot. They had to get back to Baltimore before it was too late.

CHAPTER FIFTEEN

Quinn didn't realize how tiring the last few days had been until she sat down in Clark's car and started the long trip home. As she slept, her mind was filled with fitful dreams about the egg and an ominous sense of overwhelming dread.

When Clark parked outside of O'Malley's, she woke with a start, her hand reaching for her Bowie. The last thing she remembered from the dream was a massive yellow and black reptilian eye staring at her. She gasped and twisted her head, sure it was nearby. The vision seemed so real.

"Easy, Quinn," Clark soothed, putting a hand on her shoulder. "We're home. You're safe now."

"Something tells me we're not. The dream I just had... I can't remember all of it, but it left me thinking that something awful is coming. If we don't manage to stop it, many people are going to die."

"What did you see?"

"An eye," Quinn replied. Clark raised an eyebrow and

she continued, "A big eye with a vertical slit pupil like a reptile's. Everything else from the dream is a blur."

"A big reptilian eye. Maybe a dragon's eye?"

Quinn shuddered at the thought as soon as Clark said it. "It was huge. It's not the dragon from the egg since it was too large, but the egg is important. I remember that much."

Clark opened his door. "Let's go inside. We can talk to the others about the dream, and everyone will want to see you. We all feared the worst when I couldn't find you at Gil's."

Quinn nodded, trying to put the disturbing dream out of her mind. She kept thinking there was something she was supposed to remember, but when she tried, more of what she recalled slipped away.

She nearly fell down when Taylor plowed into her, wrapping her arms around her best friend.

"Quinn, I swear, don't ever do that again. If you have to go dark, warn me so we can set up a secret way to communicate."

Quinn hugged Taylor back. She'd missed all of them, especially Taylor. "I promise, T. All I can say is, I couldn't call you first. I had no time and ran away in my underwear when the Fae trackers hit the cabin.

Naomi stood behind Taylor. "Clark mentioned them when he told us you'd contacted him. We wondered if they might be behind the thefts we had here, too."

Quinn nodded. "They were. I discovered that much before the last one died. At first, I thought it was Filippa, but it turned out to be Princess Aurora behind the attacks."

"That is a surprise," Miranda remarked. "She's always been so friendly."

"I think she had to. After all, I had her dragon egg. Once it became clear the dragon was preparing to hatch, she couldn't wait for the year to end. She had to get rid of me so the egg could bond with someone else."

"If the egg's hatching, it's the first in over two hundred years," Naomi said. "I'll have Joshua check the clan records we left with him, but I think that's right. It also is believed to portend ominous events."

"Are we surprised?" Quinn asked. "Ominous things on the horizon is what we've been dealing with for months."

She laughed as she said it, feeling more nervous about what was to come than anything. It was her way of dealing with all the stuff she'd been through. Quinn pointed to an open round table amid the other patrons in the pub. She needed food; she'd had nothing since eating breakfast at Terrence's that morning.

The group sat down, and Quinn waved to catch Juni's attention.

The waitress nodded to let Quinn know she'd seen her, finished taking another order, and came right over. "Good of you to decide to come back to the land of the living."

"It wasn't all that bad," Quinn told her. "I did work up an appetite, though. Is the kitchen still serving dinner or just late-night bar snacks?"

"What did you have in mind? I'll see if the cooks can do something extra."

"A pizza-burger platter with extra fries."

Juni laughed. "Oh, that's easy. I'll get them right on it."

After she left, Clark said, "With Aurora behind the

break-ins and the attack on Quinn, we have to be extra careful how we deal with things."

"Why?" Quinn asked. "It's not like she was all that careful with me. She sent assassins after me and burned down a friend's house in the process. I want to get some payback."

"What Clark means," Naomi said, "is that Aurora is highly placed, and not just in the supernatural leadership of the city. She is connected with the human leaders here, too. She will be well protected, especially when she discovers you're back in town."

"I guess that means going over there and storming through the front door isn't an option."

Naomi shook her head. "Not if you want to come out alive. She's made it plain, based on what you've said, that she's out for blood. In fact, she needs it at this point."

Quinn's hunger and exhaustion were getting the better of her, and she didn't see where her mother was going with this. "Okay, the front door is out. What do you propose?"

"Let me check around," Naomi said. "I seem to remember there's an event coming up for the city. It might be one of those things she'd have to put in an appearance at with some of her followers. That could be our opportunity to go to her home and get the egg back."

Quinn asked, "Why did she go to all that trouble to get the spear, too?"

Miranda said, "My guess is the two are now connected in some way, or Aurora has some other use for it. The spear is a powerful artifact in and of itself."

"Great." Quinn let out an exasperated sigh. "I went away

to learn about wild magic, and we're back at square one again."

When no one answered her, she looked up.

Taylor had frozen in her seat beside Quinn. She gripped the Huntress' arm and pointed at the club's entrance.

Quinn followed the pointing finger.

Filippa and Aurora stood inside the door.

Clark picked up on her stare and turned to see who it was. Quinn tried to get up, but Clark grabbed at her shoulder and pushed her back into the seat. "This is neutral ground, Quinn. Start a fight in here, and Paddy would have to kick us out of our arrangement."

"They broke in and stole from us," Quinn said. "How is that neutral ground?"

Clark shook his head. "We can't prove it was them, and burglary is different from violence to a person."

"That's a distinction I'd like a legal opinion on," Quinn said. "It seems a little nit-picky to me."

"Nit-picky is what the law is all about," Naomi pointed out. "Plus, the supernatural courts are run by the Fae, so you'd be fighting an uphill battle."

Taylor laughed. "Of course the court is run by them, just like they run everything else."

Taylor stopped talking as Filippa and Aurora came over to their table.

Filippa gave Quinn a passing glance, saying to Clark, "I see you found your wayward girl. I should have warned you that foundlings are notoriously unreliable."

Quinn opened her mouth to respond, but Naomi stepped behind her seat, hands on Quinn's shoulders. She gave a firm squeeze, and the Huntress stopped before saying anything.

Clark said, "What do you two want? I assume since you and Aurora have patched up your differences, you have something you needed to tell us."

Aurora smiled, though no glint of humor showed in her eyes. "My cousin and I became allies of necessity. Such is the case whenever an outbreak of wild magic occurs. We had to rally our resources so we could discover the cause of the outbreak." The Fae princess shifted her gaze to Quinn.

Quinn held her stare for a second before saying, "So, I'm the source of the outbreak now?"

"I didn't say that. I said you're the cause. In this case, that is more important."

Filippa said, "Clark, I know you understand the severity of this situation." She reached into her flowing robes and pulled out a folded sheet of yellow parchment, closed with a green wax seal.

Quinn said, "That looks official. Is it your list of grievances? If it is, I can tell you where to put it."

Filippa didn't look at Quinn, instead keeping her eyes on Clark. "This is a writ of arrest for your Huntress. It's been approved by the regional Fae court and is effective immediately in the interests of public safety."

Quinn shook off her mother's grip and pushed to her feet. "Arrest me? You've got to be kidding. I'm not the one guilty of petty burglary, assault, or attempted murder."

Aurora assumed a shocked expression and placed a hand on her chest. "Such horrible accusations. I assure you I know nothing about anything like that."

Quinn smiled. "You don't know, do you? That's a shame. I suppose I should tell you, though."

"Tell me what?" Aurora asked.

"Your man Zephyr had a fatal accident earlier this evening."

Aurora glared at Quinn, her eyebrows lowering and her lips peeling back from her teeth in the beginnings of a snarl.

"Cousin," Filippa snapped. "Control yourself."

Naomi laughed. "I see who's holding the leash now. I wonder how that happened?"

Aurora whipped her head to Quinn's mother. "No one holds my leash, vampire. Your girl has admitted to killing a member of my personal retinue. I must now insist that she be turned over to us for investigation."

"I think not," Naomi said. She moved to stand at Quinn's side. "My daughter didn't admit to anything other than finding your man dead in her travels earlier this evening. Unless you'd like to enlighten us as to what he was doing for you, there's no evidence she's done anything but found a body."

"This is ridiculous," Filippa spat. She turned around and raised her hand over her head. At that moment, the band went silent on the stage, and the crowd turned in her direction.

"People of Baltimore, I hold a lawful writ from the Fae court for the arrest of Quinn Faust, a resident of this place. I ask you to assist in her apprehension so that justice may be served, and we might end the unfortunate outbreaks of wild magic."

All eyes in the room turned to Quinn. She looked

around the room, seeing puzzled expressions turn into angry and determined ones. These people were about to turn on her, and there was no way she'd be able to fight her way free.

Miranda floated over behind Quinn and whispered, "Say you request sanctuary."

"What?"

"Just do it! You're running out of time."

Quinn didn't understand what Miranda wanted, but she then didn't understand any of this.

"I request sanctuary!" Quinn shouted.

Filippa's head whipped around. "Nonsense, girl! What do you know of the rule of sanctuary?"

Clark held up his hand. "Don't say a word, Quinn." He glanced to the side, where Paddy O'Malley stood.

The leprechaun stood by the bar, wringing his hands.

"What about it, Paddy? This is your place. Quinn requests sanctuary. What say you?"

Both Fae turned their icy glares on the bar's owner. He blanched, the blood draining from his face as he looked from Clark to the princesses and back again.

"Oh, for God's sake," Juni said from across the room. "What's the holdup, Da? If you won't do it, I will." The waitress raised her voice. "The claim of sanctuary is accepted. Quinn is safe here."

Aurora laughed. "You can't offer sanctuary, girl. Only the owner has that power. Clearly, your father knows the risk of such a move and has decided to say no."

"I am the owner of this bar, at least in part. My da and I signed the agreement over a year ago so I could take over managing the place."

Filippa shook her head. "He's the original owner, so he can overrule you."

"No, he cannot," Naomi said. "Once valid sanctuary has been offered, only the protected individual can rescind it. Paddy cannot overturn it."

Clark nodded. "She's right and you know it, Filippa. You've lost this round. I think it's time for you to leave unless you have another card you'd like to play out of turn."

Filippa glared at Paddy O'Malley, who shrank in on himself. He didn't say anything, only shook his head.

"There you have it," Naomi said. "Quinn is safe here from any writ of lawful arrest. I think it's time for you both to leave."

"Fine," Filippa said. "Come, cousin. It seems we've been outplayed."

"But we can't leave without her."

"If your man had done his job earlier tonight as you assured me he would, we wouldn't be in this mess. Let's go."

Filippa gripped Aurora's arm and swung her around, practically dragging her to the exit. Aurora glared at Quinn all the way to the door.

Taylor whooped and turned toward Miranda with her hand raised for a high-five. "All right, Miranda. Good thinking on that sanctuary thing."

Miranda stared at the raised hand, an amused expression on her ghostly face as Taylor lowered it, blushing. "I'm glad I remembered it. Inns and public houses like this were used for local courts in the old days. People sought by another court couldn't be removed if they invoked sanctuary while their case was heard. It's only temporary, but I think it bought us some time."

"Yeah, but time for what?" Clark asked. "We might have a week until the Fae court can be reconvened. After that, you know they'll overrule the sanctuary. We have to come up with a plan before that happens."

Quinn was still trying to work through the events of the last few minutes. It didn't make any sense to her that *she* was the dangerous one. "They know the egg is about to hatch, and the dragon is still imprinted on me. They can't bear to let that stand. I have to die so one of them can take control."

No one spoke for a few seconds, then Taylor said, "Well, then, we have to get the egg back and do what we can to get it to hatch. Once that happens, the wild magic situation will resolve itself, and the dragon will be Quinn's."

"Taylor," Clark said, "it's not that simple."

"But it is," the tech witch said. "Quinn's correct. The egg is at the center of this. Possession is nine-tenths of the law, and the person who possesses the egg holds the cards. We need to get the egg back. The rest we can figure out afterward."

Quinn shook her head. At this point, all she wanted to do was go to her own bed and sleep for a day or two. "Does the sanctuary cover the whole building or just the bar?"

Juni overheard Quinn's question. "You should be fine upstairs. The whole building is under the business license, including the apartment we rent out. If anyone asks, I'll say as much."

Quinn nodded. "Then I'm going to bed. We can figure out the rest tomorrow morning." She slid away from the table, then pushed her chair back in place and turned to the waitress. "Thank you, Juni. It seems I owe you my life."

"I never liked either of them. The Fae royals all think they own the rest of us. It was time for someone to remind them the world's a different place than it used to be."

Quinn smiled. She'd made many new friends over the past year, and it was hard not to see how all of them had helped her in one way or another. She'd have to find a way to make it up to the leprechaun girl.

For now, though, she wanted nothing more than a long rest to recharge. Maybe she'd come up with a plan to resolve all this before it boiled over again. She also might get a second chance at understanding that dream she'd had earlier.

CHAPTER SIXTEEN

Her sleep turned fitful again that night. When she woke in the morning, she couldn't get the giant staring yellow eye out of her mind. None of the other parts of her night's dreams remained with her, just that. It had to be a dragon, and that meant it was linked to the egg.

Realizing she was wide awake and not likely to go back to sleep, Quinn sat up. She started to talk to the egg that usually sat on the other pillow but stopped herself, glaring at the empty pillow beside her.

Anger boiled up, and Quinn jumped out of bed. It was barely six in the morning, but she didn't care. She needed to get out and work through the dream and all the jumbled feelings within her before she killed someone. She slipped on sweatpants and a t-shirt and grabbed her shoes for a run around the neighborhood.

Then she remembered the night before.

Stopping in front of her bedroom mirror, Quinn said, "I can't go out. I can't go anywhere, or the stupid Fae cops will arrest me."

Quinn shook her head and put on her shoes anyway. She didn't have to go outside. She'd go run through the Hunter tunnels beneath the pub.

Things were quiet and dark in O'Malley's when she got downstairs. It was too early for anyone to be setting up for the day. Quinn crossed the floor to the back door leading to the storerooms.

She pulled it open and jumped when she almost bumped into her mother.

"What are you doing up?" they said simultaneously, then stopped and laughed.

"You first," Quinn said.

"Getting a late snack from the kitchen before I turn in for a few hours. Paddy keeps local blood in the walk-in chiller for me. What about you?"

Quinn smiled. "I couldn't sleep. Dreams have me all worked up. This whole house sanctuary thing is going to wear thin real fast. It might as well be house arrest."

"Do you want to talk about it?"

"No. Actually, I was going to go for a run. I need to work this out of my system."

Naomi smiled. "Want some company? I promise I'll go easy on you."

Quinn grimaced. Her mother's version of easy entailed working her to exhaustion, but that might be what the doctor ordered.

"You know what?" Quinn said. "I think that's a great idea."

"Really?" Naomi asked, surprised. "I would think you'd want to avoid having me work you over in a training exercise. Who are you, and what have you done with my daughter?"

"Very funny. Honestly, I just need to keep my body occupied while my mind works through some things. Having you do all the thinking for me sounds perfect for that."

"Fair enough. Let's go."

"What about your snack? Don't you need to charge up on some fresh blood?"

Naomi shrugged. "I'll be all right. It'll still be there when we get back. Come on, let's start right now. I'll go easy for the first five minutes until you're warmed up."

Quinn nodded, and Naomi took off back down the long hallway into the darkness. Quinn invoked her night vision and took off after her, boosting her speed with a little draw from her stamina bar in the HUD.

An hour later, the two women walked back up the hall. Quinn dripped sweat. Despite her fatigue, or maybe because of it, she felt better than when she woke up.

"I can't believe you're not sweating," Quinn said to her mother after a glance at her dry pale skin.

"Undead, remember?" Naomi replied. "Believe me, I'm feeling it on the inside."

"Really? That's the first time you've ever let on about something like that. I always thought you were still raring to go after our practice sessions."

Naomi laughed. "Well, now you know it was all an act. To be honest, there were more than a few times, especially when Avery was here and working out against you, that I thought I was going to pass out."

At the mention of Avery, Quinn shifted her thoughts to

the other Huntress, wondering what she was up to. She hadn't heard from her girlfriend in almost a week. Given what she was doing, that wasn't unusual. Still, Quinn missed her. The few days they'd had together had been magical and left her hungry for more.

"I'm sorry, Quinn," Naomi said.

"Sorry for what?"

"I shouldn't have mentioned Avery. You miss her a lot, don't you?"

"I do, but her work is important. Until she uncovers the rest of Gemma's little Huntress projects, we need to be apart."

Naomi smiled and changed the subject. "Come on, let's head to the kitchen. I can get that blood bag, and you can whip up a smoothie or something."

"That sounds nice."

In the kitchen, Quinn and Naomi shared their breakfast. Quinn tried to cover her distaste for the blood snack Naomi sipped. She didn't know why it bothered her since the blood was from a living donor.

Naomi must have seen the look on Quinn's face despite her attempt to hide it. "Still grosses you out, doesn't it?"

"Yeah, it does, but it's my problem, Mom, not yours. I've got to accept this is who you are. It's not like you can change back. If I want to have you in my life, I've got to make my peace with it."

"If it makes you feel better, it took me a long time to accept who I'd become. I had a good reason to do what I did, but it was anathema to everything I'd been raised to stand for. In the early days, I had no self-control. Handon used to take advantage of that just to watch his pet hunter feed. It was horrible. I'm glad to be in a place where that's not a problem."

"How long did it take?" Quinn asked.

"To get to the point where I could resist killing someone?" Naomi replied. She continued after Quinn nodded, "Two long years, almost to the day. John had found a particularly tasty morsel for me. He was so disappointed I didn't finish her off that he walked over and snapped the girl's neck to spite me."

Quinn clenched her fists at the thought of someone being used for bait and food like that.

"I still see her startled expression right after he did it. That was when I knew I had to help you survive. You were my only chance for escape, and I wanted to make up for everything I did."

"So, I guess it worked out for both of us after all," Quinn said. She drained the last of the pineapple and banana smoothie and got up to rinse the glass in the sink. "Sorry it took me so long to come around after I found out who you were."

"It's all right. I was willing to give you the time you needed. It wasn't like I had anywhere to be. And look, here we are sharing breakfast after a mother-daughter workout."

"Let's hope there are more," Quinn said.

The door into the kitchen opened and Taylor came in, calling, "I found her," over her shoulder.

"What's up, T?" Quinn asked.

"I got up and went by your apartment. When you weren't there, I called Clark. We thought you might have gone after Aurora to retrieve the dragon egg."

"I won't say I haven't thought about it, but in this case, I think that has to be a team project. They're going to be expecting me to do it, after all."

Naomi tapped her chin. "You've been to Aurora's home, right?"

"Yes. What are you thinking?" Quinn asked.

"Well, doesn't it make it easier for Taylor to do her thing when she sends you somewhere via the VR rig?"

Taylor snapped her fingers. "That's a great idea. I'll need to code a few special additions I've had in mind. I need to get on it if you're going tonight."

The tech witch left the kitchen door to swing closed on its spring. Clark stepped in and caught it before it shut all the way.

"What was she so excited about?"

Quinn smiled. "We're hitting Aurora's in the VR tonight. It's time to get my egg back."

"She'll be expecting you," Clark cautioned. "Have you considered that?"

"Come on," Quinn replied. "Let's think about the plan. We'll need some sort of distraction outside to make it work. What Mom said last night about getting Aurora out of her house could work in our favor. They don't want to wait for the sanctuary thing to work itself out. Maybe we can give them some bait."

Naomi nodded and followed Quinn out to the restaurant. Clark fell in beside her.

Quinn smiled. For the first time in a while, she felt like things were back in her control. It was time to take advantage of it.

CHAPTER SEVENTEEN

It took Taylor all day to come up with the changes she needed to adapt to place Quinn inside Aurora's home. That was fine since it had taken all day to come up with something Clark and Naomi could do to distract the Fae princesses and their guards away from the home.

Quinn waited until well after dark and got some food down in O'Malley's to fuel up for the evening's main event. She ate the last French fry on her plate just as Clark and Naomi came into the club. She waved at them and waited for the two to join her.

"You both look pleased with yourselves. I assume that means you had some success?"

Clark smiled. "It was all Naomi's doing. She does a pretty good job of pretending to be you in a pinch. We had to wait until after sundown, but that helped our deception."

Naomi said, "At this point, you've been spotted all over the city, stirring up supernaturals to stop being pawns of the Fae and their rules."

"I can't believe it worked," Quinn said. "Didn't they realize you were a vampire?"

"Clark used Hunter magic to cover me whenever I got close to folks. It helps that most have only a vague description of you. That and our looking close in age did the trick."

Quinn's fingers came up to play with her amulet. "I hope it's enough to draw them out."

"It won't bring all of them," Clark said. "But it should get some of Aurora's security team away from the house. We said you were holding a rally downtown at the square outside City Hall. Aurora was supposed to attend an event down there with the mayor tonight. Now, Naomi has invited everyone to come down and join us to confront the Fae."

Quinn smiled. "I wish I could see the look on Filippa's and Aurora's faces when they realize it's you and not me."

"When they do, Quinn," Naomi said, "you're not going to have much time to get out. You'll have to work fast. Have you come up with a way to find the egg quickly once you're inside?"

"I hope so. The egg and I have a thing going. If it works the way I think it does, the egg will tell me where it is once I'm close enough."

At Clark's puzzled expression, Quinn explained, "I talk to it sometimes, and it sort of responds to me."

Clark chuckled. "I'm glad I didn't know you were holding conversations with it before now. I might have thought you were going off the deep end."

"It's not all that crazy," Naomi said. "Dragons are said to be very intelligent and fiercely loyal to those they consider friends. If the egg is preparing to hatch, Quinn could have a valuable ally there."

"I don't think the city needs a dragon flying around," Clark replied. "But it could explain why you're having those dreams. That dragon could grow up and cause a lot of trouble."

"We can worry about that later," Quinn said. "Right now, we need to get the egg back. My dream has to be a warning about what could happen if the egg and the dragon aren't rescued. What time do you two need to be downtown?"

Naomi checked her phone. "We need to leave soon. We came back here to check in with you and Taylor to coordinate the time of my performance. Have you talked to her?"

"A few hours ago. She was buried in some sort of programming update and didn't even look up when I came in. Miranda seemed hopeful it would be ready in time, though."

Clark shook his head. "It had better be. We won't be able to pull this off twice. They've already got guards surrounding the area to try to spot you leaving. We're going to have to sneak past them as it is."

Quinn got up. "I'm finished eating. Let's go check on Taylor."

The three of them headed to Taylor's workshop. Just before Quinn got there, a bright white flash flared from under the door, followed by a loud bang. She rushed forward and pulled open the door.

A haze of gray smoke billowed out. Quinn waved her arms and called, "Taylor, Miranda, are you two okay?"

There was no answer, and Quinn went inside. Across

the room, a standing fan in the corner switched on, and the smoke began to clear. Taylor sat coughing behind her worktable, gazing at her screen through tear-filled eyes.

"What happened?" Quinn asked.

Taylor looked up. "Huh?"

Quinn raised her voice. "I said, what happened?"

Taylor gave a half-grin and pointed to her ears. In a voice nearly as loud as Quinn's, she said, "I think the explosion affected my ears. All I hear is ringing."

Miranda floated over. "I was afraid something like this might happen."

"What did she do?" Quinn asked. The ghost heard her fine.

"She wanted to account for the wild magic episodes we'd been having so you'd be able to deal with things that came up while you were inside. I warned her it wouldn't work."

Taylor looked up from the screen. "Hey, Miranda. You were right. It didn't work."

Quinn rolled her eyes.

Clark said, "Great. Does that mean the system is down?"

Miranda started to answer, but Taylor yelled from behind the monitors, "Wow, we're lucky. The system's still working, and the code I added seems to have stuck." She looked at the others, who were staring at her. "Who's the queen of the tech witches? This girl."

"Taylor," Quinn said, "are you sure it's working correctly? I don't want to get stuck inside a wall or something."

"What?"

Quinn leaned over the triple monitors. "Can. You. Do. This?"

"Oh, no problem. Don't worry, I won't let you end up inside a wall."

Clark shook his head. "This has 'successful mission' written all over it."

"Don't be a worrywart," Naomi chided. "Taylor said it's fine."

"Yeah, but how's she going to know when to bring Quinn back out?" Clark picked up the headsets they used when Quinn was inside VR. "She can't hear the comm."

Taylor held up her wireless earbud. "I think I can jack up the signal and run it through the computer's external speakers. Miranda can relay things to me."

Clark threw his hands in the air. "She's a ghost. It's not like she can write you notes."

Quinn said. "We don't have a choice. If the system is working, I have to go in tonight. Clark, you and Naomi go downtown and do your thing. Text me when you're in place. Miranda, Taylor, and I will come up with a solution on this end."

Naomi nodded and nudged Clark. "Let's go."

He urged, "Quinn, don't go in if it looks like there's a problem."

Taylor gave Clark a thumbs-up and shouted, "Don't worry. I won't send her in if there's a problem."

Clark grumbled as he went out the door. "I'm too old for this crap."

Quinn smiled as her mother and Clark pulled the door shut. "Okay, it looks like it's going to be you and me,

Miranda. Can you make sure Taylor knows what's going on?"

"You know I'll do my best, but all I can do is try to get her to read my lips."

"Maybe the effects are temporary."

Taylor had been fiddling with the communications gear. She handed Quinn her earpiece and the small belt pack that boosted the signal. "I've got you piped through these two speakers, and I've set up this mic by the monitors so you can hear Miranda. That should do for now."

Quinn nodded and inserted the earpiece, then clipped the belt pack in place at her waist and sat on the edge of the table. "Now we wait for Clark and Naomi to get into position. In the meantime, let's come up with a system of simple hand gestures you can use to communicate with Taylor."

She picked up a pad of paper and started jotting down a few of the essential things she'd need to relay to Taylor. There wasn't that much when she thought about it. The most important thing was when she needed Taylor to pull her out. Everything else was just progress updates.

Quinn held up the pad for Miranda to read the list of phrases. "These look good to you? All you have to do is point to the one I say so Taylor can do what she needs to on this end."

"That'll work. Anything else, I'll get creative."

Taylor smiled. "Ready to go? I just need the location in the home you want to show up at."

Quinn thought about that. She'd only been in part of the house's first floor, so her choices were limited. She could appear in any of the rooms off the central hallway, but there was nowhere to hide from what she remembered. In the end, she decided on the atrium where she and Aurora'd had their sit-down. The lush foliage would conceal her if she materialized in one of the corners.

Quinn jotted down the word "Atrium" on the pad and pointed to it.

Taylor smiled. "Okay. You're the key, though. You have to keep the location firmly in your mind as you enter the system. I've set the code to meld with you as you go in. It should send you to the location you're thinking about."

Quinn nodded. It seemed simple enough.

"Ready?" Taylor asked.

Quinn was about to try to explain they were waiting to hear from Clark and Naomi when her mother sent a text.

Quinn sent back an okay and nodded at Taylor. While her friend fired up the VR system, Quinn picked up the rig and settled it over her head. She arranged the wire harness so it was out of the way as she lay down.

Taylor leaned over the monitors by Quinn's head and tapped her friend on the shoulder. "Good to go. Counting you in now."

Quinn pulled the goggles into place. As soon as she did, a tug on her mind took over. Quinn focused on the atrium's corner, opposite where she'd sat talking to the princess weeks before. The tugging turned into a sharp pull, and Quinn fell backward into the darkness.

CHAPTER EIGHTEEN

Quinn opened her eyes and crouched behind the thick foliage inside the atrium. She'd popped into the corner she'd envisioned. The glassed-in room at the back of Aurora's home was dark. Only the hall lights outside the double French doors illuminated the area.

Crouched behind a three-foot-high pottery urn, Quinn peered through a cluster of ferns growing out of it. The tips of the ferns were at least six feet above the floor.

Tapping her earpiece, Quinn whispered, "I'm in, just where I wanted to be. I'll touch base later once I get an idea where things are."

Miranda replied, "I'll let Taylor know. Be careful."

Quinn cut the connection and listened to see if anyone was close by. When she didn't hear anyone, she stood and peered around the fronds to check the hallway outside the glass doors. The corridor ran through the center of the house from the front door to the back. The staircase leading to the second floor was right next to the front door. She didn't know what else was on the first floor here or where the stairs to access the basement lay. Quinn guessed Aurora had hidden the egg either in the basement or perhaps her personal chambers upstairs.

Opening her HUD, she smiled. The wild magic icon was highlighted, proof the egg was nearby. It also meant she might have an advantage. She engaged her earth sense as she had on the mountain and it worked. She now knew where every living thing was in the home, from the four Fae guards scattered around the house to the nest of spiders nestled in the rafters down in the basement. Most importantly, she detected the dragon egg somewhere beneath her, and there was only a single person downstairs with it. She tried to identify more about them, but their signature was unfamiliar. They weren't human or Fae.

Concentrating on the four Fae guards, Quinn saw two in one room upstairs. They were playing a game, and their minds were occupied with that. Another guard stood at the corner of the house outside, watching the front door. The final one walked alone down the hallway on the second floor, away from the stairs. The way was clear for her to search for the way to the basement.

After whispering "Mist," Quinn waited until the edges of her vision blurred. Hidden in shadow now, she moved out from behind the fern to stand by the door. She kept her senses tuned to the movements of the others upstairs and froze at a slight creak from the hinges. It seemed as loud as an alarm bell to her sensitive ears.

She opened the door enough for her to turn sideways and slide through the gap into the hall. Voices near the main entrance startled her. Quinn rechecked her map, but nothing had changed. The three Fae inside were all still upstairs. After a few seconds, she realized a TV had been left on. The faint flicker of light from the living room next to the front door confirmed her suspicions. Quinn took a few steps forward and checked to be sure. The TV was on, and a cold glass of beer sat on the table next to a chair. That was why the one Fae upstairs was on the move. He must've gone up to retrieve something. He'd be returning soon, so she had to work fast to search for the stairs to the basement.

Stepping from shadow to shadow, Quinn walked across the hall and through a short passage running beneath the steps to the second floor. She passed a powder room and then entered a small living room. Another door led from there toward the rear of the house and into the home's kitchen.

Inside the kitchen, Quinn searched for something to tell her how to get to the basement. Two doors sat across the kitchen from where she stood. One was obviously the rear door to the home. She could see a narrow, closed porch through the window in the top half of the door.

The plain wooden door beside the back door might just be a pantry, but she had to check it. Quinn crossed the kitchen, passing the entrance to the dining room. She glanced inside as she passed. There was a long table in the center, with four chairs on either side but no entrance that looked like a basement door.

Quinn took two more steps and stopped next to the plain door. She leaned in to listen for any sounds on the other side and froze as soon when her skin touched the wood. Quinn's HUD popped up again, but this time, it wasn't the guards who drew her attention. It was the deep and overwhelming sadness coming from the other side of this door. It came from that person she couldn't identify down in the basement. She knew two things now from her new earth sense ability: this was the door to the basement, and someone down there needed help.

Gripping the antique ceramic doorknob, Quinn pulled it open a crack and looked around it to see the other side. An open-sided wooden staircase led down to a concrete floor below.

Quinn started down the steps, closing the door behind her. As she descended, she tested each stair tread with a toe first to avoid any unnecessary squeaks.

About halfway down, Quinn stopped. The soft sound of someone crying came from somewhere down here. The faint sobbing hadn't been loud enough for her to pick up at the top of the stairs.

Quinn crouched and bent down to peer into the basement from where she stood. She couldn't see much beyond the landing at the foot of the steps. There were shelves on either side of a door, and there was more of the concrete floor beyond. The sobbing seemed to come from behind the door.

Quinn tiptoed the rest of the way to the bottom and surveyed the area. The rest of this part of the basement had shelves lining the walls. Boxes and odd junk filled most of the storage space. To the left was a stone-walled passageway leading to the rest of the basement. The crying was more apparent now, and it sounded like a child. They were behind the old wooden door on the wall across from the stairs. She still couldn't determine what it was, only that it wasn't human or Fae.

For a split second, Quinn considered searching the basement and ignoring the crying, but the deep sadness touching her through the earth sense connection tugged at her soul. She realized she had to help whoever was on the other side. It was the right thing to do.

Raising a hand, Quinn knocked lightly on the door. "Um, excuse me. Are you all right? I heard you crying and wondered if you needed help."

The crying stopped as soon as she started talking. Someone cleared their throat and sniffled as if their nose had been running. "Who's out there?"

"May I come in? I didn't want to open the door without permission."

The person on the other side paused so long that Quinn almost asked again. "Maybe you shouldn't. My brothers tell me I scare people when they see me."

With a statement like that, Quinn felt she had to open the door. "I won't be scared. I promise. You sound so sad. Maybe I can help."

"Okay, promise you won't scream? You sound nice."

"Cross my heart," Quinn replied. "I'm opening the door now."

She wasn't sure what she was expecting, but it wasn't the huge, green-skinned form sitting in near-total darkness clutching a small, very dim flashlight in its massive hands. The creature was so large it had to sit. There was no way it could have stood up straight in the low-ceilinged basement. That put it at well over six feet tall. Sitting in the corner, its head reached three-quarters of the way to the ceiling.

A broad face lifted to squint at her through the light

streaming into the darkened room. The first things she saw were the two tusks jutting from the lower jaw to curve out and over the upper lip. The round, bulbous head was a little misshapen and not symmetrical. The eyes, though, held all the humanity of an ordinary person and were filled with brimming tears and the expectation of hope.

"Hi, my name is Quinn. What's yours?" she asked from the doorway.

"My brothers call me Theodore sometimes, but only when they are being nice. Usually, they call me worse things. They tell me I'm ugly, even for an orc."

"Hmmm, I don't know any orcs, but you look fine to me. Should I call you Theodore, then?"

The sad face broke into a half-smile at her request. "I don't know, maybe."

"Is there another name you'd prefer?" Quinn asked, smiling back at him. "What is it? If I'm going to help you, I need to know what to call you."

"My mother used to call me Tadpole when I was little. That was a long time ago. She's gone now. I've felt so alone since then." Tears welled in the big eyes again.

Quinn smiled, "Don't cry, Tadpole. It's okay. I'm here with you, so you're not alone right now. Why are you sitting down here in the dark with nothing but that beat-up flashlight?"

"My brothers went with the pretty lady to some important job in the city. I wanted to come along, but they told me I'd scare everyone and make the children scream and cry." Tears dripped down Tadpole's cheeks. "My brothers told me to sit down here in the dark where my ugly face wouldn't upset the beautiful Fae upstairs."

"That's not very nice. Is that why you were crying?"

Tadpole shook his head. "Not entirely. It's just that I have to stay here until they get back, and the flashlight is starting to go out. I don't like it in the dark, Quinn. I know I should be grown up about it, but being alone in the dark without a light scares me."

Quinn knew she had to get on with the real reason she was here, but she couldn't leave the poor guy like this. He was a little kid in a monster's body. She thought about a way to take him with her or help him escape somehow. That wasn't why she was here, though. Plus, he was too large to come back through VR with her. She didn't think he'd leave on his own to wander the city. He could've done that already.

A solution came to her, but she wasn't sure it would work. She had to check on something. "Tadpole, can I take a look at your flashlight?"

"You're not going to take it from me, are you?"

"No, silly. I just want to see what kind of batteries it takes. Is that okay?"

"Yeah, I guess so." Tadpole held out his giant hand and gave Quinn his little flashlight. It was a typical LED penlight. Based on the dimness, the batteries were nearly dead.

"It's going to get dark for a few seconds, but there's light coming from the top of the stairs, okay?" Quinn said.

He nodded, and she unscrewed the flashlight's head to reveal two AA batteries.

Quinn smiled. "I can fix this for you, but I have to call my friends real quick."

Tadpole smiled and nodded again.

Quinn tapped her earpiece. "Miranda, the belt pack for our comm gear has removable batteries, right?"

"That's correct. AA sized ones, I think. Why? Is there a problem with your pack. You sound loud and clear right now."

"Okay, I'm going to try something, and my signal is going to drop off. Don't freak out and pull me out of the VR. Hopefully, I'll be back on the comm in a minute or so."

Quinn cut the connection and pulled the signal-booster pack clipped to her belt. She turned it over and pressed on it with her thumbs to release the back cover. As soon as the lid slid off, she saw two AA batteries. She removed them and replaced them with the batteries from the dying flashlight. She held the fresh batteries in her hand while she popped the cover back into place.

She reached up and tapped her earpiece again. "Miranda, can you hear me?"

"Barely. Your signal is much weaker than before."

"Okay, but it's working. I hoped that would be the case. I'm switching off the pack until I'm ready to come out. I'll switch it back on only to tell you I'm ready to leave. Be ready when the time comes, all right?"

"What's going on?" Miranda asked.

"I'll explain later. Just tell Taylor to be ready."

"I will. Be careful, Quinn."

Quinn cut the connection and then pressed and held the small button at the end of the battery pack until the tiny red light turned off.

She smiled at the orc. "Okay, Tadpole, I think I have your problem solved." She slid the two fresh batteries into his flashlight and screwed the head back in place. Immediately the bright white LED lit up, filling the room with illumination. She handed it back to him.

"Wow, Quinn, thank you so much. Now I won't be as scared alone down here. Maybe you can come down and see me again sometime?"

"I don't know about that, Tadpole. I might not be around the next time you come out. I will be gone before your brothers return. Maybe we'll get to meet another time, though."

"I'd like that. Where do you have to go?"

"I came to pick up something that belongs to me. Once I find it, I plan on leaving right away. I don't suppose you've seen a big egg sitting around the house somewhere, have you?"

Tadpole's face lit up in a big grin. "You mean the dragon egg? The pretty lady has it locked up at the other end of the basement. It's in a hiding place there. She and her friends did some magic to it. I saw her reading from a small book and then she cast a spell. It's supposed to keep the egg from hatching until she's ready."

"You said it's locked up. How?"

"There's a secret door in the wall at the end of the basement. I watched her put it in there after she did the magic."

"Is there a key or something? I really need to get the egg back, Tadpole. The dragon inside is my friend."

"There's no key, but I know how the door works. Come on, I'll show you."

Quinn stepped back so the orc could come out. He crouched so his head didn't scrape the exposed rafters. Quinn followed him to the room at the other end of the basement. Here, as in the rest of the basement, the original stone foundation formed the walls. The room was empty except for a broken crate on the floor and an old set of wrought iron fireplace tools leaning against the wall. Quinn searched the walls, but she couldn't see where a secret room or door was located.

"You said you knew how to open it? I don't see anything that looks like a door or a hidden panel."

Tadpole picked up the rusty fireplace poker. "I saw the pretty lady. She didn't think I watched or understood what I saw."

He slid the poker into a gap between two stones in the far wall. The iron disappeared until only the handle remained in view. He turned the poker handle until there was a soft click. A rectangular section of the wall popped open, revealing a small alcove in the wall behind it. The dragon egg rested inside. It no longer sparkled with green iridescence. It seemed like someone had covered it with a dull coat of translucent plastic.

"Thank you, Tadpole. This saved me so much time. You should go back to your room. I don't want you to get into trouble for helping me."

"How will you get out with the egg? The guards upstairs will hear you leaving."

"I have a secret way to get back out. Take your flashlight and go. I'll be fine."

The big orc started to leave, then turned around and wrapped Quinn in a bear hug. When he let go, it took her a moment to catch her breath.

Quinn coughed a little and said, "I hope we get the chance to meet again, Tadpole. I'd love to introduce you to all my friends. I think they'd like you."

"That would be nice, Quinn. Be careful."

"I will."

The orc hunched over and worked his way back to the room where Quinn had found him. He turned and wiggled his thick fingers at her, then closed the door.

Quinn went to the secret hole in the wall. A small leather-bound book sat on the stones beside the egg. It looked like one of the personal journals Aurora had read from when Quinn had been here before. It might have useful information for them about what the princess did to the egg. Quinn slid it into the waistband of her jeans at the small of her back, then picked up the egg, holding it under one arm like a football.

She pressed the button on the comm battery pack with her free hand and then tapped her earpiece. "Miranda, can you hear me? I'm ready to come back."

Through a rash of static, Miranda answered from the other side. "Got it, Quinn. Get ready."

The recall came just in time. Upstairs, the front door opened, and several gruff voices announced the return of at least some of Aurora's guards and maybe Tadpole's orc brothers. She wouldn't have had much more time before someone came down to check either on Tadpole or the egg.

Quinn shifted the egg to hold it in both arms as she waited for the VR system to reach out and bring her home. A second later, the tug of the VR recall signal pulled her backward into darkness.

CHAPTER NINETEEN

Quinn sat up and looked around Taylor's workshop. She raised her hand and massaged her forehead for a second.

Miranda floated over and asked, "Everything okay? You got the egg back."

"I feel the beginnings of a pounding headache coming on, but that's just another crash translation back from VR. I didn't just get the egg. I got this." She pulled out the journal and handed it to Taylor.

Her friend took the small leather book and flipped through it while Quinn tried to relax and will the headache away.

"Quinn," Taylor shouted, "this book is strange. It's a handwritten journal on how to hatch a dragon egg. The most recent entries mention doing something to the outside of the egg to contain wild magic outbreaks."

"I found out Aurora did something to the egg. I'm glad I had the sense to bring it with me." Quinn got up to lean over Taylor's shoulder. She glanced at the journal's pages for the first time. The notes were written in a script of flowing runes. She raised her voice despite the headache and said, "How can you read that? It's in Fae, right?"

"Yeah," Taylor replied. "I've been doing an online course. I was surprised when it popped up in my search feed."

"An online course for Faeish?"

Taylor nodded and went back to flipping through the book. "The coating on the egg is some kind of magical glue or sealant. That's why it's not as shiny as it was before."

"Something to stop the wild magic is a good thing," Quinn replied. "That alleviates one problem we were going to have to contend with now that we have the egg back."

"Miranda?" Taylor asked. She pointed at one of the pages. "Do you know this series of runes? It's not familiar to me."

The ghost glanced at the journal and gasped.

"What?" Quinn and Taylor asked together.

"It's a phrase for still-birth. It reads as 'born-not-born,' but when you put it in the context of the whole passage, that's what it means. In this case, it says the coating must be removed before the dragon starts to hatch, or it will die before it gets free."

"The little dragon's in danger?" Quinn asked. "We have to do something. There must be a way to remove the coating before it is too late."

Taylor kept reading. "There is, but I don't think you're going to like it."

Quinn glanced at the journal again. "What does it say? Whatever it is, I'll do it."

Clark called from the doorway, "Do what? I don't like the sound of that."

Clark and Naomi came into the workshop.

"Did you run into any of the Fae trackers?" Clark asked.

"Yeah, they were in the house. I evaded them easily enough. She also had a huge orc down in the basement."

Clark said, "We saw a few orcs hanging around Aurora at City Hall. They all looked normal-sized. How big was the one you saw?"

"I don't know. Way bigger than a person, that's for sure."

Clark's eyes widened.

"What's the big deal?"

Naomi said, "Orcs are strictly regulated by the supernatural community. They were created by the Fae over a thousand years ago as shock troops in their wars against humans and others who threatened their sacred groves. When the initial battles were over with, everyone, including the Fae, were appalled at the carnage. It was decided then that in exchange for humans keeping away from Fae groves, the orcs, especially the enhanced warrior class, would be kept on a tight leash. If you met one, it was the first allowed out of a locked compound in a very long time."

Clark said, "I wondered why she had those orcs out with her in public. She was keeping them out of view, but they were easy to spot if you knew what you were looking for. Bringing them out is bad enough. Maybe it wasn't an orc warrior you saw."

"He called himself an orc, so I took him at his word."

Naomi's jaw dropped. "You talked to him?"

"Yeah, he was nice. He just wanted a friend to talk to. He was scared and crying, so I helped him. I hope he's all right. They might punish him if they discover he helped me take the egg."

"So, you didn't fight him?" Clark asked. "He's not dead?"

Quinn shook her head. "No, I told you. He was friendly. I don't know about his four brothers. They sounded like jerks, given how Tadpole said they treated him."

"'Tadpole?'" Clark asked.

"That's what he wanted to be called. It reminded him of his mother. She's either dead or a long way off. He misses her a lot."

Clark and Naomi stood there staring at her for a few long seconds until Quinn finally said, "What?"

Clark frowned. "I'm not sure if you're pulling our legs. You shouldn't have survived an encounter with an orc warrior. They're supposed to be vicious and nearly inde-structible."

"How do you know what they're like? You and Mom said no one has seen one in hundreds of years."

"The histories are very clear on orcs, Quinn," Naomi said. "I'll make sure Joshua brings by a few of the older tomes describing them. You have some reading to do. They're to be killed on sight."

Quinn's eyes narrowed. "If anyone hurts Tadpole, they'll have to deal with me."

Clark held up a hand to stave off any further arguing. "Let's drop this for now. What were you all talking about when we came in? It sounded like you were planning on doing something foolish."

"It's not foolish," Quinn said. "They cast a spell on the

egg to hold in the wild magic. The problem is, it can kill the dragon inside if it's not removed. Taylor and Miranda were looking at the journal I snagged to find out what the solution is."

Quinn gestured at Taylor. "Tell him what you found, T."

The tech witch cleared her throat. She must have been able to follow most of that conversation. "Here's what I've been able to translate so far about the spell to remove the coating. I'm still unsure of some of it and need to research parts to get the spell right. Basically, you have to create a paste made of fresh dragon dung and ground-up scales. It looks like you smear that on the egg and set the whole mess on fire. When you're done, the coating is burned off, and the egg will crack and start the hatching process soon after."

"So," Quinn said, "we need to get some dragon crap and ground scales. There are magic shops around that stock that stuff, right?" She glanced at the others, receiving blank stares in return."

"Quinn," Naomi said, "if Taylor's translation is right, it specifies fresh dung. That means you have to get it from a dragon's lair."

"Would Gil count?" Quinn asked. "I want to check on him anyway."

Clark said, "No. He's just a cousin to the great dragons. The lake dragons are a different breed entirely. For this, you're going to need to locate a live dragon and find a way to get close enough to steal a few loose scales and enough poop to make this paste. It's suicidal."

"Clearly, Aurora and Filippa didn't think so," Quinn

said. "They didn't put this coating on there just to let the little dragon die. They want it alive."

Miranda said, "The Fae have long had a relationship with dragonkind. I guess they know of the location of a nearby dragon or have another connection that will allow them to get the ingredients they need."

Taylor raised her hand and pointed at the journal. "Hey, did you all know the Fae have a dragon of their own? It's in a hidden cavern on an island in Chesapeake Bay. It says it's near Aurora's estate."

Quinn smiled. "There you have it, Clark. We have everything we need to get this done and save the baby dragon. I have to do this. I won't let any friend of mine die, and that little dragon inside the egg is my friend."

As if to punctuate the declaration, the egg rocked on the table. Quinn reached out and stroked the egg, making soothing sounds.

Clark's eyebrows shot up. "How long has it been doing that?"

"For a few weeks. It started just before Avery showed up. I think it's lonely, and it seems to understand me when I talk to it."

"You've talked to it?" Miranda asked.

Quinn nodded.

Naomi said, "It makes sense. We know Quinn imprinted on the egg when she first saw it. It stands to reason if the egg was mature, close to hatching, the dragon inside might have awakened enough to move like babies do in the womb."

"I've never heard of anything like it communicating with people," Clark said. "But there's a lot our young

Huntress has done that hasn't been done before. We can at least look into finding this hidden dragon. No promises, Quinn. Approaching an adult dragon is suicide in almost all cases."

"If you get me close," Quinn said, "I'll go in and get what's needed. No one else needs to risk anything."

"What about the VR system?" Naomi said. "If we know the dragon's location, we can just send her there and pull her back before it knows she's there."

Miranda shook her head. "Two problems with that. Dragons are known to have magic-dampening abilities. Even if we managed to get her in, we might not be able to get her home again. Plus, we don't know where it is. Taylor will need pretty solid coordinates to zero in on it. Quinn could end up floating in the middle of Chesapeake Bay."

"Look," Quinn said, "we've all had a busy night. Let's settle down and get some rest. We can revisit this in the morning. All I'm worried about is protecting the egg from the Fae. You know they'll try to steal it back."

"The request for sanctuary should protect us from any intrusions in the near-term," Clark said. "But you can bet those princesses are going to ask the court to expedite the case. They'll assume you were the one who left the sanctuary to retrieve it. We'll have to work fast to get everything we need before they rule against you."

They began packing up the VR rig and shutting Taylor's gear down so they could lock up for the night. Quinn took the egg with her and headed for her apartment. She wasn't sure the Fae would accept the club's sanctuary if Quinn had the egg back. She wanted it close to her at all times to make sure Aurora and Filippa didn't come for it again.

The egg vibrated like a cat purring in her arms as she headed up the stairs. Quinn smiled and stroked the shell. It no longer had a smooth pebbled surface like before. Instead, it felt tacky from whatever the Fae had used to coat it. She hoped whatever it was hadn't already harmed the tiny dragon inside.

Her worries followed her up to her apartment and led to a fitful night's sleep. Quinn checked each time she woke to make sure the egg was still there, snuggled against her side. The soothing vibrations when she curled around it helped her drift back to sleep within seconds.

CHAPTER TWENTY

It took most of the next day to lock down a boat for their trip out to the middle of the bay. By the time they did, it was getting late. They'd left Naomi and Miranda to keep an eye on the egg and snuck Quinn out through the underground tunnel system beneath O'Malley's. The passage emerged beneath a highway overpass a few blocks away. Clark waited there in his car with Taylor.

Taylor smiled at Quinn from the front seat. "It's nice to ride up front for a change with the grownups. You kids keep the noise down back there."

"Very funny," Quinn replied. "Enjoy it while you can. I call shotgun for the ride back."

"Damn, I should have done that," Taylor said. "I was distracted by getting the dragon coordinates locked down. That should count for something, right?"

"You still have to call it," Quinn said. "That's the rules."

"All right, you two," Clark said. "I've heard enough of this argument. It's fair. Taylor rides upfront on the way there, and Quinn gets to sit up here for the trip back."

Both women stopped talking but smiled at each other, eyes twinkling with delight. They enjoyed teasing Clark and knew their friendly bickering annoyed him. He'd spent too much of his life alone.

Clark drove to the outskirts of Baltimore through a series of blue-collar neighborhoods until he reached a waterfront area northeast of the city and parked in a gravel lot beside a large marina. Most of the vessels appeared to be working boats of one sort or another rather than pleasure craft.

"I'm looking forward to getting out on the water again," Quinn said.

Taylor laughed. "You used to hate it, remember? Then I made you come swimming with me at one of the city pools. You were a natural."

"I'm even better now. Wait until you see what I've learned to do," Quinn replied. She hadn't told them about everything she'd learned from Gil and Terrence.

Clark pointed at one of the piers. "Our boat's out there. The guy's a little dodgy. I'm almost certain he uses his boat for smuggling. He's a Selkie, a type of seafolk from the British Isles that settled here with the earliest European settlers. If anyone can find us a way into this dragon's cavern, he can."

Quinn and Taylor followed Clark down to the dock and out onto the pier. There weren't many people in sight, and Quinn figured most of these watermen and women got moving early in the morning and were probably done for the day in the early afternoon. At the very end of the pier, past all the others, sat an old wooden boat with a large cabin at the front and an extended open deck behind it.

As they approached, Clark called, "Ho, Jori. You there?"

A head poked out of the cabin's door. The man had thick, curly brown hair and a beard to match. He smiled, revealing a gold tooth in the front. "Clarkie, it's been how long since we saw each other?"

"It has been a while."

"I was surprised to hear from you. The last time we talked, you threatened to kill me if you ever saw me again. We Selkies take that kind of threat from a Hunter seriously."

"The last time we talked, I was pretty sure you were dealing in stolen dark magic artifacts. The original owners and I were worried about how they'd be used. You weren't very discerning when it came to buyers for one of your impromptu auctions."

"You never found anything to associate me with that heist. If you had, you would have followed through."

Quinn grew uneasy with the direction this conversation was going. She had a job to do, and they'd never find the dragon's hidden island if this guy and Clark started fighting. "Gentlemen, let's leave the past in the past. We have more important things on our table."

Jori laughed. "She's got you on a short leash, Clarkie. She your new girlfriend?"

"Ew," Taylor said. "Now I've got to get that out of my head."

"Jori," Clark said, "meet Quinn Faust, the Huntress of the new Baltimore clan."

"That's her?" Jori snorted and looked Quinn up and down. "She's a kid."

Quinn squelched the anger rising inside. She was

beginning to understand why Clark had threatened to kill this guy. "Don't let my age bother you, Captain. When you can kick supernatural ass the way I can, age doesn't matter. The question isn't whether I'm the real deal. The question is if you're the one who can help us. Having me as a friend can work in your favor, but I'm sure there are other watermen around Baltimore who'd like me to owe them."

Jori studied Quinn, one eyebrow raised. He seemed to be looking past whatever he saw at first, which was good. They didn't have time to find someone else.

"Owe me something? What might that mean?"

"I won't help you kill or harm anyone, but if you get yourself in trouble and I'm in a position to help you out of it, you can call in your marker. You've obviously heard some of what I've done around the city already. You know what I'm capable of."

Jori smiled. "I do indeed. Clark, you found yourself a live one here, didn't you? She's every bit as hard-nosed as I'd heard."

Clark shrugged. "I wouldn't cross her. You'd be wise to remember that. No marker you hold will save you if she thinks you're on the wrong side of what is right."

"I can live with that. As long as she doesn't mind a guy who occasionally walks the narrow line between right and wrong. All right, girl, what do you need from me? I assume it has to do with my boat."

"You didn't tell him?" Quinn asked Clark.

"I just checked to see if he was available. I figured it was better to tell him what we need face to face."

Jori frowned. "I don't know if I like the sound of that. What exactly do you want me to do?"

"We need you to take us out into the middle of the bay," Quinn said. "My friend here can direct you to the approximate coordinates. Once we get there, we'll be searching for something specific."

"Show me," Jori said to Taylor, who was standing behind Quinn, clutching her backpack to her chest. "Bring them in here where I have my charts."

Quinn, Clark, and Taylor carefully stepped from the pier to the boat and followed Jori into the cabin at the bow.

Jori had turned on an overhead light above a long counter with paper charts laid out on it. The boat's wheel and controls were at the far right side of the cabin.

Taylor set up her laptop and opened it. "We've localized the general area as being midway between Annapolis and the Eastern Shore south of the Bay Bridge. There's supposed to be a hidden island around there, one that doesn't show up on the regular charts."

"Damn you, Clark. You didn't say you were after Chessie. Are you insane?"

"We just need to find an entrance to her lair, Jori. That's all. No one expects you to go anywhere near the dragon."

"Wait," Quinn said. "This dragon has a name? You acted like you didn't know anything about this, Clark."

"It's an old legend. No one has seen the Chesapeake Bay dragon since the earliest days of Baltimore. Most people assume she's dead, like most of her kind."

"You could have told us," Taylor said. "I could have done a search and learned more about it."

"Why? We have all we need knowledge-wise here with Jori. I always suspected you and your family were up to no good all these years. I was right picking you for this job. You know all about Chessie, don't you?"

"Look, she's not the kind to take intrusion lightly. She's been resting for nigh on twenty years. The last time she woke up was during the purges. She took out a boatload of the bastards chasing Hunter families to even up the odds, ate a few of them, and went back to sleep. It didn't matter in the end. The fleeing Hunter families she saved were killed by attackers waiting on the far shore."

"So, this Chessie is a friend to the Hunters? That's good, right?" Quinn asked.

"She ain't a friend to anyone, girl. She's old and cantankerous and serves her own interests."

"Clark mentioned you and your family," Quinn said. "What's the connection between you all and the dragon?"

"The Selkies have always been tight with dragonkind. We frequent the same caves and underwater tunnels they do. It's one of the ways they keep their lairs hidden from the intrusions of men who'd like to steal from them. When we first came here, we sensed there was an ancient dragon in the area. My great-great-great grandda reached out to offer our services. Over the years, we've delivered things to Chessie when she needed them. That's all. She sends word when there's something she wants, and we bring it out to her."

"So, you know where the entrance to her lair is?" Taylor asked. "That's great. You can take us right to it."

Jori shook his head. "I only know the general area. She surfaces and retrieves what she wants, pays the fee, and goes back to her cave."

"So, you've never swum down to see if you could find the entrance?" Quinn asked.

Clark laughed. "She's known you for all of five minutes, and she has you pegged."

"I might have done that once upon a time when I was much younger and foolish. Chessie showed me the error of my ways." Jori lifted his sweater and t-shirt. A long line of round scars ran across his chest and back.

"What's that?" Taylor asked, gulping.

"That's where she caught me in her mouth and brought me up to the surface to return me to my father. Mind you, that's just one side of her massive jaws. At the time, the top half of my body was inside her mouth, screaming." Jori shuddered at the memory. "I can take you out there. You'll have to find the entrance on your own. I'm not going into the water out there again."

"Just get me close. I'll take care of the rest," Quinn said.

Jori looked at the deck outside the cabin. "You didn't bring along any scuba gear. How do you expect to get in there? I don't have anything for a dive operation. The entrance is underwater the whole way until you get inside the cavern."

"You let me worry about that," Quinn said. "We've talked about this enough. Let's cast off, or whatever it is you do to unpark this thing."

Jori stared at Quinn for a second and then nodded. "The correct term is 'shove off,' in case you're wondering." He smiled. "Make yourselves comfortable here in the cabin. It'll be tight, but you'll be cold and wet if you sit out on the deck this time of year."

The Selkie captain left to untie the lines holding the

craft to the pier. He returned a minute later and fired up the engine, then steered them out into the channel to the Chesapeake Bay.

Quinn wasn't quite sure about Jori or the wisdom of going into a dragon's lair like this on purpose, but she kept her misgivings to herself despite the knot of fear in her gut. She refused to turn back now. The little dragon in that egg needed her to save it. That was all that mattered. He or she was family now, just like everyone else in the clan. This old dragon wasn't going to get in the way of that.

It took them the better part of two hours to motor across the choppy waters to the correct location. Without saying a word, Jori shut off the engine and left the cabin. He walked across the deck and lifted a heavy steel anchor up and over the side, then did the same up at the stern.

He returned to the cabin. "This is as close as I'm getting. You'll have to go the rest of the way yourself."

"How far out are we?" Quinn asked.

"A quarter-mile, maybe more."

Clark said, "Quinn, you said you've got a way to do this. I don't know what you're planning, but it's time to let Taylor and me in on it."

Quinn smiled. "The plan is this. I'm going to swim down there, sneak in, take what we need, and get out. If everything goes according to plan, I'll be back in an hour or two."

"You heard Jori earlier. We don't have any scuba gear."

Jori nodded. "That and the water's pretty cold this time of year. I'm a Selkie and used to swimming in cold, choppy water. You'll die of hypothermia in ten minutes."

"Don't worry, either of you. You just make sure you're

here when I get back." Quinn started stripping out of her jeans and sweatshirt until she was standing there in a tankini swimsuit she'd put on earlier under her clothes. She bent down and reconfigured her Bowie's sheath so she could strap the belt around her waist and thigh. She also clipped a large nylon fanny pack around her waist and settled it at her back. She'd packed it with plastic zipper bags for the dung and a folded nylon drawstring bag for the scales.

Ignoring the others who stood and watched her prepare for her dive, Quinn reached out with her mind, feeling the water's power all around her. The wild magic of the sea filled her, and it was overwhelming compared to the smaller lake. Opening her HUD, Quinn clicked the glowing icon in the center and prayed the wild magic wanted what she did.

She relaxed as her body shifted around her.

Taylor gasped behind her. "Quinn, are those...gills?"

Quinn used the remaining air in her lungs to laugh and say, "Pretty cool, huh? See you in a few hours." She pushed off the deck with her flipper-feet and dove into the lower Chesapeake Bay's briny waters.

Time to find a dragon.

CHAPTER TWENTY-ONE

Quinn used her powerful legs to kick away from Jori's boat, drawing water in through her mouth and pushing it out through the gill flaps in her sides. She ignored the chill of the water since she knew she'd get used to it. As she went farther, though, unusual fatigue set in. She stopped and tried to catch her underwater breath.

As she tasted the briny salt, Quinn realized her aquatic form was fighting the difference between the freshwater lake it was used to and the alien saltwater environment. She tried to push through the difficulty using brute force of will, trying to make her body adapt.

That got her nowhere.

Quinn floated about fifteen feet beneath the water and closed her eyes, then gave in and relinquished control to the wild magic. Within seconds, Quinn's physiology adjusted to the difference. Her breathing became less labored, and her chest stopped aching.

Feeling more comfortable in the new environment,

Quinn opened her HUD map overlay. She used it to scan the surroundings nearby with her new earth sense in play. She wasn't sure what she was looking for but was over-joyed to see it worked in the water. Glowing green and yellow dots moved on the display. Quinn focused on a few closest to her. The nearest dot was a striped bass, and the remaining dots were other types of fish. The green ones appeared to be harmless. The few yellow ones on the display represented potential threats, including a lone hammerhead shark about a half-mile away. They were only dangerous if she went looking for trouble.

Quinn started to drop the map overlay, then stopped. The green and yellow dots showed up everywhere except in an area southeast of her position. She swam in that direction, and the section with no fish in it grew. In fact, nothing showed up in that area. There were no terrain features or depth indicators. It was as if it were a hole in her map.

Or maybe something blocked her abilities with wild magic there—something like a dragon.

Quinn centered her focus in the middle of the blank area and swam ahead. As she approached the boundary of the empty zone, Quinn fought a growing urge to turn around and swim away. She ignored the feeling and pressed on, drawing down her mana store about thirty percent to push back against the dragon's protection zone.

It worked. The sense of dread almost disappeared. No wonder the fish stayed away. This would keep any ordi-nary humans out of the area too, allowing a dragon to live in secret with no one being the wiser. Quinn smiled. She wasn't an average human, so the mysterious blank spot had told her exactly where to go.

Quinn passed into the blank area and dropped her HUD to scan the dark water around her. The bright moonlight overhead filtered into the upper layer of water, giving her a clear view twenty or thirty feet away. Using her best guess at where the center of the mysterious blank circle was located, Quinn swam onward. She scanned the rocky bottom beneath her for any sign of a cave entrance.

She soon reached the area she'd estimated to be the center of the dragon's protective circle. A rocky island barely a hundred yards across rose from the bay's floor to about twenty feet above the water's choppy surface. Quinn swam around, searching the underwater shelf surrounding it.

The circular cave entrance was so large it surprised her. She could never have missed it and suspected it was visible from the surface in the daytime. Of course, the repulsion spell that protected the island would prevent anyone from getting close enough to see it under most circumstances.

As she dove toward the cave's mouth, Quinn tried to gauge its size. The opening had to be about twenty feet across at its widest point. The walls were smooth rock as if bored by a drill, except at the floor right near the entrance. That area had a soft and muddy bottom. Quinn wondered if she should have asked Jori how big the dragon was, then her mind popped up the image of the bite scars the captain had shown her.

When the plan had first formed, she'd assumed she could fend it off with her Bowie if she failed to sneak in and out successfully, but if it was large enough to fill this opening, her knife would barely scratch it. Gil had been pretty large as a lake dragon, but this dwarfed him by a good bit.

Quinn checked the fanny pack behind her sheathed knife. If brute force wouldn't work, she'd rely on her ability to hide and sneak around. She'd have to work fast to avoid detection, but she didn't want to stick around long anyway.

Reaching out with her webbed hands and giving a powerful kick with her legs, Quinn dove and entered the dark cave. Quinn couldn't use her night vision underwater, so she had trouble penetrating the gloom. She ran her hand along the wall to help guide her through the tunnel.

The underwater passage angled upward after about fifty feet, which should be near the edge of the rocky island above. Quinn continued swimming until she breached the surface in a large cavern. She stifled a gasp, trying to remain as silent as possible. With the top half of her head out of the water, Quinn activated her night vision. The aquatic eyes distorted things in the open air, but she could see the cavern well enough to tell it was empty. The rough, rocky walls around her that were different from the smooth sides of the passage she had swum through to get here.

Quinn swam the last few feet to the edge of the pool and lifted herself free out of the cold water. She let the water drain from her gill flaps and the wild magic transform her back into human form, then took a few seconds to restore her lungs to breathing air, stifling coughs as she did.

She had to work fast. If the dragon wasn't here, Quinn

assumed it was out hunting and could return at any moment. She started searching for the two things she needed: loose dragon scales and a pile of crap or two. Having never seen either, Quinn had no idea what to look for until her foot kicked what she thought was a loose rock that skittered across the floor.

It was surprisingly loud in the hollow space. She bent down to peer more closely at what she'd kicked. The large, flat rock was the same color as the other rocks in the cavern and about the size of a dinner plate, but triangular instead of round. When she picked it up, its weight surprised her. It was much lighter than a typical rock that size. She brought it closer to her face to study it. Golden sparkles of wild magic danced around the edges in her enhanced vision, and her hands tingled with the energy. This was a dragon scale.

She glanced at the floor and saw dozens more. They were pretty large for something small enough to fit in this size cavern. She imagined a much larger creature would have scales this size.

Shrugging, Quinn pulled the nylon bag from the fanny pack and slid two of the scales inside. They barely fit, but she managed to get them in without tearing the fabric with the sharp edges. There was still enough room inside for both plastic poop bags if she didn't fill them too full.

Pulling the two zipper bags from the pouch, Quinn sniffed at the cavern air. She'd figured the dung piles would be the easiest components to locate, but she didn't smell anything but a slight odor of fish and the saltwater.

Since it was the only thing she had to go on, Quinn followed the smell of fish until she found a pile of large fish bones in the room's center. The bones were clean and appeared pristine in the dim light of her night vision. No dragon dung here.

Quinn began a more thorough search, walking around the circumference of the cavern with her hand lightly touching one wall. After one circuit, Quinn found nothing she could identify as the dung of a dragon.

She stopped near the water's edge and sighed, leaning against the cave wall. Taylor's translation of the book had been clear. She needed both components to save the baby dragon. Quinn had been sure she'd find what she was looking for in the dragon's lair. She was at a loss as to where to look next.

The wall where her shoulder rested shifted under her weight and the Huntress had to catch herself before she fell. She steadied herself and then froze. The cavern walls moved until it felt like the entire lair closed in around her. A gust of warm, almost hot air brushed Quinn's neck, and she spun to find herself standing in front of the giant yellow slitted eye from her dream. It glowed in the darkness and moved to follow her as she scrambled backward.

As she backpedaled, she gained the perspective to make out the triangular head pressed against the cavern wall. A forked tongue snaked out and flicked in her direction before disappearing inside again.

A voice rang in her brain like a crashing gong so loud it sent her reeling. *It's been a long time since someone found a way to get inside my home. Before I eat you, perhaps you could tell me who you are?*

I'm Quinn, Quinn Faust. I'm here to save the life of a young baby dragon, not to intrude upon your slumber.

I'm afraid you didn't succeed. I heard you as soon as you tripped over the dragon scale.

Quinn shook her head, trying to adjust to the sheer force behind the dragon's mind voice. *Is there a way you could maybe whisper or something? It's hurting my brain.*

Interesting. Most humans can barely hear me unless I use a great deal of will to communicate with them. Why are you so different? Come closer so I may taste you.

Quinn glanced at the water and tried to gauge whether she could make it before the massive head snapped her in half.

Stop. You won't make it two steps. Besides, I've moved my tail to close the entrance. See?

The water roiled and flowed away as a massive coil of the dragon's ridged tail lifted free, plugging the passage. Quinn's shoulders sagged.

That's better. Now that you know you have no choice, come here so I may taste you.

I won't die easily, dragon, Quinn threatened. She drew her Bowie and brandished it in front of her.

The rumbling chuckle of the dragon's laugher shook the whole room. *I appreciate your spunk, but I doubt I'd even feel that puny blade. Come forward as I asked—unless you'd like me to eat you now before I taste your aura?*

Oh, my aura. I thought you meant—

I only say what I mean, girl. I have no need to trick you. Come forward.

Quinn took a few halting steps forward and stopped beside the long crack that was the dragon's mouth. Once again, the tongue flicked out, slipping between two huge teeth to tickle her face and body with the feathery forked ends.

Mmmmm, I do taste a hint of an immature youngling. A sylvan green cousin of mine if I remember the taste correctly. I didn't know there were any of my tiny sylvan brethren left. It has been such a long time since I had a decent conversation with one of my own kind.

As far as I know, this is the last egg of its kind. The Fae used some kind of glue to coat it so the wild magic wouldn't leak out anymore. If I don't get the supplies we need, it won't be able to hatch, and it will die.

Wild magic, you say? I have detected flares of the arcane in the direction of the human settlement on the shore near here. How could that be, though? An egg could not manifest such power on its own. Only a mature, fully grown dragon can access that energy.

Quinn hesitated for a few seconds, trying to think of the best answer.

Out with it, girl. I don't have the patience I used to.

Yes, um, well, you see, that's sort of my fault. I think I let a powerful talisman filled with magic touch the shell. It seems to have energized the dragon inside and accelerated its access to that magic.

My, my, you are in some trouble then. You still haven't explained why the Fae didn't come talk to me themselves. They know where I am if they need to save the youngling.

I came on my own because the egg imprinted on me. It is my responsibility, and I must make this right.

So, a human with a sense of responsibility. You are a rare one, Quinn Faust. If I were inclined to let you go save this youngling, what is it you seek?

Quinn didn't miss the hint that she might still get out of this alive. Her words spilled out in a rush to explain her purpose. *I just came for a few loose dragon scales and a bit of your dung. I couldn't find out where you did your business, though. That's what I was looking for when you startled me.*

Why would you look for my excrement in the middle of my bedchamber? The flare of annoyance in the dragon's mind came through loud and clear.

I just thought—

Thought what, that I was some sort of animal who'd foul my den in such a way? Even the lowest of creatures knows better than that.

Quinn held out her hands in apology. *I meant no offense. I never learned about dragon kind and their ways.*

And yet you reek of magic and possess a core of power surprising for one so young and puny.

Quinn balked at the description of her as puny until she remembered the comment's source. Everyone was puny to this magnificent creature. She shifted gears mid-thought as something else the dragon had said connected.

Chessie had said she didn't foul her chambers. That meant she left them to do her business. Quinn remembered the soft muddy bottom outside the cavern entrance. Of course. She should have realized what it was on the way in.

I realize the error of my ways, mighty one. I will retrieve my sample outside your cave.

Once more, the rumbling chuckle shook the cavern. *You are bright for a human. Perhaps, given your commitment to this youngling, I should wait to eat you. Now that I've tasted you, I can track you across the world if I change my mind.*

Why would you let me go, only to hunt and kill me later?

Humor filled the voice echoing in her mind. *I may decide on a last-minute snack and want a bite of what you taste like. It could happen, so should I let you go, you would have to promise to submit to be my meal should I desire it later.*

I don't know. How about I agree, but only if I fail to save the young dragon? Should the youngling survive, you would consider that payment in full for my rudeness and intrusion here tonight.

The glowing eye blinked. *You think you're in a position to bargain with my generosity? It sounds as if you seek to find a way to slip out of your commitment. Tell me why I should trust you.*

You said you haven't had a decent conversation with one of your own kind for centuries. What if I agreed to bring the youngling here to converse with you regularly?

What would I have to say to an infant dragon?

Quinn shrugged. *Perhaps you could teach it to be a better dragon. You said yourself there aren't any others around to do it. If it is left to me alone, I'll have to raise the poor thing like a human.*

Bah, we cannot have that. That is no way to raise a youngling. I suppose if that is the only choice we have, it will be sufficient. I would hold you responsible for caring for the little one otherwise, though.

Oh, of course. The egg and I have become rather close over the last weeks.

Very well, Quinn Faust. You may have the scales in your sack and collect dung from outside my home. In exchange, you will return once the youngling is six months old. Understood?

Yes, your terms are very generous. I accept them. Quinn

backed up a step, hardly daring to believe she'd found a way out of this. *May I go then?*

The water roiled again as the coiled tail dropped into the water and disappeared beneath the surface. Quinn didn't wait for permission. She slid the strings of the nylon bag over her shoulder and took two long steps to dive into the murky blackness. Quinn shifted into aquatic form as soon as she submerged, kicking hard to leave the cave's confines as fast as possible. She didn't want to wait around in case the old dragon changed her mind.

Quinn reached the open water and stopped long enough to scoop the sticky mud into the two plastic bags and zip them closed. She didn't bother messing with getting them into the nylon bag on her back. She swam back toward the anchored boat's location, holding bags of dragon dung by her sides.

A shiver coursed down her spine as she realized the bargain she'd made with the enormous creature. She suspected holding up her end of that bargain wouldn't be as easy as it had sounded when she'd proposed it. She didn't relish the return to visit the dragon with the hatchling. For now, though, Quinn had to face the challenges at hand and worry about the future later.

CHAPTER TWENTY-TWO

Quinn surfaced beside Jori's boat, dropped the plastic bag of dung over the side, and clutched the deck's edge. She couldn't call out for help with a chest full of water.

After swinging the second bag over the side, Quinn pulled herself up and out of the water, heaving herself into the boat.

"Quinn, you're back," Taylor said. "Did you get everything you need?"

Quinn held up a finger while she let the wild magic shift her back into regular human form. The water drained from her gill flaps, and they closed. She gasped a few times to refill her lungs with air.

Taylor shook her head. "That's amazing to watch. I've never seen anything like it."

"You're a werewolf," Quinn said. "Why is it my shapeshifting is so unusual to you?"

"My shift is painful to the point of total distraction. I don't get to watch mine happen."

"This one isn't all that pleasant either. Picture waiting patiently and unable to breathe while your lungs fill with water or drain the water away. Not my idea of a good time, believe me."

Quinn slid the nylon bag off her back and held it up. "I got everything." She retrieved the two plastic bags and set them and the bag with the scales in the deck's center.

Clark poked his head out of the wheelhouse and smiled when he spotted Quinn. "Good, you're back. I wondered who Taylor was talking to."

"Tell Jori to head back to the marina," Quinn said. "We have what we need."

Jori leaned into view. "You made it in and out in one piece? I thought for sure we'd never see you again. I guess the old girl was out?"

"No," Quinn replied. "We had a nice chat and came to an understanding. Luckily, since you now have the location on your charts, I can use you to fulfill my end of the bargain."

"Bargain?" Clark asked. "I don't like the sound of that, Quinn."

"It's not that bad. I promised to bring the little one here from time to time for her to train it in the ways of dragonkind."

"You agreed to come back?" Clark asked.

Taylor came to Quinn's defense. "I don't think there was a choice, Clark. She knows what she's doing."

"I made the deal we needed for the young dragon to survive. That's all I care about right now. Besides, if I bring the youngling back here, maybe I can make friends with Chessie. It could come in handy."

"Quinn, dragons are dangerous," Clark warned.

"So am I. We'll get along fine."

Jori rolled his eyes. "Your girl has a suicide wish, Clarkie."

"You have no idea. Get us back to shore. We can figure out the details of this deal she made once we manage to hatch a live dragon. Until then, it's academic."

Jori nodded. "Haul in the anchors, and be careful coiling the lines when you're done." He disappeared into the wheelhouse. The boat's motor chugged to life.

Quinn and Taylor moved fore and aft to pull in the heavy steel anchors. After they finished stowing the second one, the boat started back toward Baltimore's lights to the northwest.

During the long trip back to the city, Quinn soon regretted not planning better for this excursion. Though she'd dressed in her clothes again, she hadn't packed a change of underwear and still had the damp tankini on underneath her outfit. The cold night air had chilled her to the bone by the time they returned to Clark's car.

Clark noticed her shivering as she stood beside the car, so he retrieved an old blanket from the trunk and handed it to her. "Here, I don't need to listen to your chattering teeth all the way back into the city.

"I'm fine," Quinn said.

"Just take it until I get the heat going in this old beast."

Quinn pulled the blanket around her as she climbed into the passenger seat. She was glad she had. The old heater in the sedan took almost twenty minutes to put out an appreciable amount of heat. Quinn kept the blanket wrapped around her when they got back to the secret tunnel entrance beneath the overpass. Quinn got out, and Taylor joined her.

Clark leaned over so he could see them. "Go straight back to the pub. I'll meet you there."

"Don't worry," Quinn said. "I need a hot shower, and then I'm going to bed."

Taylor and Quinn headed into the tunnel entrance while the car pulled into the night.

Clark was waiting for them beside the door back into the pub when they arrived ten minutes later. "There are two Fae by the bar. I'm not sure what they want. I wanted to warn you."

He pulled open the door just far enough for them to see inside. Two tall Fae men in quite ordinary business suits stood by the bar, talking to Paddy.

"This looks like trouble," Taylor said. "What do we do?"

"We do nothing," Clark said. "If we were outside, we might have to fight. Since we made it back inside, sanctuary covers Quinn again."

"Let's get this over with," the Huntress said. "I'm tired of running scared from the Fae."

Quinn pulled the door open and walked over to Paddy and the two Fae. "Hello, Paddy," Quinn said. "Just out for a stroll. Everything all right?"

The leprechaun wrung his hands and shifted his gaze between her and the two men. "I was just telling these two men I didn't know where you were. I'm thrilled you showed up when you did."

The taller of the Fae men said, "If we'd known you were out of the sanctuary zone, it would have made our jobs much easier. I will pass along my displeasure at being diverted from our duty by Mr. O'Malley here."

"Leave him out of it," Quinn said. "I'm the one your princesses are pissed at. What is it you want?"

The second man reached into his coat, causing everyone to tense. He paused before removing his hand, realizing they all had reached for their weapons. Even Taylor had started to shift, claws protruding from her fingertips.

"I'm reaching for the summons from the Fae court. May I remove my hand?"

"Go nice and slow," Clark cautioned.

The man nodded and slowly pulled his hand from within his jacket, removing an envelope with a wax seal. He held it out to Quinn.

"Quinn Faust, you've been served. The Fae court requires you to attend to deal with your crimes against the supernatural community."

"What if I don't take it?"

The taller Fae shrugged. "There are witnesses that we presented it to you. Take it or not. Your time of sanctuary protection is nearing an end."

Clark took the envelope and broke the seal. He unfolded the papers inside and glanced at them. "How long?"

"I believe the head magistrate gives the girl two days to present herself, along with all stolen property belonging to the Fae royal families. The location is denoted in the document."

He nodded at his companion, and the two of them

made a beeline for the exit. As soon as they left the bar, Quinn leaned in and tried to get a look at the summons.

"Where do they want me to meet them? I'm ready to take this to them and solve it once and for all. They stole from me first."

Clark shook his head. "This isn't good, Quinn. They've labeled it a court of honor."

"So? I'm honorable. They're the ones who've been shady."

"Not that kind of honor, Quinn. They plan on trying and sentencing you in one move. The court of honor will require you to fight their chosen champion under terms they set—to the death."

"What?" Taylor said. "That's barbaric. How can they do that?"

"It's my fault," Clark said. He shook his head. "I didn't plan ahead when I had Miranda tell you to invoke sanctuary. That gave them the right to open the proceedings under ancient rules."

Quinn said, "I don't care. Let them bring on their so-called champion. I've beaten the worst the supernatural community had to offer so far. I'll be the one who wins."

"They know what you can do, Quinn," Clark said. "That's what worries me. Both princesses have seen you at work in one way or another. They know you're strong and capable. They wouldn't have taken it this direction unless they had a plan they thought couldn't fail."

Taylor took the summons from Clark. "It says you're to appear at the Crystal Well with both the egg and the journal in your possession. They know you have them. They've covered everything."

"What happens if we don't agree to go along with this?" Quinn asked.

Paddy bustled over as soon as she spoke. "Don't do that, girlie. They'll come and take you by force and destroy my bar in the process. We've given you sanctuary under the old law, but now you have to comply with their orders. I cannot protect you and would be bound to help them take you into custody."

"I won't do anything to hurt you, Juni, or the bar. If they want a showdown, we'll give it to them. We've only got two days to help the egg and the baby dragon inside. That will be my focus until then. Taylor, dig into the journal and figure out what we need to do to remove that barrier Aurora put on the egg."

"Got it," Taylor said. "Miranda and I will go through the journal and pull together the details for the spell first thing in the morning."

"Good," Quinn said. "I'm going to bed. All that swimming earlier wiped me out. I'll check in down at the workshop when I wake up."

Clark nodded. "Get some sleep. I'll tell Naomi about the summons. Maybe she and I can learn more about what Filippa and Aurora have planned for you."

Quinn smiled and headed up to her apartment. The swim had done a lot more than tire her. Something about the dragon encounter left her shaken. She'd never encountered a creature that large and powerful. If Chessie had wanted to end her, she wouldn't have had a chance. It made her wonder what the Fae court would have waiting for her in two days. If they had a challenger with that level of power, she was finished.

The worrisome thoughts left her tossing and turning for almost an hour before sleep finally set in.

CHAPTER TWENTY-THREE

Quinn woke just before noon the next day without the rested feeling she usually had after several hours of sleep. She stumbled into her bathroom and stared into the mirror for a long time, trying to decide if she should just go back to bed.

After several seconds of studying the circles under her eyes, Quinn bent over the sink and splashed cold water on her face, then grabbed a towel and dried off. She glanced at the mirror again. Her reflection didn't look any more awake than it had seconds before. Quinn shrugged. It would have to do. There was a lot to accomplish today.

She made herself peanut butter toast and coffee and sat at her small table to eat. When she pulled out her phone, a message from Taylor waited for her, sent an hour before.

The message seemed ominous, considering all the worries about the court from the night before. Quinn glanced at her bedroom. Did she have time for a shower before she got dressed? She decided if it was that urgent, Taylor would have come up and awakened her. Given the previous night's activities, including the swim in the bay, she needed a shower. Maybe it would help her shake off the fatigue, too.

Rising, Quinn walked back to her room and stripped for her shower. As the hot water sprayed down on her, Quinn's mind couldn't stop going over everything her imagination could think of concerning the cryptic text message. She decided to rush through the shower despite the lure of the warm water on her tired muscles.

Fifteen minutes later, Quinn had pulled her still-damp hair back in a ponytail and headed down to see what was up. The workshop door was ajar when she arrived, and she headed inside. Taylor chatted in the corner with Miranda.

"Maybe if we grind two of them against each other, we can generate the shavings called for in the recipe?"

Miranda sighed. "They rubbed against each other in the duffel bag, but there was no sign of residue. We checked, remember?"

Taylor shrugged. "There's got to be a way to do it."

"Do what, T?" Quinn asked.

"Good, you're up. I—" Taylor stopped when she glanced at Quinn. "Did you get any sleep? You look worse than you did when you went up to your room."

"Gee, thanks. I eventually got to sleep, but it wasn't as restful as I'd have liked. Anyway, I came down in response to your message. Is what you're working on now the problem you mentioned?"

"No, this is a different issue. We're trying to create shavings from the dragon scales as called for in the spell. So far, we've ruined two expensive carbon-steel chef's knives from the kitchen and have yet to make a mark on the scales."

"Okay, if that's not the problem you texted about, what is?"

"This," Taylor said, picking up the journal and flipping through it. "I read beyond the instructions for the egg's coating in search of instructions to grind shavings from the scales. That's when I found this."

Taylor pointed to a page near the back of the journal. Quinn came over to read it, but the runes meant nothing to her.

"T, I can't read that. What's it say?"

"It refers to a secret Fae organization attempting to return the world to their control. It specifically references opening dimensional rifts to allow demonkind to rejoin their Fae brethren on this plane. Aurora, or whoever wrote this down, calls it 'righting the Great Error' or something close to that. The translation is hard because some Fae runes don't have English counterparts, especially older arcane words."

"Aurora mentioned something like that to me when I went to ask for help with Gemma."

Taylor nodded. "Did she tell you she was a member of this organization of dark Fae?"

"No."

"Well, I'm pretty sure she is."

"That doesn't make sense," Quinn said. "She helped me fight Gemma. Aurora told me Gemma worked for that same organization."

Miranda said, "Just because both Filippa and Aurora are part of the same sinister organization, it doesn't mean they don't have an intense rivalry. The Fae are famous for their court intrigue. It puts anything from human history to shame since some of these grudges have gone on for centuries."

Quinn said, "Okay, so the two of them aren't just trying to get the dragon egg back, they're also working together to destroy the world as we know it. Got it. I guess the Fae trial and court is part of all this, too, then?"

"Maybe," Miranda said. "It could be only a few members of the court working with the princesses. Others on the court may have their own agendas or owe the princesses favors. It's hard to say. The Fae magistrates have long been known to be harsh but fair in their rulings."

"Fair?" Taylor asked. "They want Quinn to fight to the death against some Fae champion. How's that fair?"

"It's a harsh form of judgment, true. But if—" Miranda stopped, correcting her words. "No, not if. *When* Quinn beats their champion, the magistrates will support the outcome as final and binding. The princesses will have no recourse since they've put things in the court's hands."

"Thanks for the vote of confidence, Miranda." Quinn sighed. "Now all we need is to find out a little about who this mysterious champion is. Then I could prepare what I need to defeat them."

"It could be anyone or anything," Miranda explained. "The aggrieved party gets to choose. After that, only the court knows who or what it will be."

Quinn shook her head. Worrying about it wasn't going to help her rest. She'd face the champion, and she'd win. She wouldn't waste time thinking about the alternative.

"Okay, so there's a secret group of evil Fae out there

that is determined to kill me. I'll deal with them when the time comes. What were you talking about with the dragon scales when I came in?"

Taylor put the book down and picked up one of the triangular scales. "The issue is that despite the deceptively light weight of these things, they're impervious to damage. Nothing we have can make a dent in them. If we can't grind them into powder or shavings for the mixture, we can't remove the coating on the egg."

"What other options do we have to try?" Quinn asked, looking from Taylor to Miranda.

Both shrugged.

Miranda said, "We've tried every tool and sharp object we can lay our hands on. Nothing has worked. We need something stronger than hardened steel alloys."

"Okay, what's harder?"

Taylor held up the scale. "The options move to ruby, sapphire, and diamond hardness scales. That makes it problematic and pricey."

"How pricey?" Quinn asked.

"Not sure," Taylor replied. "I've reached out to several industrial machine and tool companies in the area, along with some commercial construction companies. I figure there's got to be a diamond-surfaced grinder out there somewhere."

Quinn picked up the other dragon scale from the table. "How much do we need?"

Miranda said, "The spell calls for equal amounts of each key component to make a paste that will then be used to coat the entire egg."

"By weight or by volume?" Quinn asked. "These scales weigh nothing."

Taylor set the dragon scale next to the bags of dung. "We figure volume. Otherwise, we'd need a hundred or more scales to have an equal weight to the dung needed to cover that football-sized egg."

"What about the magic part of it?" Quinn asked. "Is that part hard?"

Taylor shook her head. "No, I don't think so. It seems pretty straightforward. We are going to need to do this in a safe location outdoors, though."

"Why?"

Miranda said, "Because after we coat the egg and let the layer harden, we have to set fire to it."

"What? You can't do that. Won't it cook the baby dragon inside?"

"We don't think so," Taylor said. "First, that egg is as hard as a rock. Second, my guess is that dragons, even baby ones, are pretty tough."

Miranda said, "It's a necessary step to the spell. The note on the process makes it sound like the paste mixture, once dried, becomes a sort of magical thermite. That's why we have to do this outside. It'll be hot enough to set fire to anything for a few feet in all directions."

"I'll talk to Clark and Naomi. We should be able to sneak out again, one way or another."

"Quinn," Taylor said. "I don't see any reason why we can't do this without you along. We'd just have to put the egg in a box to keep it hidden from anyone watching. Once the process was finished, we'd come straight back."

"I'm not letting that egg go anywhere outside this

building without me along to protect it. That's what this whole thing is about. I don't know what's so special about it, but those Fae women want it back for something."

"What?" Taylor asked. "Other than it being a dragon. This is the first dragon birth in hundreds of years. That's got to be a big deal for everyone."

"Yeah, T, it is. This dragon is an orphan and needs our protection. That's what makes it important to me. What I don't know is why *they* think it's so important. That's even more critical, now that we know about this dark Fae organization they're part of."

"Whatever it is," Miranda said, "I can't see them giving up easily. If you're sure you need to come along, we'll have to find some way to distract them from what we're doing. They'll be watching extra hard now that they suspect you went out once already."

Quinn smiled. "I've got an idea. My mother can go out disguised as me again."

"Do you think that'll work twice?" Taylor asked.

"I think so. They didn't catch on last time. She could lead anyone watching for me on a nice little wild goose chase. That would give us the chance to slip out, and no one would be the wiser."

Miranda frowned. "Your mother won't be happy about being away from you if trouble comes along."

"There won't be any trouble. She'll be leading the trouble away from us."

"I don't know, Quinn," Taylor said. "She might lead some of the potential trouble away, but Miranda's right. Trouble has a way of finding you."

"That's not fair. It's not like I go looking for it."

JAMIE DAVIS

"No," Miranda agreed, "it's not fair. It's also not wrong. Trouble comes wandering along whenever you're out doing something risky." The ghost held up her hands to stop Quinn's attempts to explain. "I'm not saying you can't go. I'm just saying we should be ready for anything."

A ping came from Taylor's computer at the desk beside the large work table. The tech witch walked around and checked the screen.

She smiled. "Bingo, an industrial firm that works with stone and concrete answered me. They have a diamond-grit grinding wheel made for a standard shop grinder. I'm going to go find Clark so he can take me down there to see it. I'll bring one of the scales to see if the grit can scratch the surface. If it works, we should be good to go."

Quinn nodded. "I'll go find my mom and tell her the plans for the egg and the distraction we need. That'll give her some time to get over her initial objections to the idea."

"I guess I'll stay here and mind the fort, then," Miranda said. "It's not like I can go anywhere anyway."

Taylor and Quinn laughed and left the workshop together. The plan to save the egg was coming along.

CHAPTER TWENTY-FOUR

I t took a day and a half to pull it together, but by the following evening, the whole clan stood in Taylor's workshop, prepping the final details of their plan.

Naomi and Quinn stood beside each other, wearing identical outfits. Naomi even had one of Quinn's spare Bowies hanging from her belt by her right hip.

"I'm not left-handed," Naomi complained. "It's going to be awkward to draw this thing in a fight."

"If you get in a fight, the disguise will be blown," Quinn replied. "Feel free to use that trick to pull your sword out of thin air. I still need you to show me how you do that, by the way."

"I'm not sure I can tell you. It's something we're trained in from when we're very young, with blades tied to us. They become like a fifth limb after a while."

Quinn shrugged. "We can try after all this is settled. It might be something the VR system can work around."

The door to the hallway opened. Juni poked her head in. "Two Fae trackers just came in. It wasn't hard to spot them. Quinn, you'll want to make an appearance in the bar so they see what you're wearing."

"Thanks, Juni. Seriously, I don't know how we could do any of this without you."

"Think nothing of it. I'm pissed at the way they lord their supposed superiority over everyone. These aren't the old days when they ran everything."

Clark said, "That's what's got all this happening now. They want to return to the good old days of yore."

"We're not going to let that happen," Quinn shot back. "Not if I have anything to say about it. That starts tonight, with removing whatever spell they enacted on the dragon egg."

Naomi nodded to the door. "You follow Juni back to the bar. Order drinks and bring them back here. Make sure everyone sees you. As soon as you get back, I'll sneak upstairs and go out on the roof. We know they have a team watching the building. I'll make sure they catch sight of me and then start off across the rooftops toward the center of the city."

Quinn nodded and followed Juni into the hall. She had become a good friend to Quinn and the others. Quinn hoped this sanctuary business and their plan tonight didn't blow back on her and her father somehow.

She entered the noisy club, but instead of following Juni toward the kitchen, she wove through the crowded tables to the bar. She knew many of the regular patrons at this point, so she stopped and said hi to a few of them on the way. Juni had been right; it was easy to pick out the two Fae trackers. The pair sat at a table by the entrance. Quinn made sure to wind past that side before turning to the bar to order the drinks. One of them leaned toward the other and pointed in her direction.

Perfect.

"Two beers and two sodas, Jack," Quinn said to the server tending bar. He started putting the order together and setting the drinks on a tray for her.

"You aren't fooling anyone, Huntress," a snide voice said from behind her. A crisp British accent told her it was one of the Fae.

Quinn turned slowly, keeping her hands well away from the knife at her waist. She didn't want to give anyone a reason to think she'd violated the bar's neutrality and her precarious sanctuary status. "I didn't know I was trying to fool folks. All I'm doing is ordering drinks for my friends and me."

The taller of the two trackers, dressed in black slacks and a sports coat, leaned in, trying to loom over her. "You use the old ways to gain sanctuary, but don't follow the rules. We know you've left this place. That alone should violate the terms of your protection."

"Your concern is noted. Are you here to take me in against my granted sanctuary status, or do you plan on following me when I go back out later?"

His eyebrows raised in surprise at the admission. "You flaunt your disdain for the law so obviously. I will rejoice when I see you destroyed in the court of honor."

Quinn dropped her left hand and hooked her thumb on the release, giving her quick access to the knife on her right hip. His eyes tracked to follow her hand as if daring her to pull her weapon. "I've been granted sanctuary. I have been served a summons to appear tomorrow before your magistrates. If you plan on violating things before my day in court, I might just have to kill you. Is that what you want?"

The tracker glared down at her. She thought for a second he was going to reach for whatever weapon bulged beneath his arm. A firm hand on his shoulder pulled him back.

"Leave her be," the second tracker said. "Come sit down. If she leaves, she's ours."

The first one glared at her for a few seconds longer, then went back to the table by the exit.

Juni appeared by Quinn's side. "You really shouldn't provoke them like that. We don't need the kind of bloodshed that would erupt if a real fight happened on a crowded night like tonight."

"I knew they'd back down," Quinn lied. "They have plans for me tomorrow. I'm sure they have no desire to spoil things for their mistresses."

She picked up the tray of drinks and winked at Juni. "Let me know if they take the bait when Naomi shows herself outside."

"I'll text Taylor if they leave."

Quinn navigated back through the tables to the storeroom door. Once in the workshop, she set the drinks on the table beside the egg. Quinn picked up one of the two sodas and raised it. Taylor grabbed the other. Naomi and Clark each grabbed a beer.

"To our baby dragon. May she be healthy and well after our work tonight."

Everyone tapped their glasses together. Naomi drained

her beer and laughed. "Time to go all *Freaky Friday* on those Fae bastards. Wish me luck."

Quinn wasn't sure what Friday had to do with anything. It was Wednesday. She nodded anyway. Sometimes Naomi said the weirdest things. Quinn remembered that although they looked close in age, she was twenty-plus years older than her daughter.

Naomi left, and Taylor started handing out the things she'd need for the spell. "Quinn, take this canister. It has the extra dragon scale shavings in case we need more for some reason."

"You already measured the mixture and covered the egg with it. What's this for?"

Taylor picked up the egg, now crusted in a hard slate-gray layer from the spell recipe. "The egg is coated and ready for the spell, but we'll bring along the raw materials we have left in case we need more for some reason." She picked up a square airtight plastic container and handed it to Clark. "You can carry the leftover dragon crap."

"Oh, joy," Clark said. "Just what I've always wanted."

Taylor puttered around the workshop, gathering extra odds and ends and stuffing them in a canvas shoulder bag. Taylor's phone chirped, and she held it out for Quinn and Clark to read. It was a message from Juni.

"They took the bait," Quinn said. "Let's go."

"Good luck. I'll be waiting to see how it went," Miranda said.

Quinn felt bad for Miranda. She couldn't hold a phone, so there was no way to send her messages with their progress while they were gone. They needed to work on a solution like they had when Quinn entered the VR a few days before. She filed that idea away for later and followed Clark and Taylor out the door, holding the container of shavings.

Clark and Taylor headed for the bar, while Quinn turned left to head into the tunnels. She'd meet them by the hidden exit beneath the overpass.

Clark's dark sedan pulled up under the highway bridge five minutes later.

Quinn got in the back. "Was anyone still watching the bar when you left?"

Clark pulled away from the curb as soon as she sat down. "I spotted one person, but there might have been more. I think I lost them. We'll know soon enough if it worked." He leaned forward and stared through the windshield at the rooftops around them as he drove.

"I think I can help with that," Taylor said. "Miranda has been working with me on my basic spells. I know a masking spell. It's more a misdirection of attention than an invisibility conjuration."

"Give it a shot," Quinn said. "It can't hurt."

Clark nodded, and Taylor rummaged in her canvas bag until she pulled out a small spiral notebook. She opened it and a few seconds later began muttering to herself while one hand wove an intricate pattern in the air.

Quinn didn't notice anything change as Taylor stopped her chanting.

"Did it work?" Quinn asked.

Taylor shrugged. "I cast the spell. It should be making this car unremarkable. I don't know if the Fae can counter it, but no one will pay us any notice otherwise."

Clark swerved, narrowly missing a passing car that had

pulled out directly in front of them.

"I'd say it's working. That guy pulled out like he didn't even see us." Clark shook his head. "I'll have to pay attention to that, or we'll never make it to cast the spell on the egg."

The location Clark and Taylor had chosen for the spell was an abandoned drive-in movie theater north of the city. The parking lot was paved, which would limit the spread of the fire from Taylor's mixture, and trees and a lot of overgrown brush surrounded the property, which would hide what they were doing from prying eyes in the residential neighborhood nearby. It should be perfect for their needs.

Quinn kept checking behind them for signs of someone following. She didn't see any cars staying with them for long before turning off on another street. Clark took a roundabout route, giving her ample chances to spot anyone trailing them.

Twenty-five minutes later, they arrived at the drive-in. The old movie screen jutted up behind the trees obscuring the view of the grounds. Quinn could make out that it was in disrepair, with a few holes in the white panels. Taylor hopped out and cast a spell to unlock the chain holding the gate closed, then swung it open and waited for Clark to drive through before closing it. She climbed back in the car.

Clark drove down a short lane and into the large open parking lot. The old projection house and snack stand sat in the middle of the lot, with the big screen at the far end. Clark drove around the projection house and parked midway between it and the screen.

"This should be good," Clark said. "Ready, Taylor?"

"Ready as we'll ever be." She grabbed the egg and her small spiral notebook.

"Didn't you bring Aurora's journal?" Quinn asked.

"No, I copied the spell instructions to my spellbook in English to make it easier to follow. I don't need to get hung up on remembering a word's translation in the middle of casting. Don't worry, Miranda double-checked my work."

"So, what do we do?" Clark asked.

"You two stay by the car. I need to do this alone, and I want to know where everyone is so I can protect you from what happens next."

"What is it that happens?" Quinn asked.

"Not sure. That's why you need to stay back. Just stay there, and don't interrupt me once I get started. Don't worry about me since I'll be shielded. It's part of the spell."

Quinn closed her mouth and let Taylor do her work. The tech witch set the egg down on the asphalt about twenty feet from the car, flipped through her book, and gazed at the page she'd selected for a long time before closing it. She slipped it into the shoulder bag and slid the bag around to rest against her butt.

Raising both hands over the egg, Taylor stood up straight with her legs spaced apart like she was bracing for something heavy to come down on her arms. A low droning chant flowed from her mouth as her hands and arms began moving in an intricate pattern through the air. It reminded Quinn of the hand motions she'd seen Bollywood dancers use.

It only took about ten seconds for something to

happen. The egg started spinning like a top on the asphalt, and the gray coating started glowing with a purplish light.

The explosion caught Quinn and Clark by surprise. The spinning egg came to an abrupt halt as the coating erupted in bright white flames, sending out a shockwave in all directions.

Taylor flew back and landed on the hood of Clark's car. The force nearly knocked Clark and Quinn off their feet, even though they were well removed from the source.

Quinn wanted to help the egg, now engulfed in flames, but Taylor was closer. She groaned, rolled off the hood of Clark's car, and fell to the ground next to the driver's side door.

"T, are you all right? I thought you said you had a shield."

"Yeah," Taylor groaned. "I accounted for the heat but not the force of an explosion like that." She raised up on one elbow and stared at the blazing egg. "That's quite a little fire I started."

Quinn nodded. The heat from the magical fire reached them even here, at what they'd considered a safe distance. It looked like the asphalt had melted for about a foot around the egg. Here and there, weeds poking up through the pavement flared up into tiny fires of their own and burned away.

"How long will it burn?" Clark asked. "Even with the trees around this place, that fire is awfully bright. It's sure to draw unwanted attention. I don't want the fire department showing up."

Taylor shrugged. "I don't know. It'll burn until the mixture we made has been consumed. The coating wasn't too thick, but it had to be enough to burn away whatever the Fae put on it."

The egg burned with the same intensity for nearly five minutes. Then, as if someone doused it with a bucket of water, the fire went out and darkness returned. The sole illumination came from the car's headlights, shining on the sparkling green egg sitting on bare earth. The asphalt for about three feet in every direction had been burned away.

The three of them walked up to stare down at the egg.

Taylor crouched and held out a hand over it. "Wow, there's no residual heat. It looks like the coating is gone, too. It worked, Quinn."

Quinn barely heard her friend. As soon as she got close to the egg, her HUD had popped up without her summoning it. That was strange. Stranger still was the wild magic icon glowing red at the display's top. In the back of her mind, she wondered if the Fae knew something she didn't about the egg's magic.

"Quinn, did you hear me?" Taylor asked. "I think the spell worked perfectly."

"Something's wrong. I think we made a horrible mistake." Quinn backed up as she said it, her head turning from side to side, scanning for the trouble she knew was coming.

The lights turned on in the projection house, and the screen lit up behind them. It was so bright, they all shielded their eyes from its glare. A screeching howl split the night, and a black crack appeared in the light projected against the screen.

Despite Quinn's warning, none of them were ready for what came next.

CHAPTER TWENTY-FIVE

"What the hell was that?" Quinn and Taylor said in unison as the howl faded.

Clark cursed. "Damn, the spell or the egg opened some kind of rift to the netherworld. That's got to be the howl of a hellhound. We have to close that gap, or a whole pack will come through."

Another howl sounded, and a two-headed dog the size of a horse jumped through the black crack in the screen. The pulsing icon in Quinn's HUD grew brighter as the wild magic held back by the Fae coating fueled the opening between dimensions. Quinn was their wild magic adept. She should have been ready for something like this.

The dog's two heads swiveled, searching the area for prey. They stopped, and both settled their gaze on the trio by the egg.

"Well, it's seen us now," Clark said. He drew his short sword. "Nothing will keep it from tracking us until it's dead."

Quinn drew her Bowie. "Anything special about killing one of these things?"

"You have to kill both heads, or it will keep going. Oh, and it regenerates over time, so you have to work fast."

"Good to know. Taylor, you concentrate on finding a way to close that gap. We'll keep the hellhound busy."

"I'll try. If that's wild magic at work, I can't touch it."

"Don't tell us why you can't, girl," Clark shouted as he charged at the demon dog. "Just do it. This is serious."

Quinn ran after Clark while clicking on the red icon on her display, but nothing happened. She got the feeling she was missing something important. There was no time to worry about it now, though. She'd reached the fight with the two-headed beast and forgot about doing anything but staying alive.

Despite its bulk, the hellhound was beyond fast, and with two heads, it was able to focus its attention on both Quinn and Clark. That made it hard to slip in and strike at its flanks. Quinn had to dive and roll backward after her first attempt failed to reach the hound's side.

The head closest to her whipped around so fast, it nearly caught her in its snapping maw.

The smell of smoke and brimstone emanated from the thing's mouth. Given the heat coming off it, Quinn knew the bite would do more than just cut into her.

"We have to distract it," Clark yelled.

"We need a third person," Quinn called back as she danced away from a swipe from one of the massive paws.

A black figure dashed in, moving so fast it blurred as they ran in. The newcomer slashed at the hellhound with a shining katana, and a gaping wound opened in the creature's side.

The newcomer leaped back away when the nearest head swung around to bite them.

"Need a hand?" Naomi asked, dancing back to stand next to Clark.

Quinn didn't let her mother's sudden arrival distract her. She took advantage of having the extra attacker to dart in and stab deep with her blade. She ran back to get out of the reach as one head swung toward her.

"What are you doing here?" Clark yelled. "You're supposed to be leading the Fae on a merry chase."

"That only took so long. I got bored with that game, so I lost them. Besides," Naomi said, laughing as she ran in to slash at the nose of the head on the right, "aren't you glad I'm here?"

"I am," Quinn said. "This thing is a lot to handle."

"If I recall my training," Naomi said, "the Hunters said it required five to take down a hellhound."

"Let's see if we can do it with three," Quinn said. "We're running out of time."

To punctuate Quinn's worry, a distant howl sounded from within the giant crack in the screen. As she glanced at the white expanse, the pulsing icon tugged at her awareness again. What was it trying to tell her?

Quinn shouted. "Taylor, how's the work on closing that rift coming?"

"I'm trying to get a handle on it, but I can't even see it in the normal magical spectrum. It's like it's not really there."

Quinn knew what that meant. Taylor wasn't going to be able to deal with it. This was Quinn's problem.

"T, shift into wolf form and come back here and help take out this thing. I have to do this."

Taylor didn't answer, but seconds later, a new howl split the night. Taylor bounded into the fray, her two-legged wolf form leaping at the head on the left. She slashed at its face with her claws and pushed off the head to vault over it, then ran down the hellhound's back and landed behind it.

"Go, Quinn," Naomi called. "Do what you need to do. We've got this thing."

Quinn pulled her attention away from the desperate fight a few yards away and started toward the rift on the screen.

The closer she got, the brighter the icon became until it glowed as brightly in neon-red as the white light around the gaping crack.

Forcing herself to focus, Quinn tried to remember everything she'd learned from Gil and Terrence about wild magic. She'd tried clicking the icon again, but nothing happened. She remembered with wild magic, you weren't in control. As alien as it all felt, Quinn had to relax and let it take over.

That was the struggle and why it often killed those who used it. Quinn and other casters didn't like giving up control of anything. She had no idea what the wild magic wanted of her, and without knowing, she subconsciously resisted it.

More than one howl came through the gap in the screen. They were closer now. Soon, they'd have a whole pack of hellhounds on the loose, and they'd never survive that.

Quinn fought the thing deep inside that refused to give up control. This was what had almost killed her both in the lake and when Terrence had shoved her from the ledge. She tried to remember how she'd felt falling toward certain death and recalled relaxing her hold on being in control and surrendering to the wild magic just before reaching the rocks.

As soon as she put herself in that moment, something changed inside her. The icon turned from pulsing red to gleaming silver. Quinn held out her hands and noticed she no longer held her Bowie. She gripped a long silver javelin in her left hand instead. A thin silver line attached to the javelin's end ran to a coil of silver filament in her right hand.

She stared at her hands, trying to make sense of what they were holding. A fresh chorus of baying howls drew her attention to the jagged tear in the fabric of space.

A rip. In the fabric of space.

Quinn smiled and drew back her left arm, casting the javelin as hard as she could at the top of the rift. She let the coiled line play out from her other hand as she ran to the other side of the jagged gap.

The magical silver javelin pierced the white screen next to the top of the tear and came out in the white screen on the other side.

On the ground below, Quinn ran over just in time to grab the javelin as it fell back toward her. She started to reel in the line through the holes, then stopped for a second.

She tied the end of the silver filament around the hilt of her Bowie and let it drop.

She pulled on the other end of the line, tugging hand over hand until the Bowie lifted into the air. Quinn pulled the silver thread tight as the knife came up against the small hole in the screen where the line passed through.

Grabbing the javelin in her left hand again, Quinn threw. She aimed for a spot a foot below where the line came through on her side of the tear. The javelin flew into the whiteness, emerging a second later from the opposite side.

Quinn ran for the spot where the javelin came out, catching it before it hit the ground.

She reeled it all in again, tugging the top of the tear closed as the line pulled the edges together. Quinn let out a defiant shout. "Time to stitch this baby up."

Ignoring both the fight behind her and the howls of the closing pack on the other side of the rift, Quinn ran back and forth. On each side, she used the javelin and silver thread to close the gap leading to the netherworld. Each time she pulled another section closed, the howls on the other side lessened in volume.

Quinn was down to the last stitch when a massive clawed paw reached through the remaining gap. It caught her by surprise and knocked her down while cutting deep red-hot gashes in her left arm.

Despite the pain, she didn't let go of the line in her right hand. As she lay on the ground beneath the screen, Quinn tugged with all her might to pull the last part of the gap closed.

The long leg of the hellhound reached for her through the narrowing hole in the screen. Quinn kicked it while she scrambled backward, pulling on the silver line with her uninjured arm.

She wound the line around her hand to increase her hold and strained against the pressure from the far side. Quinn dug in with her heels and gave one last effort with her whole body.

With a final yank, the gap in the screen closed. The howling from the other side was cut off, along with the end of the hellhound's leg. The severed limb fell to the pavement below the screen with a thump.

Favoring her injured arm, Quinn turned to check on her friends. They'd killed the lone hound that had gotten through. All three now ran over to her and stared at her handiwork.

Up and down the screen, the silver stitches glowed. The seam between the stitches started to disappear, and the silver threads of wild magic faded along the edges of the tear. As the last stitch faded, the light in the projection house went out, and everything went dark again. The javelin and remaining line disappeared from Quinn's hand when the light went out. Her Bowie fell from the screen to the ground with a clank.

"Quinn," Taylor said, crouching to check on her friend. "That was amazing. How'd you learn to do that?"

"It wasn't me. With wild magic, you just have to let the magic do what it wants."

"You're injured," Naomi said, reaching out to Quinn's injured left arm.

"I'll be all right. I just need to tap into some ley line power back home to heal up. Don't worry, I'll be good as new before you know it."

Clark checked the screen one more time and nodded. "Let's collect the egg and get out of here. I can't believe we haven't had anyone show up to check on the fire or the rest of the commotion."

"Maybe they'll chalk it up to someone showing a movie on the old screen," Taylor suggested.

"Let's not wait around to have to answer any questions," Clark replied.

Quinn got up with some help from her mother, and the four of them headed back to Clark's car.

They hadn't reached the vehicle before dark figures materialized around them. Sword blades and spears pointed in at them from every direction, and magical blue light appeared above them, illuminating the area around the sedan.

"We knew you wouldn't be able to resist the urge to rescue the youngling, Huntress," Filippa said from the darkness. "My cousin told me you'd tend to it immediately, and I see she was correct."

Quinn stared past the black-clad Fae trackers around her at the two tall figures standing behind them.

Aurora waved a dismissive hand. "You never took the time to get to know the girl like I did, Filippa. I told you your desire to remain above the humans had dulled your ability to understand them."

Quinn took in the situation and knew what she had to do. If any of them resisted, her friends would die, and she'd be captured anyway. The only way to stop this was to turn herself in without a struggle.

"Filippa, Aurora, tell your men to back off. I'll go along peacefully. There's no need to harm my friends."

"Quinn, no!" Naomi cried.

"Leave it be, Mom. I'll be okay."

"Yes, Mom," Filippa parroted. "Be a good sport and let us gather your daughter for her trial by combat tomorrow."

A snarl started in Naomi's throat. Quinn grabbed her mother's arm, spinning her until she was face to face with her daughter.

"I've got this. Save it for another time."

She held her mother's stare until Naomi gave the slightest of nods. Quinn looked back at the Fae princesses. "Let's go. I assume you have cars nearby?"

Hands reached in, pulling Quinn away from her clan members. They bound her arms behind her and brought her over to stand in front of the two Fae women. Both considered her for a few seconds, then Aurora flicked a finger in the direction of the lot's exit. The four trackers around Quinn marched her in that direction.

Ahead of her, headlights turned on, revealing a line of SUVs parked at the far end of the parking lot. Quinn stood straight and tall as she walked with her escort, refusing to give in to the fear rising within her. She'd gone to all that trouble to save the dragon, and now the Fae had the unhatched youngling back.

As rough hands shoved her into the back of an SUV, she wondered if she'd see another night after her honor trial the next day. At least her mother, Taylor, and Clark would live to see another day. That was something.

CHAPTER TWENTY-SIX

Q uinn woke up the next morning and stared at the sun shining in through the narrow barred window of her cell. It was evident she still had a lot to learn about the supernatural world in which she now lived. One of those things was that the Fae had a jail hidden inside an old warehouse in downtown Baltimore. Judging by the bars and stone walls, it dated back over a hundred years. It was a little chilly, and they'd taken her leather jacket from her leaving her in her jeans and t-shirt.

She sat up and ran her fingers through her tangled hair. A lot of it had pulled out of her ponytail while she slept. She didn't figure there'd be a spare hairbrush or a shower before her trial. Quinn resigned herself to detangling it as best she could before gathering it and putting it back into a ponytail.

A creak in the hall outside her stout wooden door told her someone was coming. A few seconds later, the small square panel opened in the door's upper half, and a female Fae guard peered in at her.

The woman sneered and said, "Here's your breakfast. Enjoy it. It'll be your last." A slot opened in the bottom of the door, and a plastic tray with a plate of eggs, toast, and some cut melon slid into view.

"Hey, don't I get to request my last meal? I'd expect you Fae to honor traditions like that."

The woman's face appeared in the upper panel again. "That's a human tradition, girl. The fact you don't know that is another reason you're too dangerous to be loose with the power you hold."

Before Quinn could answer, both openings in the cell door slammed shut, leaving her alone with her thoughts again. Quinn stared at the tray and considered not eating the meal, but she threw out that thought as quickly as it entered her mind. She needed food to fuel her Huntress metabolism. She had a fight coming later, and she needed her strength.

Favoring her injured left arm, Quinn picked up the tray with the other hand and returned to the cot to eat. She had tried to access nearby ley lines to heal herself the night before, but the room was shielded somehow, and she couldn't see or access anything via her map overlay. It just showed up blank, with nothing but the interior of her cell in view. If she ate, her Huntress genes would do something to heal her. She wasn't sure it would be enough before the trial by combat her captors had planned for her.

The food was gone too soon. Quinn made sure to eat every last morsel, including licking the melon juice off the tray when she finished. It would have to suffice. Her hunger didn't go away, but the edge had been taken off.

She set the tray down and thought about what had

happened the night before. She realized now they'd been fools to try to deal with the egg before the trial. There had been a chance that removing the Fae's protective coating would release another wild magic outbreak. It would have been easy for the Fae to zero in on the location when it happened, especially if they were waiting for it.

Quinn massaged her injured shoulder and flexed the fingers of her left hand. It hurt to move, but she could make a fist and pick up the plastic utensils. She wasn't sure she'd be able to use it in a fight, though. It was one thing to pick up a plastic spoon and another to hold her Bowie. She'd have to fight the Fae champion with her off-hand.

Quinn needed to figure out a way to get some healing or speed up her body's natural properties. Naomi had tried to get her to meditate a few times. She figured it was worth attempting it now. It wasn't like she had anything else to do.

She sat on the floor and crossed her legs. Closing her eyes, Quinn tried to clear her mind the way her mother had shown her. It wasn't as easy as it sounded. Anger and second-guessing the previous night's events took up her mind. Every time she came close to pushing them away, another thought drifted in, and she'd have to start all over again.

She had no idea how long she sat there working at it. A click of the lock snapped her back to awareness. Quinn opened her eyes, surprised that it looked like dusk outside her window. She'd been sitting there for hours.

Quinn stood, expecting to be stiff from being in that position for so long. Instead, she stood and stretched her arms wide, refreshed and energized. The ache in her arm barely twinged when she stretched. When she clenched her left hand, her grip was strong.

The door swung open.

Four Fae guards in black pants and sports coats stood outside. The three men waited out in the hall, one of them holding iron shackles, while the lone woman in the group entered. She met Quinn's defiant glare with a dispassionate glance.

"It is time for you to go to the trial. We noticed you meditating earlier, so we didn't interrupt you until now."

"Do I scare you so much you have to restrain me?"

The woman nodded to the doorway. "Come with us without resistance, and you will not be shackled."

Quinn stepped forward. She had no desire to try to escape. The only way out of this was through the Fae court's trial. Once that was done, she'd either be dead or vindicated.

Over the past few days, her friends had tried to hide their concern over the court's outcome from her. Quinn didn't share their fears. She had yet to meet the supernatural adversary she couldn't defeat in a fight. This time would be no different.

Quinn glared at the woman. "I won't resist. Let's get this over with. I have things to do later tonight."

One of the male guards snapped, "I wouldn't be so flippant when you get to the court. The magistrates will not be lenient on you."

"I'll keep that in mind. Thanks for the tip. Maybe I won't kill you when the time comes."

The guard's lip curled. He started to say something, but the female guard cut him off.

"Don't let the human bait you. Her insolence was what got her into this position to begin with. Bring her along."

The woman left the cell, followed by Quinn. The other three formed up to surround her. They marched her down the hall to the door through which they'd entered the warehouse the night before. When Quinn got outside, she climbed into the rear seat of a black SUV. Two of the Fae men jumped in to sit on either side of her, sandwiching her in the middle.

Quinn sat ramrod straight in the seat after buckling her seatbelt. The SUV pulled away and started toward the center of town, and Quinn followed their progress. She knew where they were headed. The court was to be held in the Crystal Well, which meant she was being taken to Federal Hill, to the home where she'd first met Filippa. She wasn't sure of the reason for the choice of that particular location. It was likely some way for Filippa to gloat about having the upper hand after Quinn had defeated Gemma there weeks before.

The SUV soon parked in back of the home, and the guards led Quinn into the basement and along the tunnel connected to the old silica mines in this part of the city. The old passages were deserted, to Quinn's surprise. She and Clark had left them in the care of the local werebadger clan. None of the small shifters were present, or maybe they were just staying out of sight. Quinn didn't expect them to rescue her, but it might have been nice to see someone she recognized. She looked forward to seeing Taylor and the others there, at least. The location and time had been on the writ the Fae had served.

They reached the chamber that housed the Crystal Well

a few minutes later. The werebadgers had done an excellent job of clearing the cave-in that had partially blocked the entrance. It was open now, and the stone floor was pristine. Quinn stared at the domed ceiling as she entered. The newly installed electric lamps wired around the circular room reflected in the cut-glass lining the chamber's roof. The crystal sparkled and sent tiny rainbows back and forth above her.

Five tall-backed wooden chairs stood in a row at the far end of the room, opposite the entrance. The carefully laid stones of the chamber floor had been swept and either mopped or polished, so they shone nearly as brightly as the glittering ceiling. On another occasion, she might have admired the restored beauty of the place. Not now, though.

There were several other Fae in clusters of two and three around the room. They all stopped talking and stared at Quinn when the guards escorted her in. She didn't see either of the princesses.

"Where are Filippa and Aurora? I thought they would want to be here for this."

"Their royal highnesses will be here soon," the female guard said. "They'll enter with the magistrates once all who wish to attend are present."

"What about my friends?"

"After their participation in your defiance of the sanctuary granted you, it was decided they couldn't be trusted to be here and abide by the court's decision. They've been detained until the matter is settled. Don't worry. They will be freed unharmed, whatever the outcome."

Quinn kept her facial muscles rigid, fearing she'd display her disappointment at not having any friendly faces in the assembled witnesses. Quinn shook off the momentary feeling of despair. She was alone, just like always—just like when she was a kid. Her guess was the Fae expected it to sap her will to live. They didn't understand how Quinn's early years had refined her streak of bold individualism. She was used to relying solely on her wits and abilities.

A gong was struck behind her, and a small formal procession entered the chamber. A quartet of guards dressed in black like her guards led the way. The two princesses came in next. Aurora wore Fae robes of nearly transparent flowing silk. Filippa was dressed in a very modern business suit, complete with pants and a tie. A single Fae tracker carried the dragon egg, still shimmering. Quinn was glad they hadn't had time to recast their spell.

A few paces behind them walked five elderly Fae in red robes trimmed with gold at the cuffs and collars. They were the first Fae she'd ever seen who looked older than thirty by human standards. She assumed it was how they'd gotten the job as magistrates over a race as long-lived as these.

The five judges took their places in the chairs. There were three women and two men, and one of the women took the taller center seat. Aurora gestured to the man carrying the egg. He walked over and placed it on the floor in front of the woman in the taller chair. He returned to his place on the wall with the others.

Once the princesses and the guards reached their final positions around the room, the chief judge raised her hand. Everyone turned toward her.

"This hearing of the Fae High Court is in session. Who brings the charges today?"

Filippa walked to stand in the center near Quinn, facing the judges. "I do, honored magistrates. A human woman has been found to be dealing with wild magic. She is a danger to herself, the city of humans in which she lives, and the balance of natural magic in the world."

"That's a bit pretentious, Filippa. Why don't you tell them the truth?" Quinn growled.

The chief judge said, "That is enough, girl. This court will ask you to speak if it desires your opinion."

"I have a right to defend myself," Quinn said, taking a step in the judge's direction.

A kick at the back of her knees sent her to the floor. The four guards were on her in an instant, pulling her hands behind her back and placing the shackles on them.

"Gag her so she doesn't interrupt the proceedings again," the chief judge said.

A hand yanked her ponytail as she lay prone on the floor, pulling her head back at an extreme angle. When a hand came into view with a wad of cloth, Quinn snapped at it with her teeth. She grinned when she managed to bite into the guard's fingers. She didn't draw any blood, but the gasp from the guard told her it had hurt.

Someone kicked the back of her head, driving her forehead into the stone floor hard enough she saw stars. Quinn wasn't sure she hadn't blacked out for a few seconds. By the time she finally gathered her wits, her mouth was filled with a wadded cloth. Another strip had been tied around her head to secure it in place.

Hands hauled her back to her feet. She was unable to

shake off the grogginess from the blow to her head. Her eyes had trouble focusing, and the electric lights had taken on a prismatic effect. A multi-colored halo surrounded the bulbs.

Quinn tilted her head back and stared at the ceiling. Everything around her grew hazy, and the glow of the reflected lights in the crystals intensified. Before she knew it, Quinn felt like gravity reversed and she fell up into the pool of light above her. She squeezed her eyes shut at the glare and awaited the pain from impact as she crashed into the intricate glass lining the ceiling.

The murmur of the Fae voices came to an abrupt stop, and everything around her grew quiet. All sound was muffled. Quinn opened her eyes, curious about what had happened.

She stood alone in the center of the Crystal Well. The electric lamps on the walls had been replaced by torches. They lit the ceiling as the electric lamps did, though the flickering flames made the effect even more beautiful. She knew she was still in the chamber, yet simultaneously somewhere else.

"Daughter, why do you fight what must happen here tonight?"

The voice was the first indication that she wasn't alone in the room. Quinn moved her gaze from the ceiling to a gray-haired woman standing directly in front of her. She wore a cream-colored dress with blue flowers embroidered across the chest and down the sleeves.

"Where did everyone go?"

"They are still here. You will return to them soon, but I needed to talk to you once again."

Quinn recognized the voice. It was the same friendly voice that had spoken to her before, showing approval or lending guidance when she most needed it.

"Are you here to rescue me or give me a way out of this trial?"

The woman smiled and shook her head. "No, daughter. You must do that on your own. Know that I have faith in you, though. Trust yourself in the trial to come. Your kind nature will show you the way out."

"That's not much help if you don't mind me saying so."

An amused smile crossed the woman's lips. "I do not. It is the way of humans to question. It was how you were fashioned. Our hope was to create a creature on Earth that could find a way to defeat the demons when they finally opened their way to return."

"I don't think the other humans know that. They don't even seem to be aware of the danger."

"Quinn, dearest, they aren't the answer we sought when we influenced creation in that direction. You and your clan are our answer to the prideful Fae and their machinations. Some of my brethren allowed them to grow too far in their hubris. They've reached the point where most no longer listen to reason about their lost cousins in the netherworld. I and others foresaw the danger. That is why you are here."

"I don't understand. I'm sorry," Quinn said. "I still don't know how this will change things. You tell me you don't know if I'll win and cannot help me. If I can't make it through this trial they've arranged, all you've worked to do with me will be for nothing. The princesses are very aware of what I can do. They will not leave it up to chance."

"Ah, but they already have, daughter. They do not

control everything. The most important variable is you. Know only that win or lose, I am proud of all you've achieved. There will be no disappointment."

"But—" Quinn had so many questions.

"There is no more time, daughter. You must go back. Do not struggle. Wait for your moment, and trust the goodness you carry inside. It will always guide you."

Quinn started to ask another question, but when she blinked, she was back amid the electric lights and the Fae court. The goddess or whoever she was had disappeared.

The court had apparently continued while she'd been elsewhere in her mind. Filippa finished listing Quinn's offenses.

"Finally, she removed the protective coating we'd placed around the dragon egg, knowing it would result in another incursion. Luckily, our trackers were able to contain the outbreak."

Quinn wanted to scream. Filippa was taking credit for Quinn's efforts to close the rift last night.

"Is there anything else you'd like to present, Princess?" the chief judge asked.

"No, Magistrate. That is all."

"Does your cousin back your testimony?"

Aurora stepped forward. "I do, Magistrate. The girl is a menace and must be dealt with."

The old woman nodded and leaned back in the chair, turning to each side as the others leaned in her direction. Though their lips moved, Quinn heard nothing of their voices. Some spell or trick covered their voices so she couldn't listen to their deliberations.

"We are forbidden from executing the human outright

as you know, but your request for a trial by combat is approved. Remove the girl's gag and restraints."

The guards untied the strip holding the gag in her mouth. The female guard pulled the wadded cloth from her mouth. Someone behind her took off the heavy shackles.

Quinn rubbed her wrists and licked her dry lips. She looked around, trying to decide who she had to fight. She liked what she saw and decided she could take anyone in the room in a standup fight. Her still-injured shoulder might tip the balance in their favor, but she figured she had an even chance.

"Do I get to choose a weapon, Your Honor?"

"No, girl. You may only fight with what the gods have given you."

"Who am I taking on, then?" Quinn clenched her fists and held them up, ready to fight.

"Your Highness," the magistrate said, "you may present your champion."

"Gladly," Filippa said. She clapped her hands, and all eyes turned toward the entrance to the chamber. An enormous robed creature entered, followed by four slightly smaller ones, also obscured by robes. The central figure had to stoop to enter the room. Quinn knew they must've had to almost crawl through the tunnels to get here.

Once inside, the robed figure stood, its face still covered in the shadows of the hood. It stood at nearly eight feet tall and was armored in leather and metal plates from head to toe. They'd stacked the deck against her this time.

Quinn recalled what the goddess had told her moments

before and searched the woman's words for some inkling of how she was supposed to defeat this monstrosity.

Behind her, Quinn overheard Filippa say to her cousin, "Let's see the girl get out of this one. She's finished for sure this time."

Quinn looked at the shadows inside the hood standing over her, trying to see who they'd brought to execute her. She couldn't pierce the darkness and make out the face of the creature. A shiver went down her spine as she prepared to defend herself against this impossible opponent.

This time, that smug Fae princess might be right.

CHAPTER TWENTY-SEVEN

Filippa called as Quinn assumed a defensive stance, "Bring the champion his weapon."

One of the hooded attendants accompanying the champion turned and left the chamber.

"Oh, come on," Quinn turned and objected to the magistrates. "This guy's armored from head to toe, and he gets a weapon?"

The chief magistrate raised her hand to stop Quinn's complaint. "What weapon would you choose?"

Before Quinn could answer, Filippa stepped forward. "She was captured with a weapon. Perhaps that will do."

"Agreed. Bring the girl her weapon."

One of the black-suited guards reached into a leather satchel and pulled out Quinn's sheathed Bowie knife. He tossed it to the floor at Quinn's feet and returned to his place along the wall.

Quinn bent down and picked up the knife, drawing the blade and throwing the sheath aside. At the other end of the chamber, the hooded attendant returned. He carried the golden spear taken from Quinn and the clan.

She shook her head. She knew the powerful magic inherent in that spear. Besides the magic, there was also the long leaf-shaped tip this monster could use to impale her before she ever got close with her Bowie. One strike with the spear could finish her. Quinn had no idea how many thrusts of her blade she'd need to take out the giant facing her.

The champion reached out a gauntleted hand to take the spear. As he gripped it, ripples of magical lightning coursed up and down the shaft. That doused the small hope that the champion might not be able to activate the spear's magic.

Quinn crouched and took a few steps forward toward the champion. To her surprise, the giant didn't advance to meet her. If anything, its body language seemed almost hesitant.

One of the attendants shouted something in a language she didn't know. The angry tone accompanying the guttural words was unmistakable. He was telling the giant to get it over with.

Quinn felt the same way. All this waiting was getting to her. "Come on, you big brute. Come and try to stick me with that thing."

The giant form shuffled forward a few steps and stopped, still not adopting anything approaching a threatening stance.

Quinn decided this was her only chance. She had to strike before the creature chose to kill her.

She tensed, prepping herself to spring forward and try

her luck at finding a gap in her opponent's armor.

"Quinn, are you mad at me?" the towering figure asked in a sorrowful tone.

Quinn relaxed and stood up straight. It couldn't be.

One of the gauntleted hands reached up and pushed back the hood, revealing an orc's tusked visage.

A broad grin crossed Quinn's face. "No, of course not, Tadpole. I didn't know it was you until now."

"My brothers said I had to come in here and kill someone. I didn't know it was going to be you, honest."

"You're way bigger than they are. Tell them no."

"I don't know if I can do that, Quinn." A single tear fell and coursed down the orc warrior's cheek.

Filippa shouted and rushed from her place on the wall to the seated judges. "Magistrate, stop this chatter. Order the champion to kill the girl."

"The champion was yours to choose, Princess." An amused tone filled the old Fae woman's voice. "Perhaps you should have chosen better."

Quinn ignored the discussion behind her. She concentrated on Tadpole. More tears followed the first. "Hey, don't let this upset you. It's going to be all right. I promise."

"But if I don't do what they want, I won't have a family anymore."

"I know how that feels. I didn't have a family of my own growing up. It was hard, but I discovered a secret. You know what I did?"

Tadpole wiped his tear-filled eyes with the back of his gauntlet. "No, what?"

"I found my own family. You can do the same thing."

All four of the hooded attendants ran up behind the

giant orc, shouting at him in guttural Orcish. Two of them had drawn their swords and poked him from behind. The giant orc winced when the sword points pricked him through gaps in his armor.

"Hey, leave him alone. He doesn't have to do what you say. If you want to fight someone, come and fight me."

Two of the orcs continued tormenting the giant. The other two turned and advanced on Quinn.

"We'll kill you if our brother won't," the leader said in English.

"You'll try," Quinn replied. She dialed up her HUD and drew off her stamina bar to ramp up her speed and strength rating. Her arm still ached, but the added boost should compensate for the lingering injury.

The two orcs stepped past their giant little brother and spread out to either side, trying to split her attention.

Quinn didn't wait for them to react. She feinted to the right, drawing the attacker on the left into attacking her exposed back.

He walked right into her trap.

Bending and spinning around, Quinn's booted foot connected with the hand extended in a lunge. The sword he held went flying and clattered on the floor. The crack that resonated up her leg told Quinn she'd broken the orc's wrist.

There was no time to relax, though. She came back up from the spinning kick, ready for another incoming attack.

The brother on her right recognized the feint and switched his block into an awkward lunge at her back. Quinn had trouble bringing her Bowie around in time to parry the incoming sword.

The tip of the sword scored a bloody line across Quinn's back and side as she completed her spin. She hissed in pain and took a step back as she recovered.

The second orc clutched his broken wrist and backed away as Quinn moved in his direction to get away from the other brother. He was out of the fight for now.

Quinn concentrated on getting past the incoming sword to finish off the lead brother before the final two decided to join the fight.

Tadpole sobbed as two of his brothers continued to poke and prod him, shouting at him in Orcish. The words seemed to be doing more damage than the swords.

Quinn batted away an incoming lunge and shouted, "Tadpole, you don't owe them anything. If they treat you like this, they don't deserve to be your brothers. I'll be your sister. My whole clan will welcome you. Come be part of my family."

The giant's eyes met hers, and she caught a glimmer of hope shining forth. She nodded and smiled despite the pain in her back and arm.

Tadpole extended his arm, thrusting the length of the golden spear out quicker than she'd thought possible for someone so large. The flat of the spear's blade flicked away the incoming sword aimed at Quinn's side. The parry struck with such force, it dislodged the sword from his brother's grip. The sword dropped to the stone floor.

"Don't hurt her."

The lead orc stared up at his brother in disbelief. "You cannot change families, you stupid oaf."

Tadpole paused and glanced at Quinn, once again unsure of himself.

"Our clan will never call you names, Tadpole. We welcome everyone."

"Theodore, I swear, if you don't listen to me now, I'll kick you out of our family, and you will never be allowed back."

Quinn shook her head. "That's not how a real family works. A real family always welcomes you back and throws a party for your return."

Tadpole's expression shifted from pain to puzzlement and then to a broad grin. He took two massive steps, pushing his oldest brother out of the way and turning to stand side by side with Quinn.

The three uninjured orcs formed up in an arc, facing the two unlikely companions. The Fae trackers came from the walls to complete the circle and surround Quinn and Tadpole.

"Enough!"

The woman's magically enhanced voice resonated through the chamber.

Everyone turned to face the chief magistrate. She stood, glowering at Quinn and those arrayed against her.

"The trial is decided. Blood has been shed, and the champion has chosen."

Aurora stepped forward. "Magistrate, the champion was to fight the accused. The girl has subverted justice, twisting the court of honor's intentions with her vile ways."

Quinn said, "The only vileness here is forcing this gentle person to fight against his will. I charge you with subverting justice, Aurora."

The princess gasped. "How dare you accuse me of

anything! You stole the egg from my cousin and me. You released the wild magic and set the hatching into motion. All of this happened because of you."

Before Quinn could answer the charges from the Fae woman, a loud crack filled the chamber, and all eyes turned to the dragon egg on the ground in front of the five magistrates. A long, jagged opening had appeared in the shell, and a golden glow emanated from it.

Quinn's wild magic icon lit up in her HUD and started flashing again. This wasn't good. A sense of impending dread washed over Quinn.

From the expressions on the faces of the others in the room, they felt something, too.

Tadpole reached out to grasp her free hand in his massive gauntlet. "Quinn, what's happening? I'm scared."

"It's going to be okay, buddy." She patted the back of his hand and pulled him back to stand near the wall. "Give me a second to figure it out. Just stay close to me, whatever happens."

The golden flows of wild magic leaching from the opening in the shell spun in a growing circle on the stone floor beside the egg. After a few seconds, the swirl's center seemed to draw downward like a whirlpool until a dark hole had opened in the center of the chamber floor. The egg rested beside it, the golden magic feeding the maelstrom.

As the opening expanded, a few of the trackers and one of the orc brothers were caught unawares. The swirling energy grabbed them, pulling them to the center and down into the abyss. Their fading screams cut off as they disappeared.

"See?" Aurora screamed over the magical roar. "The wild magic she released is expanding yet again. She's a danger to us all and must be killed."

"This isn't me," Quinn called. "This all comes from the young dragon inside. I don't think it will stop until it is born."

The chief magistrate stared at Quinn from the opposite side of the swirling energy. "This energy will continue to expand and consume everything it touches unless someone stops it. The princess is right. You are the key, girl. You must be the one to stop it. Perhaps your life, and the life of the dragonling, are the price that must be paid."

The magistrate produced a long golden dagger from within her robes and stepped forward to stand over the egg.

"No, let me try something first. If the baby dragon is doing this, it doesn't understand what is happening. We have to help it, not kill it."

"What would you do?"

Quinn didn't want to answer right away because she had no idea. She couldn't tell the magistrate she was making this up as she went, though. "Just watch and see."

She ran around the widening abyss to the egg. The magistrate nodded and took a step back to give Quinn room to work.

Quinn knelt beside the egg and stared into the crack. She couldn't see much through the flow of golden energy, but she thought she could make out something moving inside. No, not moving, she realized. Writhing. The dragon inside was in pain.

Pulling up her HUD, Quinn ignored the flashing icon in

the center, concentrating instead on her blue mana bar. She held her hand over the crack in the shell.

Taking a deep breath, Quinn lowered her hand into the golden flow, wincing as the powerful magic set off the ends of her pain receptors as if they'd exploded and caught fire. Relaxing and giving in to the wild magic instead of resisting it, Quinn drew it into herself until the blue mana bar changed color and filled.

Every nerve ending in her body burned now. Her whole being quivered with the agony that washed over her. She knew the poor youngling felt it, too. Grinding her teeth together, Quinn, reached down with both hands and gripped the jagged edges of the crack. They cut into her fingers, but she didn't let go.

Pulling with all her enhanced might, Quinn pried at the egg. At first, nothing happened, so she pulled in more of the golden energy and channeled the stores from her mana bar into her hands. She willed the redirected magic to support and sustain the young dragon inside, soothing its pain and anxiety.

The jerking motions inside the shell slowed and eventually stopped. Soon, all Quinn sensed from inside was calm and anticipation.

Outside, it was a different story.

The whirlpool of wild magic still spun, but it no longer expanded. Most of those in the room had fled. She wasn't sure, but the flow of golden energy from the dragon might have slowed. Quinn realized the wild magic was tied into the dragon's emotions. As long as she could keep it calm, the magic slowed, and the swirling pit of death in the chamber's center would stop growing.

Quinn's fingers dripped blood from the wounds caused by the shell's jagged edges. The slickness made it hard to grip the sides anymore. Her hands kept slipping, slowing her attempts to assist with the dragon's birth while causing more injury to her fingers.

She pressed forward, using the tapped power she'd accumulated to pry at the egg. It was like trying to bend steel.

Quinn drained the last of both her mana and stamina into one final pull at the shell, and a crack louder than thunder resonated through the room and up her arms. She wrenched the egg wide open and collapsed to the floor beside the halves. Quinn's hands and arms ached so much she couldn't bear it anymore. Her consciousness started slipping away.

Through her slitted eyelids, Quinn gazed at the opening. A thin snout appeared within it, and a long forked tongue snaked out, tasting the air. The scaled nose emerged, followed by the entire head.

The tongue flitted out again, this time tickling Quinn's face and nose. More of the dragon's long neck emerged, and the nose nudged Quinn's cheek. The entire head was no bigger than her fist.

Quinn smiled, licked her cracked lips, and said, "Hey, little one. It's good to meet you in person finally."

The dragon's body emerged next, followed by the long tail. The little dragon waddled over on unsteady legs and curled up beneath Quinn's chin. The tiny emerald eyes gazed into hers.

"I shall call you Sylvie. Is that all right?"

The tongue flicked out again, tickling her cheek twice.

The little head lowered to rest against its coiled body. With its vibrating warmth pressing against her, the newborn dragon folded a tiny wing over its eyes.

The swirling magical abyss abruptly shrank and winked out with a snap like a firecracker. Neither she nor the baby dragon noticed. They were both sound asleep.

CHAPTER TWENTY-EIGHT

"Sister Quinn, please wake up. I don't want to stay here anymore."

Quinn's eyes fluttered open, and she sat up and looked around. She still lay on the floor of the Crystal Well's chamber. As soon as she moved away from it, the little dragon crawled into her lap, curling back into a ball.

Tadpole sat on the floor beside her. He'd removed his heavy armor and piled it on the floor nearby. Besides the broken pieces of the shell, the room was empty again. Even the magistrates' chairs had been removed.

"Where'd everyone go?"

Tadpole pointed to the chamber's entrance. "They left a long time ago. I tried to go with them, but the old woman told me I had to stay with you. My three brothers turned their backs and wouldn't talk to me. I've been sitting here waiting for you to wake up for hours."

Quinn started to reach out and pat his arm but stopped, wincing in pain. She stared down at her fingers. The cuts in them had crusted over with scabs, making it so she couldn't move them from a claw position without breaking the gashes open.

"It's okay. I'm awake now. You ready to come with me and meet the rest of your new family? They are going to be so surprised when I introduce you."

"What if they don't like me or I frighten them?"

"Not a chance. If I vouch for you, they have to like you."

Tadpole smiled as her kind words sank in and worked their way past his doubts. Quinn knew she was going to have a lot of work ahead of her, helping him adjust to his new clan.

Gathering up the sleeping dragon into the crook of one elbow, Quinn got to her feet. "Come on, Tadpole. It's time for us to go home."

"Where's that?"

"You'll see. It's a place where there are lots of magical people like you and me, all different sorts. All you have to do is come along and be their friend like you've been to me."

"I'd like that."

"Good. It's settled. Now pick up that spear. I think it's yours for now."

The giant orc stood, grabbed the golden spear from the pile of armor, and walked beside Quinn to the room's entrance. He hunched down and ducked into the tunnel, then followed her back to the surface.

As she left the magical chamber, a familiar voice echoed in the distance.

"Well done once again, daughter. Rest for now. Build your clan. Soon, the world will require all your strength."

The Huntress Clan saga wraps up with book 6, *Huntress Defender*. With evidence that the dark Fae plot to open the gates to the netherworld is nearing completion, the Huntress, Quinn Faust, must rally all her allies for the coming battle. Old friends return and new resources and allies are discovered. Will Quinn be ready in time to take the Huntress Clan into a battle to save the world?

Extreme Medical Services: Medical Care On The Fringes Of Humanity

Monsters, Paramedics, and Street Medicine

New paramedic Dean Flynn is fresh out of the academy.

Then he learns his patients aren't your normal 911 callers.

With patients that are vampires, werewolves, fairies and more, will Dean survive his first days on the new job?

Will his patients?

Come along now with Extreme Medical Services, a supernatural medical thrill-ride with the paramedics of Elk City by best-selling author and real-life paramedic Jamie Davis.

Jump on the ambulance with Dean, Brynne and the rest of the team.

Get the first book in this best-selling service at Amazon.com.

I had the occasion to ponder the meaning of family while I wrote this installment of the Huntress Clan Saga. Most of us probably think first of those who are blood related to us. For many of us, though, the word "family" entails much more.

There are those unrelated groups in our lives we call family. Some could have a work family, or maybe a church family. There's that person in your life who you call a brother or sister even though they aren't related by blood to you. I grew up with a few aunts and uncles who weren't my parents' siblings. They were just really good family friends.

Some become part of a family when joining a profession. I'm a retired paramedic. My professional colleagues and I often referred to others in out profession as brothers and sisters from the streets. Firefighters, police officers, soldiers, and others do this as well. Family is a word with broad meaning that changes with time and circumstance.

Quinn learns this throughout the series. She starts off

with quite a negative impression of family, at least the blood relative kind or the foster kind. It's understandable. Many people have experiences like hers. For Quinn these were the people who abandoned her or tried to abuse her.

Over time, Quinn worked to build her own family, her own clan. That started with Taylor, very much a sister to the Huntress. Quinn continued adding people as they proved themselves to her. First Clark and Miranda, then she discovered her mother and Quinn added an actual blood relative to the family she'd built.

As the clan grew, so did Quinn's role. She started out a lost daughter of the clan, then became a sibling among others like herself. *Huntress Adept* marks her partial transition from sister to mother, at least in part. As I work on book six, I'll bring the series to a close and finish Quinn's journey to discovering her family and its meaning in her life.

I urge you to find your family, whatever that may mean to you. In the midst of these challenging times, it is easy to feel distant and alone now and then. Seek out (safely) those in your life who bring you joy and support you in various ways. Do something to recognize them and thank them for being a part of your various circles of family. Chances are they are looking for a connection to others, too. We're all in this together.

Until next time, thanks for reading my books. Peace.

ABOUT JAMI DAVIS

Jamie Davis is a nurse, retired paramedic, author, and nationally recognized medical educator who began teaching new emergency responders as a training officer for his local EMS program. He loves everything fantasy and sci-fi and especially the places where stories intersect with his love of medicine or gaming.

Jamie lives in a home in the woods in Maryland with his wife, three children, and dog. He is an avid gamer, preferring historical and fantasy miniature gaming, as well as tabletop games. He writes urban and contemporary paranormal fantasy stories, and LitRPG/GameLit, among other things.

He loves hearing from readers and going to cons and events where he meets up with fans. Reach out and say "hi." Visit JamieDavisBooks.com for more books, free offers and more!

Author site is: https://jamiedavisbooks.com

Facebook group is: https://facebook.com/ groups/funfantasyreaders

Twitter — https://twitter.com/podmedic

Instagram — https://instagram.com/podmedic